Language and Minority Peoples
in the Making of
Modern Thailand

泰國庶民和弱勢群體的
草根式語言學習和語言使用

李育修／著
Hugo Yu-Hsiu Lee

以雙語、多語的學習和使用
幫忙解決社會之問題

Towards Development

and Social Change

被封稱「弱勢族群的語言學家」

在泰國人眼中第一名的台灣教授

最新著作

聯合國五部門長官、美國、日本、秘魯、泰國等
當代傑出語言學家、台灣語言教育家
隆重推薦

To applied linguists, sociolinguists, foreign/second language
teachers, language educators,
nonprofit and non-governmental organizations (NGOs)
who are ready to help minority peoples
become competent and strategic
bi-/multilingual language users
hereby they stance a better chance
to achieve sustainable economic & social development

Written & Compilation @ 2019 by Hugo Yu-Hsiu Lee

First published初版2019
First Edition
Published and Printed in Taiwan
by Elephantwhite (白象文化), Taichung

泰國庶民和弱勢群體的草根式語言學習和語言使用。
(以雙語、多語的學習和使用,幫忙解決社會之問題)
Language and Minority in the Making of Modern Thailand:
Introductory Guide
(Towards Development and Social Change)

Includes bibliographical references.

Content: English (90 %) vs. Mandarin (Chinese) (10 %)

ISBN: 978-986-358-895-5

Lee, Hugo, Y-H. (2019). *Language and Minority in the Making of Modern Thailand: Introductory Guide (Towards Development and Social Change).* Taichung: Elephantwhite (Taiwan).

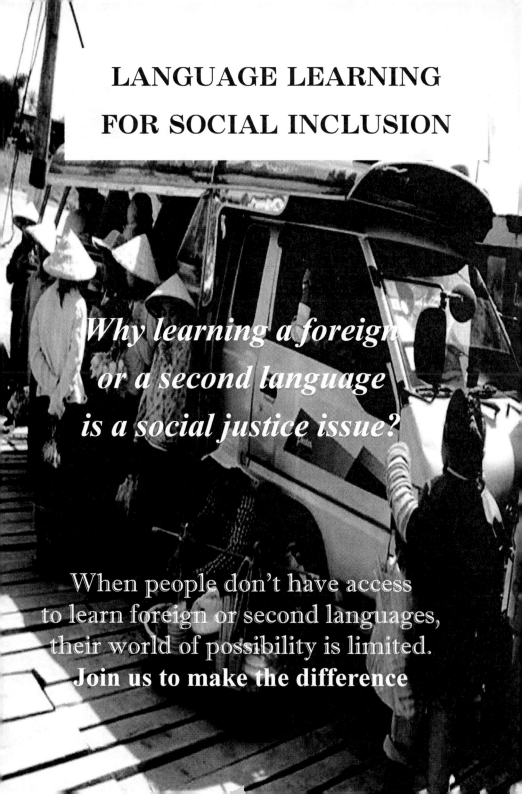

Collaboration
for Equity
in Language Learning

Hugo's logo for his research campaign (2010 – 2018)

The campaign's **vision** is: *"Language education should reduce inequality and encourage inclusive growth, and help marginalized populations achieve sustainable development goals."*

The campaign's **mission** is: *"To enable social changes towards sustainable development through an integrated language solutions approach."*

弱勢族群的語檔

與語言學習和使用

來解決社會問題的運動

2010年代最具雄心的大曼谷地區弱勢族群語言使用田野調查和語料收集計畫，當推

Collaboration for Equity in Language Learning。

截至2018年為止，共收集孤兒院殘疾院童、尋求政治庇護者、都市難民、酒吧女（愛情企業家）、按摩女、餐廳服務生、街頭青少年工作者等上百人的語言使用資料。

美國培養之台灣學者、聯合國雇員
東協之都泰國語言學界
4000天研究卷

Language and Minority

in the Making of Modern Thailand:
Towards Development and Social Change

INTRODUCTORY GUIDE

泰國庶民和弱勢群體的草根式語言學習

和語言使用。

（以雙語、多語的學習和使用，幫忙解決社會之問題）

_____

2011-2017李育修博士 原著
2018 李育修博士 更新、漢譯並校注

About the Author

Hugo Yu-Hsiu Lee earned his doctorate at the Wendell W. Wright School of Education, USA. He is an award-winning researcher at the Indiana University-Bloomington, USA (2005-2010) and the National Institute of Development Administration, Thailand (2010-2018). He is Assistant Professor of Applied Linguistics and Lecturer of Intercultural Communication and Nonprofit Marketing, ASEAN's leading International College for Postgraduate-only studies (known as ICO-NIDA). He is currently the United Nations Consultant (Since mid-2016, he was awarded the United Nations consultancy status by the United Nations, Economic and Social Commission for Asia and the Pacific). He lives in Bangkok (Thailand), Kaohsiung (Taiwan) and Bloomington (Indiana, USA) between 2005 and 2018.

https://indiana.academia.edu/YuHsiuLee

作者簡介

李育修 教授

　　1978年11月生於台灣（90年代高雄業餘街舞家），2010年美國印第安那大學語言教育博士（美國印第安那大學語言教育碩士、美國印第安那大學比較文學博士輔系畢、美國印第安那大學東亞研究博士第二副修畢、美國南方信浸會神學院同步碩士畢），曾擔任東南亞公約組織旗下亞洲理工中文項目創辦人（第一任）、曾獲得美國印第安那大學哈世迪傑出研究員獎得主、以及美國印第安那大學紀念史特蘭學者榮譽獎。（李育修博士被台灣實踐大學評選為2018年傑出校友。）

　　除了美國發展之外，也在泰國學術圈闖蕩9年，李育修博士亦被泰國語言學界認定為庶民語言學家，也是多位泰國語言專業熱血博士生「用語言促成社會改造」運動的啟蒙者。

　　目前擔任聯合國亞太經濟社會委員會（聯合國亞洲總部）人事處顧問、聯合國學習中心（聯合國會議中心3樓）團隊成員，以及聯合國官方語言中文項目（聯合國官員和雇員之中文班）導師，並出任聯合國官方語言試卷主要出題員和試卷評分員。

育修畢業的美國印第安那大學教育學院
（語言教育系碩博士班）

Photo Credit:

Author's American Mother

Sue Carolyn McClary

DEDICATION

To my loving wife, Araya Lee
and my daughter, Chayanis Lee.

Dedicated to strategic language users
across minority communities.

To all minority peoples who have sought to become competent
bi-/multilinguals for social inclusion and social justice.
Together we will achieve sustainable economic &
social development.

*I dedicate this book especially to the tens of thousands
of asylum seekers, urban refugees, orphans with and
without disabilities, bargirls, street teen labors and
street sex workers who are the most marginalized and
vulnerable in Thailand*

謹以此書獻給

我摯愛的泰國老婆和泰國女兒

和故鄉台灣高雄、屏東

的父母、親戚、朋友們

美國印第安那州教會、大學

的師長、朋友們

以及大曼谷地區基層的

雙語與多語族群朋友們

一位走進難民營、孤兒院、按摩院、

酒吧的語言教育家

初版自序　PREFACE

AS I AM writing and revising preface, the 74th session of
United Nations, Economic and Social Commission for Asia
and the Pacific (held from 11 - 16 May 2018 at the United
Nations Conference Center, Bangkok), is now in full swing to
address the issue of inequality (Theme Topic: Inequality in the
era of the 2030 Agenda for Sustainable Development).
Discussions about information and communication technology,
environment, economics, financing, trade, investment,
transport, energy are held among United Nations senior
officials and ministerial representatives during the 74th
Commission.

Nonetheless, inequality of opportunity to access basic education rights, services and resources such as suitable learning materials, pedagogy and teaching methods required for individuals and groups to communicate with foreign customers and trade partners from other countries is not addressed by the United Nations. The cost of ignoring inequality of opportunity to learn globally dominant, foreign and second languages is significant.

The book finds that inequality is on the rise in Thailand and unequal access to opportunities such as foreign and second language learning (particularly dominant-language learning opportunities) has left enormous marginalized individuals and groups behind, resulting in widen inequalities of outcomes, particularly in income.

The book also finds that to converse in a foreign/second language is closely associated with opportunity and power to increase income. This is particularly true for the urban poor and those who work in the service industry.

There is a growing recognition that strategic bi-/multilingualism in individual and group levels is good to boost economic growth. Research (as reported in the book) demonstrate that marginalized individuals and groups with high access rates to dominant, foreign, second language learning opportunities have lower poverty rates.

In other words, minority peoples who actively foster foreign/second language learning gain more rewards in their workforce.

Access to humanitarian-based language-support programs and informal foreign/second language learning resources is crucial for achieving sustainable development goals (SDGs) for different groups of minority peoples by helping reduce and combat poverty, increase employment opportunity and advance formal and informal education. In the last decade, language solutions to social problems have not yet become a central focus of research, development planning and implementation of plans by the United Nations and civil society leaders.

However, language solutions to social problems are essential to help realize United Nations' SDGs. Micro language planning, precision language education, informal language learning, competent and strategic bi-/multilingualism, for instance, help reduce poverty (SDG1) and reduce inequality (SDG10), support the development of education (SDG4) and industry (SDG9), and ultimately boost economic growth (SDG8).

FIG. Sustainable Development Goals (SDGs)
by the United Nations

Direct and Substantial Contributions

by Language Solutions Approach:

Ex. SDG 1, SDG8, SDG10

僅靠學習和使用第二語言和外語，變成「策略性」的雙語和多語者，當然還不足以解決所有經濟問題或是終結貧窮問題。可是，語言解決之道是替社會底層族群開啟一道可行之門。而且以作者在過去九年（2010-2018）走訪泰國基層和弱勢族群發展泰國「草根式」語言學習的經驗，透過這扇門走出出口，其實還蠻通暢的。

Indirect and Partial Contributions

by Language Solutions Approach:

Ex. SDG2, SDG3, SDG 4, SDG 5, SDG 11

"To prosper economically and to improve relations with other countries, Americans need to read, speak and understand other languages."

-- Arne Duncan, U.S. Secretary of Education 2010

The Next Grass-Root Language Pedagogy

For decades, earthly civil governments put their faith in the classroom-based formal, first, second and foreign language education programs and their broadly accepted teaching methods. However, against a background of foreign/second language deficit where instructional methods across public schools and colleges is in crisis to produce their graduates in a disadvantaged position largely due to the lack of foreign/second language skills, that faith has faded.

This is certainly not the first time, the author, as a meaningful member of linguistic community, is openly and seriously questioning the formal language instruction held in elementary and secondary schools and colleges. If people are unhappy about what first, second and foreign languages are taught in public schools and colleges at every level, are there alternative language pedagogies? Are there new paradigms of language curriculum? Are there novel approaches of effective self-language learning being emerged?

One might go about creating a competitor to the school-based formal language instruction so good to the point that it finally and eventually substitutes formal language education programs offered by conventional schools. However, this is not the purpose of this book.

This book is a contribution not only to an understanding of issues and challenges in language, literacy and communication faced among minority peoples in Thailand's margins (2010-2018), but also to an understanding of efforts by these disadvantaged communities through micro foreign/second language planning and learning, as well as strategic bi- and multilingual language use, to foster economic and social development from below.

This book pioneers the concepts of micro-language planning with an emphasis on strategic foreign/second language learning and bi-/multilingual language use, among others, as a means to reduce poverty, foster economic and social development, and achieve sustainable development goals (SDGs) for some marginalized groups. Drawing primarily from real-world case studies across a number of marginalized groups in Thailand, poverty reduction and sustainable development are proven not achievable unless civil society's policy makers and grass-root leaders provide language-support program, implement precision language education on critical foreign/second languages, promote informal language learning in non-educational settings and encourage strategic bi-/multilingualism for the neediest minority individuals and groups.

May 15, 2018   **Hugo Y-H. Lee**
                                                             HUAMAK, BANGKOK

International College
國際學院
National Institute of Development Administration
國家發展研究院
Bangkok曼谷, 2018

感謝　ACKNOWLEDGEMENTS

「感謝家人支持，也感謝上蒼，
　　　讓我做了這件有意義的工作。」

THE RESEARCH CENTER, the National Institute of Development Administration (Thailand) kindly granted research funds to conduct various research projects across Thailand in 2010-2018. During the 8-year period while undertaking ethnography, I was also supported financially by the Graduate School of Language and Communication and the International College at the National Institute of Development Administration. I also received extensive help from the Indiana University-Bloomington (USA) and the Language Center, the Asian Institute of Technology-Intergovernmental Organization (Thailand campus). I was associated closely with the United Nations (Economic and Social Commission for Asia and the Pacific or UN-ESCAP) as the United Nations Consultant Roster Member in Bangkok duty station.

Some parts of this book are based on materials that were previously published in referred journals and presented in conferences. I am grateful for permission to reproduce some sentences, paragraphs and pages of copyrighted material.

期刊文章和研討會論文修潤成書：

這本小書源自我在期刊發表的六篇論文以及在泰國國家發展研究院50週年校慶發表的研討會論文。

1. Lee, Hugo, Y.-H. (2011). English language teaching at expenses of Thai language teaching for urban refugee language learners in Thailand: Social inequalities related to what languages to teach. *Journal of Language Teaching and Research, 2* (4), 810-815. Reprinted with permission.

2. Lee, Hugo, Y.-H. (2011). English for communication purposes among non-native speaking heterogeneous urban refugees in Thailand: Discouragement in bilingual and biliteracy development, *Modern Journal of Applied Linguistics, 3* (2), 237-253. Reprinted with permission.

3. Lee, Hugo, Y.-H. (2012). English for the purpose of reducing the poverty of orphans with disabilities in Thailand, *Journal of Education and Practice, 3* (6), 87-99. Reprinted with permission.

4. Lee, Hugo, Y.-H. (2013). Bargirl style of language choice and shift: A tale from the land of smile. *Theory and Practice*

in Language Studies, 3 (3), 411-422. Reprinted with permission.

5. Lee, Hugo, Y.-H. (2014). Speaking like a love entrepreneur: Language choices and ideologies of social mobility among daughters of peasants in Thailand's tourist sites. *Language, Discourse and Society, 3*(1), 110-143. – International Sociological Association Reprinted with permission.

6. Lee, Hugo, Y-H. (2016). English language learning in the margins: Toward a movement to help service-industry workers in Thailand. *Theory and Practice in Language Studies, 6*, (4), 649-662. Reprinted with permission.

7. Lee, Hugo, Y.-H. (2017). Sufficiency economy and nonprofit management in the margins: A pilot study of foreign language education as a pathway to achieve sufficiency economy from Thailand's underworld. Paper presented on National Institute of Development Administration 50th Year Anniversary Conference. Reprinted with permission.

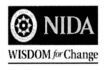 Research projects (reported as book chapters) have received funding from the National Institute of Development Administration.

Author and Emeritus President
of National Institute of Development Administration
Professor Dr. Sombat Thamrongthanyawong
**(Dubbed the "Rising World Leader"
by Time Magazine, 1974**
時代雜誌評選為1974世界領導新秀)
who constantly encouraged author to apply for
Associate Professorship, hereby author
decided to write this book as an application material

推薦序

　　李育修以一位在泰國生活的台灣人為出發點，撰寫出真實生活於當地才能體會的經驗。語言作為一個橋樑在任何地方都是不可或缺的條件，但語言並非只要講就代表能溝通，更需考量場所與情境的適用性。了解草根性語言可說是認識俗民文化的關鍵環節，更是台灣人前往泰國工作、旅遊、移民的最佳起手式。

　　相信李博士的著作定能幫助到更多現在或未來將前往泰國的台灣人，使台灣與泰國間的交流能隨著使用合適的語言更加廣泛，並期盼讀者能夠過此書的閱讀拉近台灣與泰國間的友誼，達到真正的台泰交流。

洪銘謙

台灣泰國交流協會秘書長

序于國立成功大學

推薦序

　　前瞻東協！本人創立的「香港華僑陳就娣紀念中心」，自2012年六月開始和四方報合作推出「免費學東南亞七國語言計劃」，在台灣推廣東南亞的語言文化！

　　今天大家也可以透過李博士的文章，獨特的視角觀點，認識泰國的基層社會及庶民文化！更可對東協的崛起有更深入的了解！

李三財

「就諦學堂」創辦人
序于國立台北商業大學

美國社會語言學家推薦序

FOREWORD

Foreword by USA-based Sociolinguist

作者恩師──美國印第安那大學副教授
美國賓夕維尼亞大學博士
前美國普林斯頓大學講師
Serafin M. Coronel-Molina

The social, linguistic, cultural, political, and economical reality of indigenous and minoritized people is changing by leaps and bounds around the world. The asymmetrical relationships of power, ideology, politics and economy are tremendous forces that cause a range of inequalities and injustices, and oppressions at all levels that end up increasing the gap between the haves and the have-nots.

Social phenomena such as war, famine, poverty, natural disasters, racial/ethnic cleansing, and political and religious persecutions can generate a host of displacements and diaspora movements (voluntary and involuntary migrations). Lack of opportunities for education and good health can also initiate waves of migration worldwide.

When people immigrate to a new social and physical space, they have to face the new ways of being, seeing, knowing and experiencing the world. This situation becomes even more challenging when linguistic differences are added to the cultural. For instance,

"many minorities do not possess sufficient political, economic, social or linguistic capital vis-à-vis the dominant, privileged sectors of society.

This reality puts the minority population at a disadvantage and creates some stumbling blocks in their quest to achieve linguistic inclusion and social justice.
These excluded populations are condemned to live on the margins or peripheries of society. "

In this sense, this volume entitled *Language and Minority in the Making of Thailand* by Hugo Yu-Hsiu Lee, constitutes a singular contribution that explores issues such as language poverty, language and economy, and language and development from an interdisciplinary perspective. The book is composed of seven chapters, with a primary focus on the relationship between foreign- and second-language teaching and learning, bilingualism and individual multilingualism, and the struggles of minority populations to integrate into the mainstream society of Thailand. The book also links economic disadvantages to educational disadvantages from sociolinguistic and ecological perspectives. In other words, it provides past and present accounts of the strategic bi- and multilingual language use of minorities such as orphans with disabilities, bar girls, asylum seekers, migrant workers and urban refugees in Bangkok.

In a nutshell, *Language and Minority in the Making of Thailand* encapsulates fundamental debates on language, inequality, poverty, education, economy and development. The insightful content of this book discusses pivotal topics in sociolinguistics, linguistic anthropology and applied linguistics in relation to linguistic and political economy, using linguistic ethnography as the methodology. It will be a compelling and useful read for anyone interested in language rights and language practices in contact situations, in this part of the world or any other.

Serafin M. Coronel-Molina

Associate Professor & Sociolinguist
Indiana University-Bloomington, USA
美國印第安那大學副教授
當代前20社會語言學家

泰國語言學家推薦序

FOREWORD

Foreword by Thailand-based Linguist

Hugo Yu-Hsiu Lee has been researching, documenting, and advocating for linguistic minorities on the social periphery of Thailand since 2010. Working in diverse social contexts, Hugo has correctly diagnosed

"the poverty and hardship that migrants, refugees, and other ethnic minorities, including youth and sex workers, face in Thailand."

His work has especially

"stressed the need to succeed in learning languages, whether Thai, English, Chinese, or Japanese, in order for the socially excluded to better their own situations and those of their dependents and families."

Facing up to this challenge, Hugo has promoted language teaching for social inclusion in the literature, to institutions, to the United Nations, and in his own praxis.

This volume assembles seven chapters, in part derived from Hugo's academic articles, which together document his quest to improve the lives of the marginalized by providing them with the linguistic abilities to integrate and succeed.

Hugo is based at the National Institute of Development Administration (Bangkok), and recently, the UN has recognized his commitment, awarding him consultant status with UN ESCAP. Hugo is still youthful and has decades of work ahead of him. Hopefully, as he progresses, his commitment and his direct approach to solving social problems at the coalface will be recognized more widely and emulated by others. I wish him well in his endeavors and hope Hugo's good planning and determination will see him through another decade of activism, through to a second volume of his collected works.

Faithfully and in Peace,

John Draper

Khon Kaen University, Thailand

泰國孔敬大學

日本語言學家推薦序

FOREWORD

Foreword by Japan-based Linguist

It has now been quite some years since I first met and came to know the work and activities of my friend and colleague I shall here simply call "Hugo" as I have affectionately come to know him. I have read hundreds of pages of his writings, especially those dealing with the

"minorities, the exploited, the neglected, and even the endangered who are given opportunities to acquire competence in English by those like Hugo who are willing and able to afford them these opportunities."

"Acquiring English opens the doors of opportunity to those who must have a tool such as this to survive in a harsh globalized world, a world which often seems devoid of simple compassion."

In these dark times in which we see the hatred and scorn of the "haves" of the world for migrant populations, we need to commit ourselves to bettering their lot. Do you who are reading this recall the young Syrian girl whose home area was under daily attack and who effectively used the English skills taught her by her English teacher mother, skills which allowed her by means of the Internet to be rescued along with her mother and younger brother and thereby shown a way out of the living hell of a horrifying and agonizing death for her and her family? Those like her must not be cast aside and I think Hugo has shown the way forward.

Jack M. Clontz

Emeritus Professor

Maebashi Kyoai Gakuen International College, Japan

日本前橋共愛學園國際學院

目錄　CONTENTS

第一部　導言

Part *1*　Introduction

Chapter 1

Language-Support Programs To Help Achieve Sufficiency Economy & Sustainable Development in The Margins　*62*

第一章

自給自足經濟、可持續發展、社會基層的非營利組織管理與雙語、多語之學習和使用的關聯性　*62*

第二部　殘疾孤兒的英語學習

Part 2 Issues in English Education for Orphans with Disabilities

泰國 **Map of Thailand**

緒論　INTRODUCTION

HUGO Y-H. LEE Ph.D.

National Institute of Development Administration

LANGUAGE & MINORITY
in the making of modern Thailand

THIS COLLECTION OF seven book chapters might straightforwardly have been named *Language, Poverty, Inequality and Development*. Nearly all of the book chapters are primarily concerned in one way or another with *Language and Poverty, Language and Economy or Language and Development*. Seven chapters in this book can be roughly summed up as the scientific interdisciplinary study of the specific connection between foreign/second learning, bi-/multilingualism in individual levels and economic integration and social development for those marginalized and impoverished in a developing country.

How does the language a person speaks, reads & writes affect one's opportunity to hold what types of job, and be economically successful or unsuccessful?

Lower socioeconomic status is in a negative association with adverse economic and social outcomes for minority peoples. This book links economic disadvantages to educational disadvantages, particularly with regard to disparities to access educational resources to learn a foreign/second language between those rich and those impoverished.

The Language Solutions concept has evolved from some fundamental ideas in applied linguistics research and sociolinguistics research in the grass-root level. It has combined economic and social aspects towards an integrated approach to equip minority communities with ecosystems (tools and resources) to become functional bi-/multilinguals while fostering their sustainable economic and social development.

本書目的　Purposes of This Book

This Book Calls for Minority peoples (in developing countries) are encouraged to use the power of dominant languages (particularly, English) as tools to build their futures

Language and Minority in the Making of Modern Thailand: Towards Development and Social Change is intended to provide a recent review of the past decade and a recent understanding about strategic bi-/multilingual language use among marginalized populations, labelled as minority peoples (e.g., orphans with disabilities, bargirls, asylum seekers and urban refugees), in Thailand's capital, Bangkok City. The book aims to reveal inequality in access to acquire English and inequality in educational resources to obtain fluency of other dominant (foreign/second) languages, particularly with an emphasis on Chinese and Japanese, all of which are unequally distributed to the poor, marginalized and vulnerable groups (compared to the elite class who has almost exclusive access to English and other dominant languages to legitimize their status in the social hierarchy).

This book is also used as a databank on descriptions of language and poverty, language and minority peoples, language and economic growth, and language and development complied for the past decade (2010-2018) in Thailand.

Chronic low-income and long-term poverty in individual, family and national levels remain a constant issue to overcome. This book helps understand the mechanisms through which foreign/second (bi-/multilingual) language competence in the individual level affect one's economic, social and sustainable developments. Understanding these above-mentioned mechanisms might have policy, research and practical implications for educational and social policy in national, regional and international levels.

Mainstream English and other dominant languages (e.g., Chinese) to overcome poverty and attain development for the marginalized and vulnerable groups in developing countries

This book invites readers to join an important debate in which economists, linguists and development agents are often at odds to the relationships between language, inequality, poverty, education, economy and development.

Rationale to Write This Book

Over 24 years ago, William Smalley's (1994) book titled *Linguistic Diversity and National Unity: Language Ecology in Thailand* (published by the University of Chicago Press) was considered well-written, at that time, to provide the most comprehensive and the best account of sociolinguistic situations in Thailand. 24 years have passed since the publication of William Smalley's landmark book (1994), writing in mid-2018, I face the challenge of finding relevance from William Smalley's book chapters and a fair number of one-off articles (published from 1990s to 2010s by, for example, Taylor and Francis Group, Elsevier, Routledge, Sage and Willey-Blackwell) to my own applied linguistics research and sociolinguistics fieldwork undertaken in Thailand (2010-2018). I would argue that William Smalley's oft-cited classic is incomplete because it largely does not take account of the poor and marginalized, vulnerable socioeconomic groups who do not fit into the category of Thailand's ethnic minority but are considered the urban poor (e.g., orphans with and without disabilities, bargirls, masseuses, restaurant waiters and waitress, street teen workers, domestic workers, asylum seekers and urban refugees, all of whom have contributed to form a lower-income social class in the contemporary Thai society). More than two decades after the publication by the father of Thailand's sociolinguistics (William Smalley, 1994) and at the time of writing this book, it is witnessed that the rapid pace of change in the contemporary Thailand, particularly with increasingly new and dynamic changes brought about conjointly by forces of globalization, regionalization and so on, deserve a new investigation.

本書使用的理論框架和研究方法
Theoretical & Methodological Approaches

Seven chapters in this book represent a broad range of studies in bi-/multilingualism, foreign/second language learning and sociolinguistics fieldwork, in association with political economy (theoretically) and linguistic ethnography (methodologically). Drawing on theoretical approaches from political economy and methodological approaches from linguistic ethnography, the book has included empirical and interpretative ethnographic research (also widely known as sociolinguistics research and linguistic anthropology research) in bi-/multilingual contexts: Orphanages (English-speaking western Christian missionaries versus Thai orphans with and without disabilities), bars/workplace settings (expatriates versus Isaan-dominant bargirls), and refugee centers, just to name a few examples.

Political economy (see definitions by Susan Gal in her pioneer work in 1989; also see a recent update by David Block in 2017 for the linkage between language and economy), particularly the issue of inequality (ample or limited opportunities to access English and other dominant languages) in relation to social class, is adopted as the conceptual frame for research and implications throughout the book. Viewed from the political economy perspective (Gal, 1989; Block, 2017), linguistic skills (individual or group levels) in English and other dominant languages are regarded as economic resources and valued competences. Thus, skills in these dominant languages including English, in effects, have been commodified and have become mediators to jointly contribute to the inequality in employment opportunities (job markets), income disparities and upward mobility in societies.

Grounded in Hymes (1974), the author of this book enacts as a linguistic ethnographer and analyzes linguistic data, aimed to develop in-depth understandings of small communities studied, as well as to draw implications to societies at large.

本書結構

Overview of Chapters & Suggestions of Reading this Book

CHAPTER 1-7 Cooperative projects undertaken in Thailand (2010-2018) from three different groups of minority peoples are included in this book.

CHAPTER 1 One introductory chapter (part 1: chapter 1) provides a context for the nonprofit and NGO's social work (Teaching English is a fundamental component of their social work) to help Thailand's minority peoples achieve sufficiency economy and sustainable development.

CHAPTER 2 One of the projects (part 2: chapter 2) was completed in various orphanages in 2012 where Christian English teachers helped Thai orphans with (and without) disabilities learn English, as a means to increase opportunities for orphans' employment.

CHAPTER 3-5 Projects reported in Chapter 3-5 (part 3) offer an analysis of income disparities in the service sector (with a particular focus on workers in massage parlors and bars) between those who learn dominant languages (e.g., English, Chinese and Japanese) or those who do not.

CHAPTER 6-7 In addition to addressing these challenges faced by national and domestic minority groups (e.g., orphans, massage therapists, bargirls and love entrepreneurs) in Thailand, this book turns to address issues in language learning (language education) and language use (communication) for refugees resettled to Thailand in early 2010-2011's (part 4: chapter 6-7). As it turns out, refugee children, youth and adults face additional challenges in accessing dominant/foreign/second language learning opportunities and resources than those who are considered domestic minority peoples.

本書收錄了李育修博士有關泰國曼谷基層社會人士語言學習和使用的七篇文章，透過策略性雙語和多語等第二語言和外語學習進而達成可持續性發展目標，將語言和經濟、社會發展之間的關聯性做了詮釋。

　　本書的第一章就整個〈充足經濟、可持續發展、社會基層的非營利組織管理與雙語、多語之學習和使用的關聯性〉做個基本概論，並且綜述非營利和非政府組織提供的英語教學以達到自給自足經濟為目標。

　　第2部〈孤兒和少年殘疾人的英語學習〉〈從有特殊需要（殘疾）的孤兒來看學習英語對減少貧困的承諾〉一文中探討基督教宣教士替孤兒院（殘疾和非殘疾）院童提供英語教學活動的影響，雖數據不具絕對性，本稿確認其能改善院童長大後的實質經濟狀況。

　　第3部〈基層服務業和特種行業雇員的語言學習和使用〉〈按摩師、餐廳服務生的雙語、多語之學習和使用〉一文則是嘗試個案分析和比較第二語言、外語對幾位服務業基層人士的不同程度的影響，本稿顯然提出雙語和多語能力有利創造更多就業機會、促進職場升遷、發展個人經濟實力等有力證據，不容否認。

　　第4部用兩章的篇幅〈第六章　難民孩童的的語言教育議題〉〈第七章　成人難民的語言和溝通議題〉講述在公元2010年代早期，到曼谷尋求政治庇護的難民面對的語言教育問題和語言溝通使用議題。

參考文獻 REFERENCES

David Block

1. Block, D. (2017). Political economy in applied linguistics research. *Language Teaching, 20* (1), 32-64.

Susan Gal

2. Gal, S. (1989). Language and political economy. *Annual Review of Anthropology*, 18, 345–367.

Dell Hymes

3. Hymes, D. (1974). *Foundations of sociolinguistics.* London: Tavistock.

William A. Smalley

4. Smalley, W. (1994). *Linguistic diversity and national unity: Language ecology in Thailand.* Chicago: The University of Chicago Press.

PROLOGUE

從台灣籍美國學者，成為泰國當代「草根語言教育家」和聯合國顧問

近代東協語言學界最神的神話之一
The Years Everything in My World Changed

I AM A global citizen. In relatively early age, I have lived and worked in the world's developed and developing countries in North America, East Asia and Southeast Asia. First, I was born and raised in Taiwan (1978-2005) and educated in USA in my early twenties (2005-2010). When I was a young adult, two particular experiences in Kaohsiung (Taiwan) and Bangkok (Thailand) helped to shape the person I am today. Back in 2004-2005, I was accidentally involved in providing informal language education for the first time as a potential solution to social problems in Taiwan. I got involved my language teaching as social work with a teenage lady with a number of disabilities from birth (e.g., heart attack symptoms), because she often washed my hair in a barber shop & hair salon. She never completed her primary education in Taiwan, largely because of her disabilities. By the time she turned to her 15-17, she was earning a living in this barber shop & hair salon where she washed my hair and came up with an idea to receive a certificate of equivalent middle-school education without going through a formal education. The first thing I did was to provide free English tutorial lessons in her barber shop & hair salon preparing her to take the examination, thereby she could obtain an equivalent middle-school education certificate. To be born with multiple disabilities and was in desperate need to learn English in a barber shop & hair salon to be certified with a basic (secondary) educational attainment is not something to wish on anyone. Across my life journey in three countries and United Nations, what began in a barber shop & hair salon of Taiwan has become a lifelong calling. My experience in this barber shop & hair salon in 2004-2005 was my first step in a journey over the past fifteen years to advocate micro language planning, informal and self-paced foreign/second language learning, competent and strategic bi-/multilingual use to solve social problems (such as poverty, lower educational attainment and unemployment) that continues to this day in 2018.

Back in the early 2010, I moved from Bloomington, Indiana (USA), to live in Bangkok, as a son-in-law of Thailand's Chachoengsao. Starting in August 2010, my first job in the Kingdom was to teach research methodologies in applied linguistics (language and communication major) for doctoral students in Royal Thai government's postgraduate-only institute. This is the second time in my life I was involved in addressing issues in poverty, because poverty was all over minority communities across the Bangkok City where I have lived for the past 9 years. In contrast with Taiwan and USA, poverty and hardship are seemed rather apparent to the middle and lower-class of Thailand. I found it increasingly a difficult task to lecture some old-school theories and practices in the field of language education, applied linguistics and sociolinguistics in the high-tech classroom with Thai PhD students while the minority communities across Thailand outside my classroom were in need of possible language solutions to their economic and social problems. Later, I found out that I felt the emptiness of theories and practices of conventional language education studies, applied linguistics and sociolinguistics I learned from Indiana University (USA) and journals (e.g., Routledge). After I asked myself, it seemed to me that all that I was trying to do was to undertake ethnography on micro language planning, practical language pedagogies and informal language learning resources that emerged from the peripheral world and helped minority populations learned foreign/second languages (e.g., English, Mandarin and Japanese) and became competent and strategic bi-/multilingual language users. Finally, I decided to create a database that indexed the ways in which orphans with and without disabilities, Isaan bargirls from peasant families in Thailand's impoverished North-east, asylum seekers and urban refugees (from Sri Lanka, Congo, Myanmar, Pakistan and

Somalia), and children and adolescents born of cross-cultural families (from Bangladesh, Nigeria and Philippines) learned and used foreign/second languages as a means to help them achieve sustainable development goals. I succeed in creating a database to show that increasing income and ultimately achieving sustainable development by strategic bi-/multilingual language solutions is not as difficult as what is imagined by the general public.

反映庶民生活和社會基層民眾的語言學理論在哪裡？

2005年到2018年是我對社會問題態度和看法的關鍵轉折期。2005年，我到美國印第安那大學讀研究所，主修語言教育。我讀的書和期刊從Chomsky以降，許多大師（從早期的Dell Hymns、John Gumperz、Joshua Fishman到近代Alastair Pennycook等人）都提出語言教學、第二語言習得、社會語言使用等理論。

2010年，當時我畢業後在位於泰國曼谷的國家發展研究院任教，擔任語言和溝通學院博士班質性研究方法論的講師。在課堂上教授當代應用語言學和社會語言學時，我才發現西方學界的教科書和期刊文章老早就對幾乎所有課堂上的語言教學和語言學習等議題都有既定的解答和學術理論來作解釋，即便今日大多數研究語言教育的學者，大都以教室內的學習為主，缺乏教室外的深度田野調查，這種針對局部性語言教學和學習的研究,是無法得知全貌。

一旦走出教室，使用田野調查的方法探索真實庶民和底層民眾的語言學習方法和使用方式，西方的理論和觀念卻常常使不出力來。

我才知道我必須暫時和西方為主的語言學習理論抽離，才能真實地了解所謂弱勢雙語、多語者的世界。我開始走訪了曼谷的弱勢群體，蒐集語料，並試著由他們的眼光來了解第二語言和外語在生活扮演的角色。原來變成雙語和多語者是擺脫貧窮、發達經濟的辦法。且在有侷限的資源當中，不同社會基層群體仰賴不同學習模式來習得第二語言和外語。

本書基於這些基層的田野調查經驗，另立新說。

International College

國際學院

National Institute of Development Administration

國家發展研究院

Bangkok曼谷, 2018

第一部　導言

Part 1. Introduction

CHAPTER 1

Language-Support Programs To Help Achieve Sufficiency Economy & Sustainable Development in The Margins

non-profits & NGOs

FROM THAILAND'S UNDERWORLD

第一章

自給自足經濟、可持續發展、社會基層的非營利組織管理與雙語、多語之學習和使用的關聯性

A KEY CHALLENGE to nonprofit organizations and non-governmental groups (NGOs)today is to develop the economies and societies for minority peoples.Traditionally, nonprofits and NGOs have relied on humanitarian-based programs (for instance, medical services),but recently many of them have turned to foreign/second language-support programs and explored the possibility of offering the English language courses. In this light, the view that sufficiency economy is one of the prospects for change adopted by nonprofits and NGOs toward today's minority peoples has long been uncontroversial.Yet, research into nonprofit management has historically and consistently failed to adopt a sufficiency economy perspective to fully understand the extent to which informal and private foreign/second language-support programs (provided by nonprofits and NGOs) play a crucial role in helping minority peoples achieve the sufficient economy goals. The present study (as reported in the chapter), which draws on data from the fieldwork of nonprofits and NGOs in Thailand, examines a form of private education – informal foreign/second language-support programs – that adopt the sufficiency economy approach.

GLOBALLY, MARGINALIZED GROUPS have not equally benefited from the mainstream (formal) foreign/second language education programs. Increasingly, inappropriate formal foreign/second language education is regarded as one of the key factors in the persistence of marginalization of minority peoples. Notwithstanding the documented progress in the mainstream applied linguistics of formal foreign language education over the past decades, there is little understanding of the extent to which a lack of appropriate informal foreign/second language learning affects minority people's lives to achieve the sufficiency economy goals. Despite these aforementioned challenges and knowledge gaps, the study found that there have been a number of promising practices of sufficiency economy philosophy by nonprofit organizations and NGOs. Informal foreign/second language-support programs are adopted as a tool, thereby some programs have gone out of their way to help realizing sufficiency economy of minority peoples.

ACKNOWLEDGMENTS

The original study reported in chapter 1 was peer-reviewed by organizing committee members of Research Center, National Institute of Development Administration for Foundation-Day Conference 2017.

摘要

　　非營利組織和非政府組織（NGO）面臨的主要挑戰是如何促進社會底層弱勢民眾的經濟和社會發展。傳統上，非營利組織和非政府組織一直採行人道主義的方案（例如說醫療服務），但最近已轉向外語培訓項目,尤其是探討對一些社會基層弱勢民眾提供英語課程的可能性。自給自足經濟 (Sufficiency Economy) 的觀念是非營利組織和非政府組織對當今社會基層弱勢民眾採取變革前景之一的觀點，這早已在學界不存在爭議。然而，研究非營利組織管理的學者在學術文獻上甚少使用自給自足經濟的視角來充分理解非正式外語教學之項目(Informal Language Education)：由非營利組織和非政府組織所提供語言培訓項目(Language-Support Programs)，旨在幫助社會底層弱勢民眾實現自給自足經濟目標所需要發揮關鍵作用的雙語和多語能力。本章透過蒐集泰國非營利組織和非政府組織的實地調查數據，探討了一種非正規外語教育計劃,採用非正式語言教育形式，來達成自給自足經濟方法。

　　學校裡面失敗的正規外語教育被認為是社會基層弱勢民眾持續邊緣化的關鍵因素之一。儘管過去幾十年研究正規外語教育的應用語言學界取得了不錯的進展，但此學術圈內的學者缺乏對非正規外語教育和其對社會基層弱勢民眾實現自給自足經濟目標的關聯性還不甚了解。本章報導透過非正規外語教育為一種工具，某些非營利組織和非政府組織已經為社會底層弱勢民眾達到了一些自足經濟目標的實踐。

Introduction 導論

A KEY CHALLENGE to nonprofit and nongovernmental organizations (henceforth NGOs) today is to develop the economies and societies for minority peoples. Traditionally, nonprofits and NGOs have relied on humanitarian-based programs (for instance, medical services), but recently many of them have turned to foreign/second language-support programs and explored the possibility of offering the English language courses.

Nonprofit insights into sufficiency economy issues relating to informal foreign language learning, in a nutshell, are the focal point of this chapter. In this light, the chapter stresses the need to refine our current understanding, theories and practices around applied linguistics in foreign/second language education, which could be in connection to nonprofit management of sufficiency economy philosophy (see His Majesty King Bhumibol Adulyadej's sufficiency economy philosophy in Grossman & Faulder, 2011, p. 162-165, 187, 262, 265-279).

Background & Problem Statement
研究背景和問題陳述

Across the globe, formal foreign/second language education programs are at crisis (for instance, see Lu, 2012, for Hong Kong; see Skorton and Altschuler, 2012, for USA). On the one hand, all too soon attacks on formal foreign/second language education have grown intensely. It is in part due to that it fails to provide appropriate pedagogies for 1minority peoples. On the other hand, the mainstream applied linguistics researchers and formal foreign/second language teachers, consciously or unconsciously, have conspired to make the interdisciplinary study of nonprofit management in connection to informal foreign language learning less developed than it should have been. It is not surprising that the modern and western applied linguistics and the formal foreign language education sector have not arrived at an advanced theory to explicitly define terminologies and sufficiently provide conceptual lenses that distinguish and describe the social moment of teaching foreign languages (English, in particular) for social inclusion. Efforts by nonprofits and NGOs with an explicit goal to make the learning of privileged foreign/second languages, with a focus

---

[1] Criteria for the identification of minority peoples are in the sub-section of site and sample of the methodology section.

on English, more approachable, accessible and equitable for minority peoples are defined as **Teaching Foreign/Second Languages for Social Inclusion** and/or **Teaching English for Social Inclusion** in the present chapter.

Education, an essential part of people's lives, is the departure point of this chapter. In many developing countries, it is widely agreed that government schools play a crucial role in a country's educational sector and Thailand is the case at point. While the public school system has conventionally been a primary source of education for a country's general public, it should also be recognized that the informal education programs provided by nonprofits and NGOs serves a complementary role. Globally the non-public and informal education (also referred to as 'private education,' 'private schooling,' 'low-cost private schools') for minority peoples is rising (see The Economist: "For-profit education," 2015) and the view that a vibrant informal educational sector has a positive effect on a country's development economically and socially has long been accepted. Let's turn to Thailand. The public school system (provided by the government sector) is traditionally the largest source of education, but the role of education offered by nonprofits and NGOs particularly with regard to the informal foreign/second language education has increased over the years.

Speaking of formal (public) vis-à-vis informal (private) education, foreign/second language programs in formal and informal education sectors are generally known to be one of the most important development strategies for developing countries. Despite the significant role of foreign/second language education in a country's economic and social development, there is a long-term failure by academia to recognize the substantial heterogeneity across the formal educational sector and the informal counterpart. While there has been an upsurge in applied linguistics research to explore the formal foreign/second language education, few attempts have been made to explore the informal language education programs offered by nonprofits and NGOs that address the needs of minority peoples.

It is no overstatement to claim that hundreds of nonprofit and NGO development agents throughout developing countries are involved in development planning and implementation of such plans as **Teaching Foreign/Second Languages for Social Inclusion** and/or **Teaching English for Social Inclusion** through the teaching of privileged foreign/second languages and English in particular to minority peoples. A view that the mainstream applied linguistic perspective (for instance, views, theories and practices published by the *TESOL Quarterly* and the *RELC Journal*) continues to prevail in the informal educational sector designed for minority peoples and the teaching models produced by the mainstream formal foreign/second language teachers are followed universally by the nonprofit and NGO sector has not been critically examined and criticized. However, it is evident that researchers who produced the mainstream applied linguistics literature have not paid significant attention to informal foreign/second language teaching programs offered by nonprofits and NGOs for minority peoples (probably because such efforts are seemingly a daunting project). These development agents from the nonprofit and NGO sector devote to the language-support program (as their social movement) with an ambitious goal: to create more equal accesses and opportunities for communities and groups in the margins, defined as minority peoples in the present chapter, to learn privileged foreign/second languages and, particularly, English. In so doing, they might be one step close to achieve the sufficiency economy goals for minority peoples.

Purpose Statement 目的聲明

The purpose of the chapter is manifold: First, the introduction of this chapter explores the ambitious plans (or the daunting project) from these development agents – nonprofits and NGOs, and examines their strategies and efforts in informal foreign/second language-support programs from the perspective of nonprofit management in relation to the sufficiency economy philosophy (Grossman & Faulder, 2011, p. 162-165, 187, 262, 265-279).

Second, the chapter is a report of current actions, some promising practices and achieved progress to the sufficiency economy goals of a number of nonprofits and NGOs. Third, it also serves to offer concrete suggestions and policy recommendations for policy makers and practitioners.

Some possible approaches to accomplish these ambitious goals by nonprofits and NGOs are through nonprofit management, in conjunction with sufficiency economy philosophy (ibid), an inclusive perspective (see a more detailed explanation in literature review section), which acknowledges both developed and developing countries, placing Thailand within a more appropriate context of study. The present chapter is based on the premise that the informal foreign/second language-support programs offered by nonprofits and NGOs is beneficial for minority peoples and, as such, the experience of these development agents in Thailand has stood out as extraordinary examples of the extent to which sufficiency economy (ibid) might better be achieved for Thailand's minority peoples and there are important implications for elsewhere.

Reviews & Critiques of Literature
對既有文獻的評論與批評

The Current State of Applied Linguistics Literature in Foreign/Second Language Education
應用語言學文獻在外語教育領域的現狀

Increasingly, critiques are launched against traditional studies in applied linguistics and formal foreign/second language education that include those relating to minority peoples based largely on the mainstream classroom settings, instead of the informal educational settings (Mohanty, Panda, Phillipson, and Skutnabb-Kangas, 2009; Lee, 2016).

The formal foreign/second language education across mainstream public schools and colleges are something all of us are familiar with from our schooling experiences. Asian high school students and college students, for instance, take English as a foreign language. So does the majority of American high school students take Spanish as a foreign language. As such, the pedagogies for educating youth and young adults to become proficiency bilinguals and multilingual by means of public schooling are well documented by classroom-based research. Nonetheless, the mainstream foreign/second language education is a failed experiment for the majority of minority peoples. It is due to that the majority of the minority peoples (indigenous/tribal populations, immigrants, ethnic minorities and so forth) are not provided with appropriate foreign/second language education that would enable them to succeed in the school setting and the real world (Mohanty, Panda, Phillipson, and Skutnabb-Kangas, 2009).

> In his own words as Hugo Yu-Hsiu Lee (2016) noted, *"conventional research frameworks in language studies, and policies and practices in the language-education sector, have given little regard to language learning in the margins"* (p. 649).

The majority of classroom-based research on applied linguistics and formal foreign/second language education from 1970s until the early 2000s was outright 'minority blind.' Over the past forty years or so there have been a massive number of publications in the broadly defined field of applied linguistics detailing formal foreign/second language education for non-minority students in the mainstream classroom settings (There are some good examples from the *TESOL Quarterly* and *RELC*). Minority blindness means that there is neither recognition nor a response to the needs of the majority of minority peoples by the mainstream applied linguistics researchers and formal foreign/second language teachers. The resulting suffering for minority peoples is sobering – tens of millions of minority peoples are left behind with foreign/second language deficiency (reference to be added in the subsequent section). Such minority blindness is largely attributed to that the majority of mainstream applied linguistics researchers and formal foreign/second language teachers are from the predominantly Research I Institutes and the public school system, with little or no regard for low-income and vulnerable minority peoples' needs (Own Fieldwork, 2010-2017).

Nonetheless, there are only few exceptions to this trend as some publications discussing underprivileged groups in informal foreign/second language educational settings, including orphans with disabilities (Hugo Yu-Hsiu Lee, 2012), immigrant women (Hugo Yu-Hsiu Lee and Coronel-Molina, 2011), asylum seekers and refugees (Hugo Yu-Hsiu Lee, 2011), bargirls and love entrepreneurs (Hugo Yu-Hsiu Lee, 2013, 2014), street teenage workers (Hugo Yu-Hsiu Lee, 2016) and Christian missionary teachers and students with lower socioeconomic backgrounds (Wong and Canagarajah, 2009).

The Current State of Development Studies Literature

發展研究領域文獻的現狀

Over recent years, the modern development studies literature has come to address issues of inequality, poverty (Errico, 2017), irrigation and farming, inadequate infrastructure, gender and transportation (Kusakabe, 2012), urbanization and unemployment (Resnick and Thurlow, 2015) and so forth. Nevertheless, the development studies researchers might risk failing to address the foreign language deficit of the poor, marginalized and vulnerable (minority peoples), resulted largely from the poor formal foreign/second language education.

Scholarly literature related to development studies (development planning, sustainable development, social policy, sufficiency economy and so on) and applied linguistics of foreign/second language education in developing countries has not begun to incorporate with a greater extent of the former to the latter. Despite its importance, formal and informal foreign/second language education is often excluded from national and regional development planning. As such, the classic development studies literature provides fewer insights into what constitutes planning and implementation of informal foreign/second language-support programs in the nonprofit sector. There is a general neglect of **Teaching Foreign/Second Languages for Social Inclusion** and/or **Teaching English for Social Inclusion** among the mainstream development studies researchers and even the ground-level development agents assigned by the central governments and intergovernmental organizations. The reasons leading to the neglect of **Teaching Foreign/Second Languages for Social Inclusion** and/or **Teaching English for Social Inclusion** in the informal foreign/second language educational sector probably lie in that they are regarded as underground activities conducted by nonprofit organizations, but not in the to-do list (infrastructure, transport, and so forth) of central governmental agenda, in collaboration with intergovernmental organizations (the United Nations (UN), the World Health Organization (WHO) and the International Labor Organization (ILO) and so on).

Theoretical Frameworks 理論框架

The Adoption of Economy Sufficiency and Its Implication for Nonprofit Management

經濟自給自足理論的採用及其對非營利組織管理的啟示

Teaching Foreign/Second Languages for Social Inclusion and/or Teaching English for Social Inclusion are terminologies created by the author of the current chapter to describe efforts, movements and pedagogies that make the learning of privileged foreign/second languages and English in particular more approachable, accessible and equitable for individuals and groups in the margin (those most in need), otherwise known as minority peoples, by utilizing resources derived from nonprofits and NGOs. Enacting and participating in Teaching Foreign/Second Languages for Social Inclusion and/or Teaching English for Social Inclusion essentially means that informal foreign/second language teachers from nonprofits and NGOs provide the equal access of privileged foreign/second languages, with a focus on English, to certain lower-skilled groups and individuals in the margins, recognized as minority peoples, who do not traditionally access to these privileged foreign/second languages (e.g., English) and educational resources.

Moreover, with regard to the theoretical approaches adopted for the chapter, the conceptual shift (from 'mainstream' or 'center' to 'minority' or 'peripheral') moves its focus away from analytical frameworks that exclude minority peoples' interests and towards more efforts to meet minority peoples' needs. It is in spite of two lines of theoretical underpinnings seemingly run parallel to one another, one premised on nonprofit management and the other premised on sufficiency economy (see His Majesty King Bhumibol Adulyadej's sufficiency economy philosophy in Grossman and Faulder, 2011, p. 162-165, 187, 262, 265-279). They are interrelated components as analytical frameworks and intertwined in a dynamic fashion in the present chapter. In so doing, the adoption of the philosophy of sufficiency economy (ibid) as part of the nonprofit management has been identified as particularly an important consideration to help nonprofits and NGOs achieve their development goals.

In a time when the dominance of western economic theories continues to prevail in developing countries, nonprofit and NGO development agents have followed western development theories framed by western epistemologies and terminologies rooted in claims of universal relevance. The economy sufficiency philosophy (ibid), however, arises from a growing awareness that there is an urgent need for the adoption of a national - regional development approach that is grounded in the local context. Thus, the economy sufficiency philosophy (ibid) emerges by considering development of economies and societies must proceed from lower to higher stages, with a focus on the adoption of the 'secure foundation' ready and operational by the majority of participants who are likely to become contributors of the economic growth. As it turns out, the economy sufficiency philosophy (ibid) plays a fundamental role in transforming more than 23,000 villages throughout Thailand as a pathway to a more sustainable prosperity.

Method 研究方法

Research Questions
探討的問題

The chapter pursues the answer to the question poised below: To what extent the sufficiency economy philosophy is adopted by nonprofit and nongovernmental organizations (NGOs), and by means of what approaches and methods they achieve the sufficiency economy goals?

Sites and Samples
田野調查的地點和樣本

The primary investigative site is the state capital of Thailand – Bangkok. The site is selected in part largely because the majority of international nonprofit organizations and NGOs stay in Bangkok (headquartered in Bangkok), despite some of their presences are nearly everywhere throughout Thailand. Moreover, semi-urban and semi-rural areas (bordered with Bangkok) are also surveyed in the study reported in this chapter.

TABLE 1.1: Key characteristics of the database
used in the analysis of sufficiency economy and nonprofit
management in the margins of Thailand

Variables	Database		
Time Coverage	December 2016 – March 2017 (pilot study) April 2017 – ongoing (subsequent study)		
Spatial Coverage Sample	Thailand: Bangkok City; Central Region; Northern Region; and Eastern Region		
Data sources: Personal Interview Surveys and Conversations	Nonprofit Organizations and NGOs: 7	Minority Peoples: 100 +	Scholarly articles (Documents; journal articles & book chapters)

The participants of the study in part are nonprofit professionals from nonprofit organizations and NGOs who have resided in Thailand for at least 5 years. The sample of nonprofit professionals is made up of 7 participants consisting of 2 Americans, 1 Singaporean, 1 Swedish, 1 Taiwanese and 2 Thais. All nonprofit professionals who participate in the study vary in regards to their age, educational attainment, socioeconomic status and years of stay in Thailand. The demographic profile and data of the participants from the nonprofit and NGO sector are in TABLE 1.2.

TABLE 1.2: The demographic data
and profile of nonprofit and NGO participants

Nationality	Age Group	Gender	Years of Stay in Thailand	Number of minority peoples s/he helps with	Informal Classroom Setting
American	60 + 65	Man	40 +	Hundreds	Slums
American	60 + 65	Man	30 +	Hundreds	Slums
Singaporean	45 - 50	Woman	20 +	Hundreds	Orphanages
Swedish	50 - 60	Man	20 +	Hundreds	Orphanages
Taiwanese	35 - 40	Man	7	10 - 20	Bars; Streets
Thai	25 - 30	Woman	25 + (Native to Thailand)	30 - 50	Slums
Thai	About 30	Woman	30 + (Native to Thailand)	30 - 50	Slums

Advocates who foster their commitments in support of **Teaching Foreign/Second Languages for Social Inclusion** and/or **Teaching English for Social Inclusion** would agree that this aforementioned social movement might be an individual activity by one or two individual development agents (even the only individual development agent who conducts planning and implemented these efforts is affiliated with a global-wide nonprofit organization). Field-site visits are paid to 7 nonprofit and NGO professionals, who are poised to designate informal foreign/second language-support programs for the purpose of making privileged foreign/second languages and English in particular more approachable, accessible and equitable to minority peoples across vulnerable communities. Unless otherwise specified, the chapter takes greater account of minority peoples and they are classified and defined according to a combination of criteria, including those of socially excluded populations and lower-income persons. A survey of over 100 minority peoples is also included in the database.

TABLE 1.3: Criteria for identification of minority peoples
附表 1.3: 弱勢族群的定義

李育修製表

Meanings of 'minority'	
Minority1: (aspects of ethnicity and race)	The politics of not belonging (one who has a sense of not being a member of the dominant ethnic group within a nation state)–'involves constructing and keeping in public view its negative counterpart of not belonging,' defined by the social majority and the differentiation is based on some noticeable appearances and characteristics, e.g., ethnicity (ethnic looking), wealth, among others.
Minority2: (social and economic levels)	Social and economic marginality ('inability' of the 'socially excluded' to access ostensibly 'normal' and routine services and aspects of our shared cultural life) -- collective rights or civil rights that are not equally accessible to some impoverished and disenfranchised members in a society.
Minority3: (formal educational settings)	The extent to which minority children and teens are prevented from achieving their full potentials in schools or being forced to be out of schools when their lives and cultures are labeled as marginal in formal educational settings -- deficit thinking is the ideology and the discursive practice of holding lower expectations of academic achievements for students with demographics that do not match the traditional

85

	school system (e.g., low-income, culturally and linguistically diverse students, and out-of-school street children and teens).
Minority4: (value attribution of languages)	Marginalized in language learning -- inequality in a 'symbolic' linguistic 'market,' linguistic hierarchy and 'linguistic imperialism,' difficulty in foreign/second language learning, and language education (of prestige standard varieties) only accessible for elites.

Sources: Bourdieu, 1991; Pickering, 2001; Shields, Bishop and Mazawi, 2005; Winlow and Hall, 2013; and Lee, 2016

It should be noted that there are different terms adopted to refer to the poor, lower-skilled groups and vulnerable minority peoples at the national and international level, ranging from "socially and economically disadvantaged people," "students with lower-income backgrounds," or simply "minority," "minorities," "minority groups," "minority individuals," to "marginalized groups".

Research Instruments, Procedure of Data Collection and Analysis

研究工具、資料採集程序和資料分析方法

The study reported in this chapter adopts the qualitative approach in data collection and analysis. More explicitly, interviews and conversations with the nonprofit professionals are recorded and transcribed. The primary data for the study are gathered from a 20-topic interview administered to 7 nonprofit and NGO professionals in the Bangkok City. The data, reported in the present study are collected over a period of 4 months (December 2016 – March 2017). To speed up the data collection, the principal investigator (author) adopts the convenient sampling strategy by requesting assistance and help from his affiliated nonprofit organizations and NGOs. The data collected is analyzed adopting the content analysis convention.

Results 研究發現

Informal Foreign/Second Language Education for Minority Peoples Gain Momentum as Informed by Sufficiency Economy Perspective

The most significant theme that emerges from the data analysis is that the sufficiency economy philosophy is strongly in connection to the legacy of nonprofits and NGOs. This can be summarized as follows. It has become clear that despite most of the nonprofits and NGOs surveyed have some key features in common, they are all, with no exceptions, intended for the poor, lower-skilled, marginalized groups, labeled as minority peoples, to achieve the individual self-sufficiency economy goals. Yet, achieving sufficiency economy for minority peoples in Thailand requires a wide range of economic activities. However, they focus on engaging minority peoples to the informal foreign/second language-support programs in order to create, for instance, the English-speaking competitive advantage for minority peoples. These aforementioned foreign/second language-support programs in private and informal settings provide a way of defining the meaning of sufficiency economy, as seen from the perspective of nonprofit management. Following capacity planning and implementation of plans to promote foreign/second languages as part of the development process termed 'capacity building,' nonprofits and NGOs that are studied emphasize explicitly at varying degrees the teaching and the learning of English, or Chinese (Mandarin), or Japanese. To that end, nonprofit and NGO professionals who adopt sufficiency economy frameworks are against the backdrop of the failure of formal foreign/second language educational programs across public schools and colleges.

In the result section, the author compares different informal English language programs implemented by different nonprofits and NGOs. Data demonstrates that in a general sense, nonprofits and NGOs that support orphanages and help orphaned children and youth outperform those support and help slum children and slum youth. It is unfortunate but true that some slum children and slum teenagers are placed in the informal English language courses by their parents with the wrong financial incentives. These aforementioned children and youth in the slum are to cater nonprofit and NGO English teachers in order to give their parents a chance to exploit resources and materials brought in to the slum by nonprofits and NGOs. By contrast, social workers and volunteers in collaboration with nonprofits and NGOs in orphanages show higher integrity and benevolence than those parents of slum children and slum teens.

PHOTO 1.1: *Debbie Crist*

Executive of Central Thailand Mission (NGO)

gave a lecture in English with Chinese translation from the author

March 10, 2018

圖1.1：泰國CTM非政府組織創辦人（右邊）的英文專題演講
由本書作者（左邊）擔任中英翻譯
2018年3月10日

Discussion and Conclusion
討論和結論

Discussion 討論

The calls for a locally-driven approach are echoed in the present study. The sufficiency economy philosophy provides a better sense of how local nonprofits and NGOs are managing their foreign/second language-support programs for the marginalized groups and individuals. I shall proceed by summarizing the essence of these activities here.

Despite some of the informal foreign/second language education programs surveyed in the study continue to generate a number of positive results, their programs proceed with developmental stages. This result derived from the study resonates the sufficiency economy philosophy (see His Majesty King Bhumibol Adulyadej's sufficiency economy philosophy in Grossman and Faulder, 2011, p. 162-165, 187, 262, 265-279) in part because it clearly states that progress from a family and a community to a country and its economies and societies are made by stages. English teachers from these nonprofits and NGOs surveyed adopt the 'middle-path' pedagogy by identifying stages-of-development with regards to their students' learning goals. The sufficiency economy, along with its implication for teachers, stresses moderation with limited lesson content and lesson delivery in order not to overwhelm students from lower-income families and marginalized groups. English teachers studied as research participants report that they begin with teaching alphabet and how to count one to ten, but never expect a deeper understanding of the English language within months.

Even as children and youth studied as research participants face learning challenges such as a lack of educational resources in their homes, communities and schools, they are rewriting traditional career paths to join newer business opportunities (tourism and transportation in particular), empowered by their English language proficiency with the help of nonprofits and NGOs. Despite they do not achieve a higher-level English proficiency, their moderate command of English is equated as part of the 'foundation' building as referred to in the sufficiency economy philosophy (ibid). Their English learning is essentially aimed at their (individual) long-term career development and is closely related to their self-sufficiency goals, despite their present-time lower-level English is viewed as a mere 'enough' to the long-term sustainable development in individual levels.

Conclusion 結論

Implications & Recommendations
本章的啟示和對未來這領域研究員的建議

Sufficiency economy is arguably one of the most important philosophies adopted by these nonprofits and NGOs in the study as reported in the current chapter. It is therefore argued here that, in developing countries, there is a need for significant attention paid on nonprofits and NGOs originated from or informed by the sufficiency economy philosophy, which pertains to informal foreign/second language-support program (with a focus on the teaching of the English language) for those at risk of being left behind.

Both historically and currently, there have been calls from the scientific community throughout the world for a search of alternatives away from the mainstream, modern and western perspective. In developing countries, such calls are most vocal in the nonprofit and NGO sector, among others. The exploration for non-western alternatives is gaining momentum where the local context appears to be disparate than the western settings. Data by nonprofits and NGOs in Thailand, for instance, shows that building on local experiences is of imperative and at the same time local experiences echo the locally-driven sufficiency economy philosophy. Sharing local language solutions from the perspective of nonprofit management and sufficiency economy philosophy result in better theory and practice in social sciences (applied linguistics of foreign/second language education is the case in point), and to actions for more inclusive and just society. In so doing, we might move closer to achieve equality, self-sufficiency and sustainability for the disadvantaged groups.

For further information about this chapter (if you want to discuss with the author), please contact:

Hugo Lee, Faculty Member

International College

National Institute of Development Administration

18th fl., Navamin Building, 118 Seri Thai Rd,

Khlong Chan, Bang Kapi, Bangkok 10240

Hugo Lee, Consultant Roster Member

United Nations

Economic & Social Commission for Asia & the Pacific

3rd fl., United Nations Conference Center, ESCAP HR

United Nations Building, 76 Rajadamnern Nok Ave

Bangkok 10200

T. 088-607-2560

E. hugoclubheart3@gmail.com   f Li Y-h Hugo

W. https://indiana.academia.edu/YuHsiuLee

參考文獻　　REFERENCES

Pierre Bourdieu

1. Bourdieu, P. (1991). *Language and symbolic power.* Cambridge: Polity.

United Nations
– International Labor Organization (ILO)

2. Errico, S. (2017). *The rights of indigenous peoples in Asia.* Geneva, Switzerland: International Labour Organization.

The Economist

3. For-profit education: The $1-a-week school. (2015, August 1). *The Economist.* Retrieved March 17, 2017,
   from:
   http://www.economist.com/news/leaders/21660113- private-schools-are-booming-poor-countries- governments-should-either-help-them-or-get-out.

4. Grossman, N., & Faulder, D. (2011). (eds.). *King Bhumibol Adulyadej: A life's work.* Singapore and Bangkok: Editions Didier Millet.

Kyoko Kusakabe

5. Kusakabe, K. (2012) (ed.). *Gender, roads and mobility in Asia.* Bourton on Dunsmore, Rugby:　Practical Action Publishing.

Hugo Yu-Hsiu Lee (李育修)

6. Lee, Hugo, Y.-H., & Coronel-Molina, S. M. (2011). Exploring biliteracy practices among immigrant women in Taiwan, *Internet Journal of Language, Society and Culture, 33,* 73-83.

7. Lee, Hugo, Y.-H. (2011). English language teaching at expenses of Thai language teaching for urban refugee language learners in Thailand: Social inequalities related to what languages to teach, *Journal of Language Teaching and Research, 2* (4), 810-815.

8. Lee, Hugo, Y.-H. (2012). English for the purpose of reducing the poverty of orphans with disabilities in Thailand, *Journal of Education and Practice, 3* (6), 87-99.

9. Lee, Hugo, Y.-H. (2014). Speaking like a love entrepreneur: Language choices and ideologies of social mobility among daughters of peasants in Thailand's tourist sites. *Language, Discourse and Society, 3* (1), 110-143.

10. Lee, Hugo, Y.-H. (2013). Bargirl style of language choice and shift: A tale from the land of smile. *Theory and Practice in Language Studies, 3* (3), 411-422.

11. Lee, Hugo, Y-H. (2016). English language learning in the margins: Toward a movement to help service- industry workers in Thailand. *Theory and Practice in Language Studies, 6,* (4), 649-662.

12. Lu, D. (2002). English medium teaching at crisis: Towards bilingual education in Hong Kong. Gema Online Journal of Language Studies, 2 (1). Retrieved March 16, 2017, from: eprints.ukm.my/223/1/GemaVol2.1.2002No5.pdf

13. Pickering, M. (2001). *Stereotyping: The politics of representation.* New York, NY: Palgrave.

14. Resnick, D., & Thurlow, J. (2015). *African youth and the persistence of marginalization: Employment, politics, and prospects for change.* London and New York: Routledge.

15. Shields, C. M., Bishop, R., & Mazawi, A. E. (2005). Pathologizing practices: The impact of deficit thinking on education. New York, NY: Peter Lang.

16. Skorton, D., & Altschuler, G. (2012, August). America's foreign language deficit. *Forbes.* Retrieved from: www.forbes.com/sites/collegeprose/2012/08/27/ameri cas-foreign-language-deficit/#115990dc4ddc

17. Skutnabb-Kangas, T., Phillipson, R., Mohanty, A. K. *(2009). (eds.). Social justice through multilingual education (Linguistic diversity and language rights). Bristol: Multilingual Matters.*

18. Winlow, S., & Hall, S. (2013). *Rethinking social exclusion: The end of the social.* Los Angeles, CA: SAGE Publications Ltd.

Suresh Canagarajah

19. Wong, M. S., & Canagarajah, S. (2009). (eds.). *Christian and critical English language education in dialogue: Pedagogical and ethical dilemmas.* New York: Routledge.

第二部 殘疾孤兒的英語學習

Part 2.
Issues in English Education for Orphans with Disabilities

Chapter 2

The Promise of English to Reduce the Poverty for Orphans with Special Needs

orphans with disabilities

第二章

從有特殊需要（殘疾）的孤兒

來看學習英語對減少貧困的承諾

IT IS NO overstatement to claim that hundreds of development agents throughout Southeast Asia are involved in development planning and implementation of such plans as 'equity of language learning', mostly through the teaching of the English language. However, researchers who produce the mainstream applied linguistics literature do not pay significant attention to such informal English language teaching activities carried out by non-profits and NGO (probably because such efforts seem like a daunting project). These development agents have an ambitious goal: to create more equal accesses and opportunities for communities and groups in the margins to learn English. This chapter explores the ambitious plans (or the daunting project) from these development agents as nonprofits and NGO, and examines their strategies (e.g., micro language planning) and efforts of English language teaching from the perspective of nonprofit management.

THIS CHAPTER EXAMINES the English teaching/learning practices of Christian missionaries who teach Thai orphans with disabilities with a view to developing skills that will enable them to overcome their impoverished condition. The researcher (author) found that older Thai orphans (>14 years) with disabilities evinced higher levels of awareness of their disabilities and are accordingly more engaged in learning English than the other orphans examined. This is largely because they believe the acquisition of English skills will prove *compensatory in view of the paucity of survival skills they now command, thereby enhancing employment opportunities in spite of their disabilities. Conversely, the researcher (author) found that younger Thai orphans (<14 years) with disabilities exhibited lower levels of awareness of the consequences of having disabilities and scarcely saw the need to learn English for the sake of becoming more employable. As a result of demonstrating the role of awareness of disabilities as a major motivating factor for learning English, the researcher (author) concludes that Thai orphans such as those studied can be encouraged to learn English by heightening their awareness that their job opportunities are limited by their disabilities and that becoming skilled in English can provide a feasible means whereby they can obtain suitable employment. The results of this study (as reported in the present chapter) should prove beneficial to those engaged in sustainable English education and practice in Thai orphanages.*

ACKNOWLEDGMENTS

The original study reported in chapter 2 was edited and proof reading by Jack Clontz (PhD, University of California, San Diego, USA), Emeritus Professor, Maebashi Kyoai Gakuen International College, Japan (日本前橋共愛學園國際大學). It was peer-reviewed by editorial board members in *Journal of Education and Practice*, New York (ISSN Paper: 2222-1735 & ISSN Online: 2222-288X).

摘要 1.

　　毫不誇張地說，整個東南亞地區有數百個非營利和非政府組織(NGO)等發展機構(development agent)透過英語教學活動對基層的民眾來增加所謂「平等的語言學習」機會。然而，貢獻主流應用語言學文獻的學者並沒有對非營利組織和非政府組織的這類英語教學活動給予高度重視（可能是因為這種努力看起來像一項艱鉅的任務）。這些發展機構有一個雄心勃勃的目標：透過學習英語為社會邊緣的群體創造更多平等的機會。本章探討這些發展機構作為非營利組織和非政府組織的雄心勃勃的計劃（或艱鉅的項目），並從非營利組織的角度審視了他們的英語教學策略和努力。

摘要 2.

　　泰國貧寒的孤兒院院童不是讀不了書,無法待在學校好好學習英語,而是因為經濟因素,逼著他們只能待在孤兒院提供的教室,或是繳不起學費從學校輟學,因此從來沒有機會好好學習英語,改變自身的命運。有幸的是還有一群基督教的宣教士,在提供免費英語教學給這些孤兒院院童。而英語,大大的改變了少數孤兒院院童的命運,有些沒有殘疾的,長大了離開孤兒院後擔任輕軌(MRT)和天車(Skytrain)等大眾運輸交通公司的雇員,都需要基本英語對話能力來應對美國、歐洲和東亞的觀光客。論英語對孤兒的幫助,相較之下,有殘疾的孤兒卻很少成年後因為英語能力而獲得工作機會。即便會說英語,僱主們卻因為他們殘疾的外觀不給予工作機會。

本章探討基督教宣教士對泰國殘疾孤兒提供的英語教學活動，旨在培養能夠克服孤兒面對貧困的謀生技能。研究人員（即作者）發現，有些年齡較大的殘疾孤兒（14歲以上）對殘疾的認識水平較高，也知自身受限於殘疾的身體，因此與其他沒有殘疾的孤兒相比，殘疾者更願意學習英語。這是因為他們認為，鑑於他們缺乏掌握生存的技能，獲得英語技能可被視為補償性質，可是從而增加了就業機會，儘管他們的殘疾令大多數雇主不願意雇用。比較之下，研究員（作者）發現，有些年輕的孤兒（14歲以下）對殘疾造成的工作機會侷限有較低的警訊，且在本文研究的幾間孤兒院幾乎沒看到14歲以下的院童主動用心學習英語，以提高其就業能力的行為。本文證明孤兒院童意識到自身殘疾到的結果是學習英語的主要動力。研究人員(作者)總結認為，可以適時鼓勵泰國孤兒，以不傷害他們心靈的方式，也就是他們可接受的教育模式，提高他們對自身殘疾的認識，認為他們的工作機會受到殘疾的限制，轉而將熟練掌握英語技能視為一種很可行的方法，從而獲得工作。這項研究的結果應對那些在泰國或是其他地方的孤兒院從事英語教育的社工之義舉有肯定作用。

Introduction 導論

PROJECT OBJECTIVES

Purpose of this Study
研究目的

THE OBJECTIVE OF this inquiry is to examine the English teaching and learning practices (in spoken and written modalities) involving Christian missionaries as English teachers and Thai orphans with disabilities—whether late and early adolescents or younger children—as learners of English. The English teachers are engaged in the task of providing these disabled orphans and healthy orphans with a marketable skill on the assumption that otherwise they will have an unremittingly impoverished life, because of being largely unemployable. Even though such endeavors may appear small in the overall scheme of things, it still seems well to examine how English language learning can become a beneficial tool in addressing severe socio-economic problems and human suffering. To address this task it is first incumbent to understand what educational practices would prove fruitful in teaching English to such students. Once we have a firm understanding of the situational logic of teaching English to such students, we can consider whether developing English skills can indeed be a useful adjunct to alleviating problems of poverty, especially those stemming from physical conditions prohibiting ordinary employment, on a sustainable basis. The next section provides context in which is necessarily briefly discussed questions of disability, poverty and the sustainability of ameliorative programs in regard to Thai orphans. The following section provides a highly selective review of the expanding role of English learning techniques as applied to Thai orphanages. Finally, the literature review section provides a selective review of the literature pertaining to context awareness theory.

Disability, Poverty & the Sustainability of Ameliorative Programs for Thai Orphans

泰國孤兒的殘疾、貧困、可持續性發展和改善計劃

The impoverishment of orphans with disabilities is at crisis level on a global scale. In Thailand, 4.7 percent of children from ages one to seventeen are orphans with disabilities (according to the UNICEF 2006, p. 51). These children are afflicted with a huge variety of disabilities stemming from a vast array of causative agents or factors. For example, Thai children have been variously diagnosed as suffering from Prader-Willi Syndrome (PWS), other genetic disorders, cognitive disabilities, hemiplegia, traumatic brain injuries, hearing loss, limb disabilities and impaired vision. This somber state of affairs has become a large social issue in Thailand, as is shown by the copious literature bearing on this issue as it impinges upon the problem of orphans living in impoverished conditions (National Statistics Office Thailand, 2007; Manzanares & Kent, 2006; Maier, 2005). Thai society is confronted with an enormous challenge in having to develop sustainable ameliorative programs for such children. Tragically, children, adolescents, and young adults with disabilities face tremendous obstacles toward actualizing whatever potentialities they have. Recent statistical compilations show that approximately ten percent of Thais with disabilities are not employable, nor do they complete formal K-12 schooling (National Statistics Office of Thailand, 2007). According to official reports from the National Statistical Office Thailand (2007) and the International Labor Organization (ILO), it is estimated that 3 percent of the total population— almost two million Thais in Thailand—have one or more disabilities (Pozzan, 2009). The untoward upshot is that incapacity and absence of skills condemns most of the disabled to lives of poverty since they either cannot be gainfully employed or are at best have to endure being severely underemployed. Moreover, those employed among the disabled population earn less than one tenth of Thailand's earned income and own less than one percent of the nation's wealth. This is why reducing the levels of poverty for those children and youth with disabilities has been at the core of social welfare development programs. There are numerous possible answers and potential solutions to issues and problems concerning education, schooling, and training programs designed for people with disabilities in Thailand and elsewhere. However, the current chapter addresses only the opportunities provided by English education and practice for orphans with disabilities to learn skills necessary for sustaining themselves in the Thai society. The idea of teaching the English language to orphans with disabilities in Thailand is innovative and can potentially contribute to ameliorating the impoverished conditions of life for at least some orphans with disabilities for their short or long-term sustainable economic and social development.

English Teaching Projects for Thai Orphans Leading to Amelioration of Poverty
幫助泰國孤兒脫離貧困的英語教學項目

The connection between English language learning and Thai orphans with disabilities has scarcely been addressed by researchers until Hugo Yu-Hsiu Lee (2012). After an exhaustive search of the extant literature, no official Thai government reports have been found that the rate of unemployment of Thai orphans declines in tandem with such orphans having studied English with Christian missionaries or other English teachers. As such, there is a need to conduct nationwide research concerning putative percentage-point declines in unemployment of orphans with disabilities and English language training. This lacuna in the literature is the *raison d'etre* for the current investigation. Generally speaking, English ability helps one become more employable in Thailand's service sector, not least because tourism is a major industry in Thailand. Thais working in the tourism industry must normally communicate with foreign tourists in English (or Chinese). If so, it is reasonable to infer that Thai orphans with disabilities who learn English thereby enhance their employability. However, it must be owned that there are observers that hold that English language ability does very little by way of enhancing employment opportunities for orphans with disabilities. While acknowledging this negative assessment, the researcher (author) does not consider its full evaluation to be within the scope of the current undertaking. A contrary view is held by Christian missionaries, who accordingly find it important and invaluable to teach the English language to orphans with disabilities, thereby bolstering the view of optimistic observers that such teaching will mitigate the problem of poverty which so often blights the lives of orphans with disabilities. However, the researcher (author) suspects that this common missionary belief is much too simple, inasmuch as one can find both support for and evidence against such beliefs. As such, this discrepancy warrants further inquiry, the upshot of which may change the way we think about English teaching/learning practices in such cases. Today, being able to communicate in English is a necessary condition for successful international communication (e.g., international conferences and events that require intercultural communication) in addition to providing safeguard measures for the maintenance of economic prosperity and the ensuring a better quality of life on the personal, national, and transnational levels (McCrum, 2010). As already mentioned, it is in this context that English language competence seems obviously fundamental to furthering employment opportunities and in turn reducing poverty for orphans with disabilities in Thailand according to the beliefs of hundreds of Christian missionaries. To help children and adolescents with disabilities to become more employable as adults, some Christian missionaries rely on more than traditional vocational skills training programs. If resources for providing English education accompanied by vocational skills training are made available, it is believed a young orphan with disabilities can grow up safer, become more economically independent and self-sustaining in the Thai society. With the assistance rendered to them by Christian missionary English teachers, it is believed that Thai orphans with disabilities can lift themselves out of poverty and ultimately become agents of change and masters of their own destiny. Hundreds of volunteers and paid or unpaid English teachers from English-speaking countries (e.g., Americans and Canadians) and non-English-speaking countries, organized by Christian ministries and corporations (e.g., Future For Five, Global Service Corps, and Openmind Projects), are sent to Thailand every year and place their faith in the magic of the power of English. Thus, this type of English teaching practice has expanded in orphanages across Thailand (and even throughout the mainland Southeast Asia). There is currently every indication that the number of Christian missionaries will continue to grow. Below are given statements from Christian missionaries who consider this widespread belief in helping Thai orphans to learn English as a remedy for poverty.

TABLE 2.1: Selected quotations from English speaking Christian missionary teachers in Thai orphanages

A Christian English teacher in a Thai orphanage	*"Many of them have physical disabilities, but that does not hold them back from their ability to learn and do well in school. They live in Thailand and yet are surrounded by a huge tourism industry that craves individuals who can speak English. Learning the English language opens up many new job opportunities to the Thai person. For the children at [the name of orphanage removed for confidential reason], it would allow them to one day become independent by giving them a very valuable skill set."*	**Source:** Future For Five, n.d., available online at its website
An advertisement to recruit English teachers for Thai orphans	*"English language skills are increasingly important all across the world. This is especially true for people in developing countries, where having good English skills can open up many new job and education opportunities."*	**Source:** Openmind Projects, available online at its website

The Theory of Awareness Context
情境意識理論

Teaching the English language to Thai orphans with disabilities involves complex practical and ethical issues for Christian missionaries. The management of care for Thai orphans with disabilities requires compassion, a service-oriented mindset, a co-operative approach, love, openness and more from Christian caregivers. The Christian English teachers deal with strong emotions, obstacles to advocacy, boundaries and professional responsibilities and moral duties. Information concerning disabilities should be given with care and sensitivity when interacting with Thai orphans. One theory that explores how individuals react to emotive ethical issues and sensitive news is the theoretical approach of awareness contexts. Believing that English ability can help Thai orphans with disabilities find better jobs, Christian missionaries cannot always be certain that Thai orphans know why they need to learn English in view of their disabilities and limited job opportunities. Thai orphans are not always certain that the reason why Christian missionaries teach English to them is because of their disabilities and limited job opportunities. Thus, both parties are uncertain whether the other party is aware of the connection between disabilities and English language learning. Many proposals have been put forth by theorists to explain learning practices within, external to, or below the threshold of consciousness. Because this school of thought considers the principal causes of one's learning behavior to be forces within the individual, the researcher (author) views the major determinants of English learning by Thai orphans to be their awareness of disabilities, which leads to limited job opportunities in Thailand's labor market brought on by the disabilities. Competing views are acknowledged by the researcher (author) as well. Nevertheless, the scope of this chapter does not permit discussion of learning external to or below the threshold of consciousness. Such issues are too large to receive fuller treatment here in spite of being important. The bibliography suggests sources which do justice to the approaches not considered here. The traditional term "awareness" is adopted as a convenient umbrella term (with several subtypes relating to brain-based, behavioral-based, psychological-based, and psycho-social components) to designate "knowledge or perception of a situation or fact" (as defined online by the Oxford dictionaries) in Thai orphans' minds that lead them to seeing or not seeing a need to learn English (defined so as to suit the context of this chapter). Awareness is not an all-or-none occurrence (Bandura, 1977). Awareness has been shown to facilitate behavioral changes in learning. If awareness is measured at long intervals, it precedes changes in behavior (Kennedy, 1971). The term "awareness context" was coined by Glaser and Strauss (1964, 1965) to indicate that an interactant in a setting knows about another person with whom h/she or interacting. Awareness includes one's own identity as viewed in the eyes of others. To be aware entails being informed, conscious, knowing and realizing. Awareness relates to the degrees and levels of understanding and knowledge of facts. It has to do with one's psychological acceptance of one's own self. Individual awareness is under the influences of cultural, ideological, political and social forces, as well as society as a whole. Awareness of contexts is by no means fixed. Awareness of contexts changes and transformations result from interactions (see Glaser & Strauss, 1964, 1965, for a more detailed treatment).

These proposals concerning the contexts of awareness as originally put forward by Glaser and Strauss (1964, 1965) include: 1) Closed awareness, when an interactant does not become aware of his or her impending situation of extreme deterioration (e.g., terminal illness, cancer, HIV/AIDS, disabilities), despite everyone else in his or her social context being fully aware; 2) Suspicion awareness occurs when an interactant suspects that others are aware of his or her deteriorating situation. S/he tries to confirm his or her suspicions; 3) Mutual pretense awareness occurs when both an interactant and others are aware that her/his situation is getting worse. However, each pretends that the other is not aware. 4) Open awareness occurs when both an interactant and others are aware that his or her situation is getting worse. They both have the same knowledge. They both act in a relatively open fashion in respect to the factual situation. Glaser's and Strauss's (1964, 1965) theory of awareness context was modified by Timmermans (1994) so as to include: 1) Suspended open awareness occurs when an interactant and others ignore information/bad news; 2) Uncertain open awareness occurs when an interactant disregards bad news and holds on to the chance of a good outcome;

3) Active open awareness occurs when an interactant and others are fully informed and receptive to the bad news. They all act accordingly. Timmermans' modification of this theory (1994) recommended that open awareness should be divided into three different contexts. These three different open awareness contexts do not unfold temporally or seriatim in stages. They generally shift back and forth between suspended, uncertain and open awareness of contexts.

Research Methods 研究方法

Research Questions & the Central Hypothesis (prediction)

Regarding the objective of this study (as reported in the present chapter), this investigation seeks to pursue answers for the primary research question along with three sub-research questions. The primary research question asks: **Is awareness of disabilities predictive of engagement in English language learning for Thai orphans with disabilities?** In congruence with the primary research question asked, the central hypothesis is formulated and tested. As a short-hand convenience for the present discussion, the researcher (author) has drafted a diagram (Fig. 2.1) showing the hypothetical relationships between awareness of disability and enhancement of employability.

I Awareness of disability →
II Constraints in job markets →
III Engagement in English learning →
Enhancement of employability

Explanations for the central hypothesis
I. Awareness of disability leads to the realization of constraints in job markets.

II. Constraints to job options lead to engagement in English language learning.

III. English language learning leads to enhancement of employability.

FIG. 2.1: Diagrammatic view of the central hypothesis

(prediction)

The central hypothesis is stated as the effects of awareness of disability on engagement in English learning. Although awareness of disability is likely only one of the several factors affecting engagement in English learning, it may operate as a fundamentally crucial mechanism consequential to multiple predictor variables. Further, to take the discussion of the effects of awareness of disability effect on engagement in English learning to a higher logical level—even though Fig. 2.1 illuminates important dimensions of the association between awareness of disability and engagement in English learning — it should be noted that the main predictor (awareness of disability) used to predict the complex criterion variable (engagement in English learning) is based on a combination of three consequential predictor variables (i.e., multiple prediction equations, not a single prediction equation). These include (a) context awareness theory, (b) the realization of constraints in job options caused by disabilities, and (c) the belief that the learning of English can somehow compensate for the lack of skills caused by disabilities. First, after applying context awareness theory in this manner, the examination of the effects of awareness of disability on engagement in English learning should be supplemented by the results of a literature review of (a) the theory of awareness contexts (Glaser & Strauss, 1964, 1965; Timmermans, 1994). Secondly, the sense evinced by orphans that their disabilities influence their judgment of job opportunities must be taken into consideration. Hence, it is not surprising to assume that (b) disabilities lead to constraints in the seeking of jobs. Lastly, we should consider (c) the belief that lack of survival skills caused by disabilities can be compensated by English ability when seeking jobs. Moving beyond the main predictor (awareness of disability) along with a combination of three other predictor variables (i.e., (a), (b), and (c)) consequential to the main predictor, we should not neglect the fact that the criterion variable (engagement in English learning) is also influenced by multiple intervening and compounding variables outside the multiple prediction equations formulated in this central hypothesis.

How awareness (e.g., awareness of disabilities) is related to learning (e.g., English learning) is a question that has received many answers from literature and real-life examples. From the outset, the reliability of this hypothesis seems to be questioned, because it lacks a robust, standard and structured model. Acknowledging the limits of rationality, however, there is a plethora of research investigating the effects of awareness on one's actions. The researcher (author) searched online databases, refereed journals, and reports which documented and measured the effects of awareness on actions, behaviors and learning experiences. As such, in elaborating this line of thought, we begin by discussing seeing-a-need for learning through awareness-raising. For instance, a selective overview of the process of its manifestation in our human behavior (adapted from Eker, 2005: 18-19) follows: Awareness (concepts, thoughts, thinking, ideas and the like in our mind) lead to feelings and emotions. Feelings and emotions lead to actions (Eker, 2005, suggested that one responds to emotions and feelings faster than thoughts and ideas). Actions lead to results or outcomes. The same holds true for Thai orphans with disabilities who were studied in this investigation. Likewise, Friedland and Truscott (2005: 550) have asseverated that "tutoring helped adolescents develop a greater sense of awareness as learners, which led to greater commitment to and perseverance" in learning to read and write. As it turns out, adolescent students achieved learning outcomes (literacy skills) by raising awareness as committed learners (through tutoring). In another study, affective awareness is shown to be associated with a positive affective stance to work (see Helson & Pals, 2000, for more details).

Additionally, framed by the central hypothesis, three sub-research questions along with three corresponding sub-hypotheses are formulated and tested. They are stated as follows. *Sub-research question 1:* Are there any differences between Thai orphans with and without disabilities who were studied in regard to their degrees of engagement in English language learning? By the same token, the same question can be asked: do the Thai orphans with disabilities studied more likely to see a need to learn English than those without disabilities (because healthy Thai orphans have more job options than their disabled counterparts)? *Sub-hypothesis 1:* disabilities will lead to greater degrees of engagement in English learning. The corresponding null hypothesis to *sub-hypothesis 1:* there will be no differences between Thai orphans with and without disabilities studied on the levels of engagement in English language learning. *Sub-research question 2:* Among the disabled Thai orphans studied, are those who exhibit higher levels of awareness of their disabilities more likely to see a need to learn English language than those who displayed lower levels of awareness of their disabilities? *Sub-hypothesis 2:* the Thai orphans studied with a stronger sense of disabilities are more likely than those with lower-awareness of disabilities to engage actively in English language learning. *Sub-research question 3:* Among the disabled Thai orphans under study, do those who were reminded of their disabilities in English classrooms (independent variable/treatment: toward open-awareness) appear to be more likely engaged in English language learning than those not reminded (toward closed awareness)? *Sub-hypothesis 3:* Among the Thai orphans with disabilities studied, those who received reminder treatment (toward open-awareness who were reminded of their disabilities with sensitivity and care) will be more likely to engage in English language learning to a greater degree than those not reminded (toward closed-awareness).

Data Collection & Research Participants

資料蒐集和研究參與者

TABLE 2.2: Data Sites and Data Sources

10 data collection sites	Multiple data sources
4 orphanages in urban, cosmopolitan & slum areas of Thailand	Internet data/information from Web Sites Visual data: photography *Survey data*: Demographic information, orphan student beliefs and practices questionnaires (*n= 90*), and missionary English teacher beliefs and practices questionnaires (*n= 30*)
6 orphanages in rural areas of Thailand	*Interview data*: Orphan student interviews (1-on-1 interviews, follow-up Interviews & focus-group interviews), missionary English teacher interviews *Field-notes*: Researcher field notes (from participant observations and nonparticipant observations), reflective notes (after field visits) Audiotapes, digital recording, and transcripts of classroom discourses

Note. Thai orphans with severe disabilities (e.g., serious hearing impairment, cognitive disabilities, speech impairment, visual impairment), or who are "lost souls" (e.g., glue sniffers, "runners" for drug dealers, alcoholics) are not included in this convenient but biased sample. Thus, any generalizations derived from this chapter should be made with all due caution.

PHOTO 2.1：Front Gate of an Orphanage in Bangkok

February 11, 2012

圖 2.1：泰國曼谷一間孤兒院的大門口

2012年2月11日

TABLE 2.3: Tabulation of Thai orphans with disabilities
(among selected orphan informants assessed)

	Number	Percentage
With disabilities	70	77%
Without disabilities	20	23%
Total	90	100%

TABLE 2.4: Tabulation of treatment (among selected orphans
with disabilities studied)

	Number	Percentage
Received kind reminder Treatment (open-awareness)	35	50%
No Treatment (closed-awareness)	35	50%
Total	70	100%

Anchored in the field research involving visiting multiple orphanages (i.e., 10 research sites in various geographic location) across Thailand, this inquiry delved into the lives of 90 Thai orphans (given the relatively low sample size, the results must be interpreted with caution) and 30 Christian missionary English teachers. Informants were selected by snowball and cluster sampling strategies, and consented to take part in the survey, interviews, and observations on the basis of their accessibility to the researcher and their willingness to collaborate in this study. Participants (*N*=*120*) chosen represent three different pre-defined groups, i.e., 70 Thai orphans/English learners with disabilities, 20 Thai orphans/English learners without disabilities of varying ages ranging from six to eighteen and 30 Christian missionary English teachers. Externally defined measures, such as physical or mental disabilities, albeit obvious to the researcher (author) and site administrators, may or may not be relevant to the informants when they are in closed-awareness of their disabled condition. The researcher (author) also sees a need to sub-categorize Thai orphans with disabilities studied (*n*=*70*) by combining objective/etic and subjective/emic approaches to their categorization, because some (physically or mentally challenged) might not be aware of their disabilities. Field-site administrators are consulted by the researcher (author) to compare objective/etic and subjective/emic profiles of disabled informants regarding their awareness of disabilities.

Data were collected through a questionnaire (i.e., responses derived from beliefs and surveying practices) and interviews, descriptive and reflective notes from on-site observations, and excerpts from websites. Self-reported assessments of perceived degrees of awareness of disability and engagement in English learning were assessed to determine informants' degrees of hypothetical association (positive or negative) between awareness of disability and engagement in English learning. To measure the association between degrees of awareness of disability and degrees of desire to learn English, the following are examples of self-reported survey questions and interview questions: To what extent does the context awareness of the disabled condition, relate to, affect, influence or shape English learning by Thai orphans with disabilities? To what extent can reminders of context awareness of the disabled condition as an English instructional intervention better serve, encourage or contribute to Thai orphans' English learning? What ideas do Christian English teachers hold about future job opportunities as measures to reduce the poverty levels of Thai orphans with disabilities in the course of English teaching/learning practices and how do these ideas affect their English teaching? What ideas do Thai orphans with disabilities hold about their future employment opportunities leading to reduced poverty by English learning and how do these ideas affect their English learning?

PHOTO 2.2：Christian Missionaries organized a Christmas
celebration for orphans

February 4, 2012

圖 2.2：基督教宣教士替泰國孤兒院院童舉辦聖誕節慶祝活動

2012年2月4日

Data Analysis
資料分析方法

The qualitative data gathered was analyzed using three lenses:
1) research purpose, 2) research questions, and 3) existing
typologies and constructed categories informed by the central
hypothesis. Quantitative data obtained were tabulated using
SPSS. To determine the effects of awareness of disability on
the Thai orphans studied *vis-à-vis* their English learning
behaviors, the researcher (author) hypothesized that those
informants with higher degrees of awareness of disability differ
from others with lower degrees of awareness of disability. To
quantify awareness of disability, a score between 1 and 3 is
assigned to every valid response made by orphans (*n=90*
including 70 with disabilities and 20 without disabilities) to
each question in the questionnaire and interview. Accordingly,
1 represents a range from the least to a lower awareness of
disabilities; 2 represents an intermediate or mixed degrees of
awareness of disabilities; and 3 represents a range from a
higher degree to the maximum degree of awareness of
disabilities. In the same way, when measuring degrees of
informants' engagement in engagement in English learning, 1
represents a range from the least engagement in English
learning to a lower level focus on English ability; 2 represents
an intermediate engagement in English learning; and 3

represents a range from a higher level engagement to a maximum involvement in English learning. For example, when eliciting data concerning the degree of awareness of disability, informants who self-reported themselves as having a lower level of awareness of their disabilities received a score of 1; those who identified themselves as sometimes aware but other times not received a score of 2; and those who responded at a higher level or maximum level of awareness of disabilities received a score of 3. Likewise, when asked degrees of engagement in English learning, informants who reported themselves at the least or lower engagement level received a score of 1; those who identified themselves as between the lower and higher levels of engagement in English learning received a score of 2; and those who responded at a higher or maximum level of engagement in English learning were assigned a score of 3. By averaging their responses across the questionnaire and interview questions, a mean awareness of disability index score and a mean engagement in English learning index score for Thai orphans with ($n=70$) and without disabilities ($n=20$) assessed were obtained.

PROJECT OUTCOMES

Results & Discussion
發表研究成果與討論

Data analysis demonstrably suggested "yes" to the array of primary and sub-research questions. However, this claim must be qualified to some degree and limiting conditions stated. Evidence seems to appear that there is an increase in engagement in English learning when Thai orphans are aware of their disabilities, despite the association being weaker for younger orphans with disabilities studied (<14 years) (indicating a lower positive relationship or no relationship) than their older counterparts (>14 years) (indicating a relatively higher positive relationship). By the same token, awareness of disability is reliably a strong predictor of engagement in English learning for older Thai orphans with disabilities (>14 years) under study.

PHOTO 2.3: Author donated children's books
to an orphanage in Bangkok

February 4, 2012

圖 2.3：作者在曼谷一間孤兒院捐贈泰文童書

2012年2月4日

PHOTO 2.4: Author donated children's books
to another orphanage in Bangkok

February 11, 2012

圖 2.4：作者在曼谷另一間孤兒院捐贈泰文童書

2012年2月11日

The Hypotheses Confirmed

The mean degree of engagement in English learning index score for older orphans (>14 years) studied ($n=30$) divided by higher (3), intermediate (2) and lower levels (1) of awareness of disability confirms a small but significant, linear and positive relationship. Correlations between awareness of disabilities ($M=1.47$, $SD=1.4$) and engagement in English learning ($M=2.04$, $SD=0.89$) among Thai orphans studied, at modest but significant levels, were statistically significant, suggesting a "yes" answer to the primary research question (i.e., Is awareness of disabilities predictive of engagement in English language learning for the Thai orphans with disabilities studied?). Moreover, Thai orphans with disabilities studied displayed higher levels of engagement in English learning than those without disabilities, suggesting a "yes" answer to sub-research question 1 (i.e., Are there any differences between Thai orphans with and without disabilities studied in regard to their degrees of engagement in English language learning?).

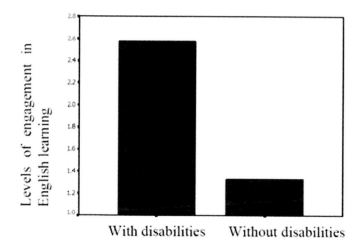

FIG. 2.2: Bar charts for differences
in engagement in English learning
between Thai orphans with and without disabilities assessed

TABLE 2.5: Percentage of hypotheses supported and unsupported by respondents

Percentage of self-reported responses to the central- and sub-hypotheses

		N=70 orphans with disabilities	N=20 orphans without disabilities	N=30 Christian English teachers	N=120 total number of respondents
Hypothesis confirmed & supported	Strongly Agree	85	20	66	70
	Agree	7	80	16	21
Hypothesis disconfirmed & unsupported	Undecided	0	0	0	0
	Disagree	8	0	7.5	8
	Strongly Disagree	0	0	0	0

Additionally, data suggest a "yes" answer to sub-research question 2 (i.e., among disabled Thai orphans studied, do those who exhibited higher levels of awareness of their disabilities more likely to see a need to learn English language than those who displayed lower levels of awareness of their disabilities?), thereby confirming the sub-hypothesis 2 (i.e., Thai orphans studied with a stronger sense of disabilities are more likely than those with a lower-awareness of disabilities to engage actively in English language learning). Computation utilizing chi-square tests gives a value of 90.940, with an asymptotic significance or probability value of .00, thereby indicating a positive relation between the level of awareness of disability and the degree of engagement in English learning. This also means that—as based on chi-square computation—the probability of this distribution having occurred by chance to be less than .00. Further, data analysis suggests a "yes" answer to sub-research question 3 (i.e., among disabled Thai aware of their disabilities in English classrooms (independent variable/treatment: toward more open-awareness classrooms) appear to be more likely engaged in English language learning than those not reminded (toward closed-awareness classrooms)?), thereby supporting sub-hypothesis 3 (i.e., among Thai orphans with disabilities studied, those who received reminder treatment (toward open-awareness: reminded of their disabilities with sensitivity and care) will be more likely to engage in English language learning to a greater degree than those not reminded (toward closed awareness)). When measuring the correlation between awareness contexts (open-awareness and closed-awareness) and engagement in English learning, data are revealed that informants who received open-awareness treatment more likely demonstrated higher degrees of engagement in English learning than those in closed-awareness classrooms.

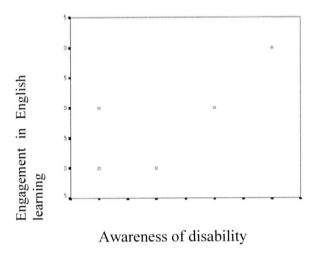

FIG. 2.3: Scatter plot chart showing a positive relationship between awareness of disability and engagement in English learning

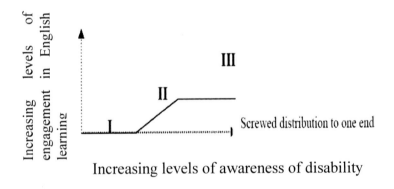

FIG. 2.4: The pattern of bounded awareness of disability effects on engagement in English learning, stretched in a reversed "z" shape for Thai orphans with disabilities studied (n=70)

I: The flat portion at the bottom left of Fig. 2.4 is the period during which younger orphans/informants studied (<14 years) are not aware of their disabilities and do not consider English ability to compensate disabilities as militating against future employment.

II: The slopping portion is the period with which older orphans/informants studied (>14 years) at different ages become aware of their disabilities and considered the possibility of compensating for their disabilities by obtaining English ability prior to seeking employment. This confirmation also implies that the increase of awareness of disability effect on engagement in English learning is linear and continuous.

III. The flat portion at the top right is the period in which the ceiling effect commences, because some older orphans/informants studied (>14 years) displayed the maximum level of awareness of disability. By the same token, since they do not perceive they have any other options, they rely solely on their developed English ability to compensate for the skills they lack caused by disabilities when seeking employment in the job market. This finding also implies that the effects of awareness of disability on engagement in English learning may not continue to increase as the subjects grow older.

Significance of the Study
本章的重要意義

Previous studies have been extremely limited with regard to their direct assessments of the effects of awareness of disability on engagement in English learning. However, this chapter has provided a relatively large number of insights into the myriad ways and available avenues in which we can provide assistance to Thai orphans with disabilities to learn English as a means of reducing the poverty they would otherwise be forced to endure. The findings of this study as reported in the chapter, at a modest but significant level, attempted to show that engagement in learning the English language can be enhanced through elevating the levels of awareness of disability among older Thai orphans with disabilities with care and sensitivity. This formula means that Thai orphans with disabilities can be encouraged and assisted to overcome poverty in a manageable way with care and sensitivity, on the condition that awareness-raising *vis-à-vis* disabilities leads to English learning and English learning leads to poverty reduction. This view implies that this type of English teaching/learning practice in Thailand's orphanages can be sustainable and it is hoped can be reproduced at other orphanages across Thailand and even across the mainland Southeast Asia. A more positive and productive way to look at English teaching/learning practices regarding Thai orphans with disabilities studied is to view the phenomenon from a compensation perspective. This explains why awareness of disability is linked with engagement in English learning. That is to say, some Thai orphans with disabilities under study attempt to make good use of their English ability to compensate for their lack of employments skills in confronting the job market. Although there are divergent results between older (>14 years) and younger Thai orphans (<14 years) with disabilities assessed, the good news is that it is now more likely the younger orphans studied will become engaged in English learning by the time they become fourteen years old. This means that after some period of time, orphans under the age of 14 years old now have a chance in the future to reduce the levels of poverty which they would have to endure, so long as they become more aware of their disabilities and start to see the need to learn English in order to compensate for their disabilities as they enter the job market.

The Hypotheses Questioned: Limitations of the Study

本研究的侷限性

In view of the evidence provided by relatively few items of data, the effects of awareness of disability on engagement in English learning are observed to be comparatively moderate in some cases.

Challenge one: Development of skills other than English

第一個挑戰

Slightly more than 85 percent of the participants (*N=120*) studied support the hypothesized claim. Nonetheless, this view does not go unchallenged. A claim like this is contested by opposite claims. Data also seem to suggest that higher levels of awareness of disability also lead to development of skills other than English (e.g., washing car windows, selling flowers in traffic intersections, and selling drugs), because they do not see an immediate benefit from learning English. Based on the data, this counter-example occurs roughly about 8 percent of the time in regard to 70 Thai orphans with disabilities assessed. Some of the orphans with and without disabilities attended kindergartens run by NGOs, followed by completing a few years of government primary schools. They learned to read Thai and count. However, they showed no or little interest in learning English. Then, they started earning their living on the streets. For some, numbers are far more important than English. Counting quickly in card games, gambling, taking cities buses by recognizing bus numbers, and selling lottery tickets are survival skills, but English is not. Being poor at counting means you go hungry even if you are good at English.

While English may have long-term relevance to their lives, it has no immediate relevance.

Challenge two: Uncertain open awareness

第二個挑戰

Some Christian missionaries, albeit aware of their students' disabilities, maintain closed awareness in English classrooms. Some pretend that disabilities do not exist and hold positive view toward their students' learning outcomes (cf. uncertain open awareness, defined by Timmermans, 1994). For face-saving reasons (maintaining-face is normative in Thailand; however, space limitations prohibit addressing this cultural component here), orphans are usually not reminded of their disabilities in public unless they are in a close relationship with missionaries who might kindly remind [not in public] them to study English harder (out of good intentions) because of limited job options caused by their disabilities. Some interactions between Christian English teachers and Thai orphans are identified as uncertain open awareness interactions (in view of Timmermans, 1994). They both know that orphans need English ability to increase job options because of disabilities, but they pretend not to observe the disabilities. However, other interactions are identified as active open awareness (in view of Timmermans, 1994). They both are open to discussing the orphans' disabilities and act in accordance with the truth without pretense. Even if the hypothesized claim is held to be true (see Fig 2.1), data are revealed that the majority of Thai orphans studied are not reminded of their disabilities in English classrooms located in orphanages. Thus, orphans studied, most of them (50 out of 70 assessed), will have to become self-aware. This might potentially bring a crisis to the sustainability of the English teaching/learning practices in these orphanages.

Challenge three: A different agenda
第三個挑戰

The hypothesis (see Fig. 2.1) might become more contestable if one single truth is revealed as follows. Despite most Christian missionaries studied believing that teaching English helps Thai orphans with disabilities find jobs and reduce poverty, (66%, strongly agree; 16%, agree) they ($n= 30$) have a different agenda in mind. On the one hand, Thai orphans with disabilities benefit from learning English and English ability has a potential to reduce poverty. At the same time, the ultimate goal of Christian missionaries, on the other hand, is to convert Thai orphans to Christianity (Protestants hold this view more strongly than Roman Catholics). Instead of learning to speak Thai, it might be easier for Christian missionaries from English-speaking countries to teach English. After Thai orphans understand more English, it will become easier to understand biblical teachings in English. It is logical to speculate that this conversion mindset of Christian missionaries who are also English teachers might affect their teaching outcomes. That is to say, the focus of their teaching might be on the English necessary for understanding biblical passages (this would be, of course, a different form of English teaching/learning than the one assessed in this article) rather than English for finding-a-job purposes or learning English for the sake of poverty reduction.

Challenge four: Multiple causes & Confounding variables
第四個挑戰

In combination with the aforementioned limitations, it is reasonable to suppose that there are multiple causes and experiential variables in addition to the one this research investigation considers (illustrated in Fig. 2.1). The researcher could only confidently argue that the degree of engagement in English learning is, to a large extent, because of the awareness of disability of the Thai orphans studied (estimated 85% strongly agree, $n=70$ orphans with disabilities; 66% strongly agree, $n=30$ Christian missionaries). Some informed readers might list many factors other than awareness of disability effects on engagement in English learning. While they might accuse the author of this article of being naïve and occasionally careless, we cannot deny that the argument proposed in this present article has empirical support. The claims and supporting evidence presented in this study are important in the end, but we must still look at the available evidence to the largest extent feasible. The formula— awareness of disability has effects on engagement in English learning—certainly explains the phenomenon of English teaching practices in Thailand's ten representative orphanages, but this phenomenon is too complex for a single explanation. This formula holds true in many cases, but not in all. Readers may think that the argument overlooks, ignores and misses key factors that cause Thai orphans to be active or not in learning English, including but not limited to such independent variables such as the orphanage's location (e.g., urban or rural), characteristics of caretakers (e.g., educational attainment, single or married, teenager or adult) and support available for orphans (e.g., educational, emotional/psychological, material, medical and social support). Readers might consider some causes deserve more attention (e.g., missionaries using activities that are "fun" for the Thai orphans to stimulate their engagement in English learning) than the ones the researcher proposed in this study. Readers are likely to think of counterexamples (e.g., Thai orphans without or with little awareness of disability learn English intensively, because 10 out of 20 (50%) orphans without disabilities studied showed strong interest in English learning) and exceptions that undermine the thesis presented in this paper. The researcher acknowledges these counter-examples, alternate explanations and other points of view. Therefore, the author will welcome any feedback and comments, whether adverse or not.

Conclusions 結論

Synthesis of the Study
本研究總結

We now take a step back from the limitations acknowledged in section 3.3 and consider the main conclusions of this study. It was tempting to conclude that awareness of disability emerges as a strong predictor toward degrees of engagement in English learning for Thai orphans with disabilities studied. It should be noted that the awareness-of-disability effects on engagement in English learning seems to only persist across the age span from fourteen years upward, but are restricted for orphans studied under fourteen years of age. Awareness of disability leads to engagement in English learning for older Thai orphans (>14 years) assessed, because English ability is believed to help them find jobs. This study indicates that a multiage group (14+) of older participants (85%, $n=70$ orphans with disabilities, strongly agree; 7%, $n=70$ orphans with disabilities, agree) agree with this claim. It is observed that English language learning by Thai orphans is in relation to their awareness of disability. That is to say, greater engagement in English learning by older orphans (>14 years) concerned with their disabilities shows they take into account that English language ability can be a survival skill in competing in future job markets so as to escape poverty.

Drawing the strands together, this study sheds light on awareness of disability in Thai orphans' experience of engagement in English learning, thereby reporting the possibilities and challenges of English teaching/learning practices in Thailand's orphanages. By acknowledging the role of awareness of disability in engagement in English learning for the purpose of poverty reduction, Thai orphans can be encouraged to learn English with care and sensitivity. It is the author's hope to examine the English teaching/learning practices in a wider range of different orphanages in Thailand. Thus, on the basis of this better understanding, we can further help disabled Thai orphans, who are currently living in poverty, to change their life for the better and help these English teaching/learning practices become more sustainable.

Future Studies for English Teaching/Learning Practices in Thailand's Orphanages

對未來泰國孤兒院英語教學實踐研究的建議

The study as reported in this chapter provides suggestions and recommendations for further refining and strengthening English teaching/learning projects carried out in orphanages across Thailand. Follow-up and longitudinal studies are recommended to investigate the progress of Thai orphans with disabilities who exhibited different levels of awareness of disability as measured by different techniques other than those used in this study. This article demonstrates that Thai orphans with disabilities studied showing higher levels of awareness of disability are better engaged in their English language learning by virtue of believing that English ability can compensate for disabilities in the job market (reported 85%, *n=70* orphans with disabilities, strongly agree; 7%, *n=70* orphans with disabilities, agree). However, this one-point-in-time study can hardly determine if this association is still in evidence at different ages, varying growth patterns, an array of maturation levels, work-place status and so forth for orphans studied. This initial association might appear stronger, but may not last over a long period of time. Conversely, for those who initially demonstrate weaker association between awareness of disability and engagement in English learning, this association might produce much stronger and longer effects from a longer term perspective. The English teaching/learning practices reported herein have proved to be amenable to training older Thai orphans with disabilities (>14 years) and developing their English abilities so as to increase their job opportunities. For the sake of helping Thai orphans reduce the levels of poverty they must endure and to encourage English teaching practices by Christian missionaries at orphanages in Thailand so as they shall be more sustainable, it is hoped that this study will provide useful scaffolding for future studies (albeit comparisons and generalizations might differ from study to study).

（本文原稿於2012年發表在《教育和練習期刊》第三卷第六期）

For further information about this chapter (if you want to discuss with the author), please contact:

Hugo Lee, Faculty Member International College
National Institute of Development Administration
18th fl., Navamin Building, 118 Seri Thai Rd,
Khlong Chan, Bang Kapi, Bangkok 10240

Hugo Lee, Consultant Roster Member
United Nations
Economic & Social Commission for Asia & the Pacific
3rd fl., United Nations Conference Center, ESCAP HR
United Nations Building, 76 Rajadamnern Nok Ave
Bangkok 10200

T. 088-607-2560
E. YL15@umail.iu.edu   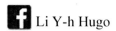 Li Y-h Hugo
W. https://indiana.academia.edu/YuHsiuLee

參考文獻 References

1. Bandura, A. (1977). *Social learning theory*, Englewood Cliffs, N.J.: Prentice-Hall, Inc.
2. Cowleys, S. (1991). A symbolic awareness context   identified through a grounded theory study of health visiting, *Journal of Advanced Nursing, 16*, 648-656.
3. Eker, T. H. (2005). *Secrets of the millionaire mind: Mastering the inner game of wealth*, New York: Harper Collins Publisher.
4. Friedland, E., & Truscott, D. (2005). Building awareness and commitment of middle school students through literacy tutoring, *Journal of Adolescent and Adult Literacy, 48*, 550-562.
5. Future For Five, n.d.
   <http://futureforfive.com/Their_Stories.html.>
   Retrieved 23.01.12

Barney Glaser and Anselm L. Strauss
6. Glaser, B.G., & Strauss, A.L. (1964). Awareness contexts and social interaction, *American Sociological Review, 29* (5), 669-679.
7. Glaser, B.G., & Strauss, A.L. (1965). *Awareness of dying.* Chicago, IL: Aldine.
8. Glaser, B.G., & Strauss, A.L. (1967). *The discovery of grounded theory: Strategies for qualitative research.* Chicago, IL: Aldine.

9. Helson, R., & Pals, J. L. (2000). Creative potential, creative achievement, and personal growth. *Journal of Personality 68* (1), 1-27.

10. Kennedy, T.D. (1971). Reinforcement frequency, task characteristics, and interval of awareness assessment as factors in verbal conditioning without awareness, *Journal of Experimental Psychology, 88*, 103-112.

Father Joseph Maier

11. Maier, J. (2005). *Welcome to Bangkok slaughterhouse: The battle for human dignity in Bangkok's bleakest slums*, Bangkok, Thailand: Asia Books Co., Ltd.

12. Manzanares, J., & Kent, D. (2006). *Only 13-the true story of Lon*, Bangkok, Thailand: Bamboo Sinfonia Publications.

13. McCrum, R. (2010). *Globish: How the English language became the world's language,* New York City: The Viking Press.

14. Morrissey, M.V. (1997). Extending the theory of awareness contexts by examining the ethical issues faced by nurses in terminal care, *Nursing Ethics, 4* (5), 370-379.

15. National Statistics Office Thailand (2007). The 2007 disability survey. < http://web.nso.go.th / > Retrieved 23.01.12

16. Open Mind Projects (n. d.). Volunteer teaching English abroad. <openmindprojects.org/volunteer-projects/volunteer-teach-english-abroad-volunteer-teaching-opportunities-in-thailand-laos-cambodia-and-nepal> Retrieved 23.01.12

17. Oxford Dictionaries (n.d.).
<oxforddictionaries.com/definition/awareness?q=awareness>
Retrieved 03.11.11

United Nations – International Labor Organization (ILO)

18. Pozzan, E. (2009). Inclusion of people with disability in
Thailand. International Labour Organization (ILO).
19. Timmermans S. (1994). Dying of awareness: the theory of
awareness contexts revisited, *Social Health Illness*, *16,* 323–39.

United Nations – The United Nations Children's Fund (UNICEF)

20. UNICEF (2006). *Thailand Multiple Indicator Cluster Survey
December 2005-Feburary 2006 Final Report*, Thailand Country
Office.

第三部　服務業基層人士的語言議題

Part 3.
Issues in Language Learning and Language Use for Service-Industry Workers

Chapter 3

Service Industry could be a Game-Changer for Language Learning: Another Challenge for Thai Masseuses, Restaurant Waiters and Waitress

domestic migrants

service-industry workers

restaurant waiters and waitresses

massage therapists

第三章

按摩師、餐廳服務生的雙語、多語之學習和使用

THIS CHAPTER EXAMINED the largely unexplored effects of exposure to foreign customers' language (e.g., English) as informal learning for service-industry workers, a pattern common in developing countries where resources to learn English were not widely accessible to lower-status workers in the labor market. It also pointed out the paucity of research on service-industry workers' language development in applied linguistics and sociolinguistics literature. This study, as reported in chapter 3, adopted two analytical tools, the magnet of trend's model and the concept of "quadrant," to highlight the English learning opportunities provided for the service-industry workers in a developing country, and explored how the development of their language abilities enabled them to expand and navigate more quadrants. Field visits and qualitative interviews were undertaken to gather data from the sample, consisted of 200 participants. Broad content analysis conventions were deployed to interpret interview data and field notes derived from observations, aimed at combining both emic and etic (interactional) data.

The chapter reported the role of English-speaking customers as informal tutors to facilitate these workers' English language development. This chapter turned to different case studies of exemplar workers who reported following the English-for-customer pattern, because they illustrated two themes common across the sample studied. The results revealed that, among these workers, (1) educational background and (2) exposure to English-speaking customers in an informal educational setting may contribute to fostering the learning of English.

摘要

　　有很多很多社會底層的人，對於體制不滿可是想要掙扎、發聲甚至抗議的餘地都幾乎沒有。在泰國的觀光產業這個體系裡，基層服務業人員學習並且使用外語，尤其是英語、日語和中文，是升遷和扭轉改變命運的有效辦法。

　　在所有職業當中，服務業工作者接觸外國客戶口說的語言進而學習這些語言（尤其是英語、日語和中文）是發展中國家（特別是東南亞以發展觀光業為導向的國家）普遍存在的一種「非正式」外語學習模式。但是當代應用語言學和社會語言學的文獻中對服務業工作者透過和顧客溝通互動來學習語言的研究卻很少。本研究案建立一個資料庫,它清楚明白地告訴我們兩個主要影響泰國服務業人員英語學習和使用的因素：

1. **教育背景：**泰國大曼谷地區服務業工作者在過去學校當中受到正規英語教育的經驗，會影響他們現在在服務業工作地點對英語的接受度和使用英語的能力。過去在學校裡面英語學的基礎好的，比較容易在職場上使用英語。
2. **「非正式教育」的環境：**在工作地點接觸講英語的顧客有助於促進泰國服務業從業人員的英語學習。

　　在泰國進服務業這一行的，多是家境貧寒的子弟。以下幾個外語學習成功和不成功的案子從作者資料庫裡提出來講：

芳（匿名）是一位難得有受過大學教育的女按摩師，大學畢業後創業開餐廳倒了，才來按摩店的。比起大部分只有小學、初中和高中畢業的按摩師同行，芳的英語口說能力可算是流利。除了待在一間大路旁的按摩店被動地等待說泰語為主的客人上門，透過英語溝通的優勢，她也主動出擊去一間五星級賓館FREELANCE給歐美、香港、新加坡、台灣、中國大陸等客人，大大增加了她的收入。

懷（匿名）坦言說，在離開泰國以前根本就不會說英語。可是曾到過泰籍母親在南非經營的餐廳去工作，由於常住在南非，在餐廳工作的緣故，從客人以及南非的前男友身上學習不錯的英語口語溝通能力。

可是回來泰國之後，目前在這間以泰國顧客為主的按摩店，還不能發揮她的英語長才。果然當了女按摩師不到半年後，就另謀出路。希望這次能用她英語溝通長才，找到更高薪的工作。我在此祝福她。

點（匿名）在馬來西亞當按摩女打工期間，和馬來人顧客學習了口說英語。要是她當年沒有離開泰國，她可能也是一句英語也說不好。本來收入也不錯，可是常常有馬來西亞警察來臨檢她工作的按摩店。回到曼谷後，暫時待在一間以服務泰國男客為主的按摩店。她的英語能力暫時還派不上用場。

嫻（匿名）有不錯的英語口說能力，歸功於之前學校的教育和她自己的興趣。可是怨嘆學歷不如人，英語程度好還是找不到高薪工作（她說：雇主不只看英語能力，也會看雇員的學歷和工作經驗），只能待在這間按摩店當按摩女。

杯（匿名）在來到這間酒吧餐廳擔任坐檯聊天女之前，在柬埔寨做了一陣子賭場女服務生。只有高中學歷的她，目前社區大學休學當中。她在高中學的英語只足夠她看懂我傳給她的手機英文簡訊，可是透過電話或是面對面英語口語溝通就完全不行。她靠得是她的年輕貌美來賺錢，幾乎都是泰國男客捧她的場子，她通常只能說泰語來坐檯，遇到說英語（非泰籍）的顧客就不敢出場了。所幸泰國男客捧場她，目前她尚未計畫好好學習英語，來賺外國遊客的坐檯費。

蓮（匿名）是從小沒見過親生父親（被伯父收養長大）且連小學也沒有讀完一學期的街頭性工作者。嫌在卡拉OK餐廳當服務生賺得少，以她的條件而言，視街頭攬客為謀生賺錢的最佳工作。基本上，蓮連一句完整的英語句子都不會說，可是令人訝異的是在夜晚和半夜在Chatuchak公園和Lumpini公園找上她的大部分客人都不是泰國人。蓮說她的客人大都是待在曼谷一段時間，可以用泰語口語和她溝通的Expat（美國人、日本人等）。她最近讓一位日本客人包養，可是她總是說她沒受過正規教育，不懂如何學習外語，她依舊還是說泰語和她有錢的日本乾爹溝通。

171

ACKNOWLEDGMENTS

The original study reported in chapter 3 was edited and proof reading by Jack Clontz (PhD, University of California, San Diego, USA), Emeritus Professor, Maebashi Kyoai Gakuen International College, Japan（日本前橋共愛學園國際大學）. It was peer-reviewed by editorial board members in Scopus-indexed and Scimago-indexed (Q2) *Theory and Practice of Language Studies*, Finland and London (ISSN 1799-2591).

Introduction 導論

THE LACK OF previous research on the effects of English-speaking foreign customers on service-industry workers in developing countries is surprising (please see Endnote 1.), because more than half of developing countries have shown the benefits of this form of informal learning. English-speaking customers play a vital role in providing exposure to the English language for Thai service-industry workers in the labor market. The aim of this study is to examine the strategies Thai service industry workers utilize to support the learning and the development of the English language in Thailand whereby the pattern of their language-learning-and-language-use is known as English-for-customer and/or English-as-an-additional-language-for-work.

Sociolinguists utilize the concept of "trends" to describe the association between everyday language-learning-and-language-use and globalization, regionalization and so forth. This chapter thus re-conceptualizes the notion of "trends" by extending the notion of "magnets" (Fig. 3.1) and their implications to language-learning-and-language-use. Using this method, "magnets of trends [model]" (Fig. 3.1) along with the concept of "quadrant" (Fig. 3.2), this chapter provides an analysis of the service-industry workers in Bangkok, helping understand how they approach the task of the learning of English.

Conventional research frameworks in language studies, and policies and practices in the language-education sector, have given little regard to language learning in the margins characterized as the dominant-language-speaking minority (for a similar line of study for the dominant-language-speaking minority, of relevance to the concern herein, see Blommaert, 2010; Draper, 2010; Gal, 1978; Lee, 2013, 2014b; Smith-Hefner, 2009, to name just a few). Traditionally, scholars (researchers and language educators) and practitioners (language teachers) in their research and practices tend to emphasize global-, prestigious-, standard-, foreign- and second language learning experiences of classroom students, indigenous and immigrant communities. The present chapter attempts to contribute to scholarly conversations around one of the silences in the aforementioned research paradigm by reporting an alternative (theoretical and methodological) framework for a development plan that has been termed 'equalizing language learning or 'equity in language learning' (henceforth ELL, as abbreviated throughout the chapter) targeting learners labeled as ethnic and socio-economic minorities in developing countries.

Three pro-ELLers involved into the research team undertaking the present survey and challenged traditional policies and practices in the foreign/second language education sector that widen the gap between mainstream foreign/second language learners including classroom students and their dominant-language-speaking minority counterparts in non-educational settings. Pro-ELLers also point out one problem in the academic discourses that deal with issues in applied linguistics and educational linguistics, which is that it has become increasingly non-dialectal with dominant-language-speaking minority individuals and groups. They encourage a stance whereby teaching global-, prestigious-, standard-, foreign- and second languages to dominant-language-speaking minority is central to the research, policies and practices.

A defining characteristic of this chapter is about broadening language repertoires for minorities as part of a movement termed 'equalizing language learning' or 'equity in language learning' (ELL) – what it is in the context of Thailand and how to do it with development strategy's implementation by means of formal and informal (language) learning. This chapter commences with the premise that an equal access and more opportunities to global-, prestigious-, standard-, foreign- and second languages should be created not only for typical marginalized populations (e.g., aborigines and immigrants), but also for less typical ones (e.g., dominant-language-speaking minority). By making such a claim, the chapter examines informal (language) learning phenomena of the dominant-language-speaking minority labeled as marginal (with particular reference to Standard Thai dominant speakers in the service industry including barbers, bargirls, bus fare collectors, massage therapists, restaurant waiters and waitress, street vendors, taxi drivers and street child/teen labors, among others) in Thailand. Meanwhile, it also reviews a vital issue of marginality and language learning neglected by mainstream language studies academia and classic language learning literature by arguing that most scholars, either explicitly or implicitly, neglect the range of marginalized dominant-language speakers and of their issues in global-, prestigious-, standard-, foreign- and second language learning.

Social Campaign (ELL Development Plan): A Bourdieusian Framework

平權語言學習的社會運動

Inequalities & Equalizing Language Learning

This chapter approaches the term inequality as the resources, power and wealth held by the elites and the rich, thereby unevenly distributed. 'Equalizing' or 'equity' is a general term that describes specific actions of making "the quality of being fair and impartial" (Oxford Dictionaries).

It is truism that the capitalist globalization has widened the economic inequalities within the civil society, and in local- and international levels (Hobsbawm, 2007; also cited in Blommaert, 2010, p.153). "Inequality between the rich and the poor has reached its highest point in the past thirty years" ("inequality," 2014 by OECD, as cited by Channel News Asia and BBC World Service on December 9, 2014). Put directly, major population in a modern nation-state have little or no access to resources that provide opportunities for upper social and economic mobility, while the elites have such access for the pursuit of power (Hobsbawm, 2007; also cited in Blommaert, 2010, p.3). For instance, language learning across numerous modern nation-states and civil societies has been characterized by both the enduring discrepancies between the higher success of learners from wealthier families and the consistent under-achievement of learners from lower-income families both in mainstream schooling settings and non-educational settings (own fieldwork, 2007-2015). In other words, there is an issue of uneven distribution of language resources.

The chapter described herein was drawn from a social campaign vis-à-vis the author's research network which begins with the slogan: Collaboration for equity in language learning. In line with the 'equalizing language learning' or 'equity in language learning' (ELL) movement, the campaign and the strategy move toward a comprehensive planning that addresses current foreign/second language learning opportunities and challenges marginalized populations are facing. As ELL stems from a Bourdieu's tradition (1991), it inaugurates with a capacity analysis of language learning resources accessible to marginalized populations in individual and societal levels, and creating 'symbolic capitals and powers' for them by offering opportunities to learn more 'capital' languages, particularly English. ELL refers to the processes of activities and social premises involved in the facilitation of foreign/second language learning and implementation of intervention to individual and group language learners characterized as marginal. The study reported in this chapter is in an attempt to realize ELL research methodology and ELL strategic intervention as an alternative framework and paradigm from which pro-ELLers purport to improve foreign/second language learning outcomes for the marginalized populations. To do this, pro-ELLers enact as the research team and survey the pilot areas by examining dominant-language-speaking minority's access to prestige varieties of languages and prestige forms of multilingualism (e.g., international Standard English and Chinese) during the phase of capacity analysis.

Understanding ELL development plan begins with issues in language learning dominant-language-speaking minorities are facing. Many of the world's minorities have little or almost zero access to learn global-, prestigious-, standard-, foreign- and second languages. Although it is well-known that language learning affects one's level of economic development, the association between them, and successful and unsuccessful stories of dominant-language-speaking minority's language-learning-and-language-use, have been largely neglected by scholars. It is not surprising that scholarly work on minority and language learning has been focused on typical minorities. It is likely that global-, prestigious-, standard-, foreign- and second language learning experiences of 1). aborigines, 2).

immigrants and 3). classroom students are key issues in the mainstream academic and policy-making fields, informed by applied linguistics, educational linguistics and sociolinguistics literature, among others. Less typical minorities –dominant-language-speaking minority populations– are often neglected. ELL development planning aims to better understand the current opportunities and challenges the dominant-language-speaking minority language users face in the context of Thailand.

The research team, consisted of pro-ELLers, has not reached a consensus concerning the specific steps to realize ELL. However, there is an agreement of fundamental principles and basic steps in ELL. ELL is consisted of three-stage development plan: (i) (present) capacity analysis is an approach beginning with identification of existing capacity – evaluation of multiple factors that affect current practices of language-learning-and-language-use (tools adopted for capacity analysis are, for instance, standardized English proficiency tests and informal assessment based on English-medium interview) – determining the maximum language learning outcomes, (ii) capacity planning and predictive (future) capacity analytics are process of determining the maximum capacity of language leaning outcome needed to meet the demand to compete in the job market, and (iii) implementation of capacity development).

It is unfortunate but true that pro-ELLers in the wake of ELL campaign are unable to ask for equal distribution of language resources among the rich and the poor in a society. However, pro-ELLers increase language resources minorities gain access to, particularly in respect to basic vocabularies and phrases needed to understand and/or for effective communication in global-, prestigious-, standard-, foreign- and second languages.

Literature Review 文獻綜述

Applied linguistics, educational linguistics and sociolinguistics on minority have been active disciplines and have drawn attentions for the previous decades around the world. The chapter has been informed by the work of scholarship in language studies, primarily drawing on the disciplines of applied linguistics, educational linguistics and sociolinguistics, with particular reference to language education/learning, 'development linguistics,' or 'language and minority [studies]' (For lack of a better term, this is what the researcher of the present chapter might call). Over the past 50 years, scholars concerned with applied linguistics, educational linguistics and sociolinguistics in regards to global-, prestigious-, standard-, foreign- and second language learning have shown growing interests in three particular researched groups, namely 1). classroom students, 2). aborigines and 3). immigrants. Thus, considerable pieces of fabric of studies consist in efforts to develop a body of work within the mainstream applied linguistics (e.g., Wei and Cook, 2009), educational linguistics (e.g., Hornberger, 1989, 2003, 2004) and sociolinguisitcs (e.g., Blommaert, 2010; Fishman, 1991, 2001).

Yet, linguistic communications and issues in foreign/second language education of the aforementioned three groups have been explored by the dominant intellectual tradition in a variety of (theoretical, experimental and empirical) settings across the globe. Most prominent researchers stemming from these old (established) and new (emerging) traditions, to a more or lesser degree, emphasize the interplay between a country's state language and indigenous languages (e.g., Coronel-Molina & Rodrı´guez-Mondon˜edo, 2012; Fishman, 1991, 2001; Hornberger, 1989, 2003, 2004; Romaine, 2009; Sallabank, 2013). Some explore the interplay between a country's state language and immigrant languages (e.g., Blommaert, 2010; Cohen, 1987; Fishman, 1991, 2001; Hornberger, 1989, 2003, 2004; Lee, 2010, 2014a; Manosuthikit, 2013; Morita, 2007; Mukherjee and David, 2011). Others have been concentrated on the interplay between a country's classroom students and their foreign/second languages (e.g., Abhakorn, 2013; Draper, 2012; Saksit, 2012, 2013; Wei & Cook, 2009). There is by now sufficient knowledge (generated by scholars currently informing the analysis in language learning studies) to understand the extent to which indigenous- and diasporic communities, and classroom students, cope with challenges in foreign/second language learning.

However, despite all this, less attention has been paid to address the inequalities for the dominant-language-speaking minority to learn global-, prestigious-, standard-, foreign- and second languages. The lack of scholarly interest is that most dominant-language-speaking minority, who are not labeled as aborigines, immigrants and students, have lived in linguistically homogenous communities and operated in the quadrant of localization (Fig. 3.2). As a result, there is no growing demand for the vast majority of them to acquire global-, prestigious-, standard-, foreign- and second languages. However, some dominant-language-speaking minority language users who work in the service industry are highly expected to encounter effects of globalization and regionalization (Fig. 3.1), because they are often in direct contact with foreigners in the workplace.

Against the academic backdrop described above and in the sections that follow, the chapter attempts to bridge this gap. To this end, the chapter formulates two interrelated and correspondent theoretical–activity (integrated) models (termed the magnet of trend's model and the LANGUAGES quadrant) of 'development linguistics' or 'language and minority [studies] that are markedly utilitarian to understand the extent of issues in foreign/second language learning among marginal populations labeled as the dominant-language-speaking language users.

Theoretical Frameworks
理論框架

In parallel fashion, the two correspondent theoretical frames, of the magnet of trend's model and the LANGUAGES quadrant were regarded as infrastructures for the ELL campaign. There was little fundamentally and principally wrong with the utilization of these two theorized models to help realize ELL. One would wish to argue that, for instance, Hornberger's (1989, 2002, 2003) landmark continuum of biliteracy model (or other established models) were utilitarian to help the ELL movement. However, one would also find it difficult to argue that the two interrelated models, proposed in the chapter, were not utilitarian given that they provide visual perspective, emphasize the local conditions of language phenomena, and they are self-explanatory and accessible to participants. More importantly, what pro-ELLers had of the two conceptual-activity models was a product of studies on a broad variety of contexts (e.g., globalization, nationalism, and urbanization) and informed by robust theories.

The Magnet of Trend's Model
用磁鐵來解釋趨勢的模型

In the early 2010s, a conceptual framework termed 'the magnet of trend's model' (For a detailed review, see Lee, 2015) was proposed and implemented in author's fieldwork and classroom teaching, originally conceptualized to account for the experiences minorities encounter in language contact situations and language use (practice). This model was accompanied by the LANGUAGES quadrant in the present chapter. It should be acknowledged that both the magnet of trend's model and the LANGUAGES quadrant were not another attempt of formulating alternative framework to account for the existent traditions of scholarships in language studies but complementary to theoretical conceptions stemming from the emerging tradition ('sociolinguistics of globalization') started, in part, by Blommaert (2010), among others.

To be sure, the two interrelated and correspondent models (the magnet of trend's model and the LANGUAGES quadrant) that underpinned the study reported in the chapter, as introduced below, can be seen as both conceptual frame (for analysis) and activity model (for implementation of planning, strategy and intervention) that were theoretically grounded and empirically derived model of scientific inquiry. They could be adopted as a thinking frame to help scholars develop more informed views of language contact, opportunities and challenges in language learning, and be used to intervene and build capacity of foreign/second language learning for individual and group minority learners.

Magnets, in this model, were utilized metaphorically as forces to create invisible magnetic fields that pull on language users from their first-language (L1) speech communities. In this model, globalization refers to economic, financial, geographic, political and societal drive for the global circulation, flow and mobility of capital, goods, human resources and knowledge (Lee, 2015). Global centers (e.g., developed economies and global cities) are magnets to attract capitals and foreign talents from global peripheries. In this model, globalization requires the increasing role of English as *Lingua Franka* within and across the three economies (e.g., English is utilized when Thailand exports canned fruits to USA).

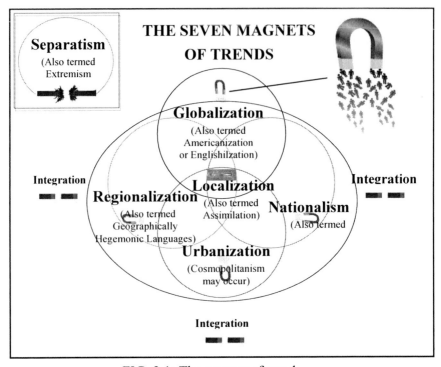

FIG. 3.1: The magnet of trend

Sources: Expanded from Kosonen, 2008, informed by Kaku, 2012; p. 171; Fishman, 1998/1999; and modified from Lee, 2015

Regionalization, in this model and in Thailand's context, refers to the increasing role of hegemonic languages from developed and developing economies in South-east Asia and/or Asia-pacific region, notably Chinese (Mandarin), Japanese and Korean. Regional centers (regionally strong economies and cities) are magnets to attract exports and foreign talents from neighboring countries.

Nationalism, in this model and in Thailand, refers to the increased use of the state language, Standard Thai. Urbanization, in this model and in the context of Thailand, refers to the increased use of urban languages. Urban centers are magnets to attract populations from semi-urban and non-urban areas. Localization, in this model, refers to people who are either not attracted by magnets such as global centers, national centers and urban centers or those who are attracted by these centers but fail to survive in these centers. Integration, in this model and in Thailand's context, refers to a regional economic integration, known as ASEAN Economic Community. Separatism, in this model and in the context of Thailand, refers to community-based language users who intentionally separate themselves from magnetic fields created by these forces introduced above.

Minority
弱勢族群

It is imperative to define what it means by minority itself in Fig 1 and in the present chapter. This sub-section provides operational definitions of 'minority' (with a focus on 'the politics of not belonging,' 'marginalization,' 'social exclusion,' and 'deficit thinking') in the present research context. The word 'minority' or 'minoritized' has been defined in numerous ways throughout the decades. In its general sense, the term 'minoritized' is most commonly deployed as shorthand to describe an unequal access to resources (causes) and consequences of growing social and economic inequalities in individual and societal levels.

The following literature refers to the power disparity and focuses on whether in the numerical (population size) majority or minority, many of these individuals and groups become subordinate and are subjected to oppression [and discrimination] by ideologies and activities derived from the dominant discourse, in that they continue to be socially excluded and pushed to margins in their respective state and civil society. In the utilization of the term 'minoritized,' the chapter applies the same understandings as Pickering (2001),

Winlow and Hall (2013), and Shields, Bishop and Mazawi (2005).

Pickering (2001) employed the words to describe "the politics of not belonging" ("involves constructing and keeping in public view its negative counterpart of not belonging," p. 107). From this view, the term 'minority' or 'minoritized' or 'marginalized' is defined by the social majority and the differentiation is based on some noticeable appearances and characteristics, e.g., ethnicity (ethnic looking), wealth, among others. Put it more directly, the term minority refers to those who have a sense of not being members of the dominant ethnic group within a nation state. It should be noted that Kammuang (Northern Thai) and Lao/Isaan (Northeastern Thai) language users are regarded as type I minority in the present chapter.

Further, Winlow and Hall (2013) adopted the term for social and economic marginality ("inability of the 'socially excluded' to access ostensibly 'normal' and routine services and aspects of our shared cultural life," p. 20). Departure from this view, the term 'minority' or 'minoritized' or 'marginalized' is referred to collective rights or civil rights that are not equally accessible to some impoverished, discriminated and disenfranchised members in a society. It should be acknowledged that lower-status workers in the service industry and labor market are viewed as type II minority in the present chapter.

Aligned with the above, Shields, Bishop and Mazawi (2005) utilized the term in formal educational settings ("how minority children are prevented from achieving their full potentials in schools when their lives and cultures are labeled as marginal"). In their writing, Shields *et al.* argue that deficit thinking is the ideology and the discursive practice of holding lower expectations of academic achievements for students with demographics that do not match the traditional school system (e.g., low-income, culturally and linguistically diverse students). In Thailand, out-of-school street child/teen labors are seen as type III minority in the present chapter.

The tradition of scholarship in language studies has been focused on typical minorities such as aboriginal communities, underprivileged diasporas (migrants) in contemporary urban metropolis, and students in formal schooling settings whereby targeted occurrences are richly accessible to researchers.

TABLE 3.1: Definitions of Minority
附表 3.1: 弱勢族群的定義

李育修製表

Minority1: (aspects of ethnicity and race)	The politics of not belonging (one who has a sense of not being a member of the dominant ethnic group within a nation state) – 'involves constructing and keeping in public view its negative counterpart of not belonging,' defined by the social majority and the differentiation is based on some noticeable appearances and characteristics, e.g., ethnicity (ethnic looking), wealth, among others.
Minority2: (social and economic levels)	Social and economic marginality ('inability' of the 'socially excluded' to access ostensibly 'normal' and routine services and aspects of our shared cultural life) -- collective rights or civil rights that are not equally accessible to some impoverished and disenfranchised members in a society.
Minority3: (formal educational settings)	The extent to which minority children and teens are prevented from achieving their full potentials in schools or being forced to be out of schools when their lives and cultures are labeled as marginal in formal educational settings – deficit thinking is the ideology and the discursive practice of holding lower expectations of academic achievements for students with demographics that do not match the traditional school system (e.g., low-income, culturally and linguistically diverse students, and out-of-school street children and teens).

Minority4: (value attribution of languages)	Marginalized in language learning -- inequality in a 'symbolic' linguistic 'market,' linguistic hierarchy and 'linguistic imperialism,' difficulty in foreign/second language learning, and language education (of prestige standard varieties) only accessible for elites.

Sources: Bourdieu, 1991; Pickering, 2001; Shields, Bishop and Mazawi, 2005; Winlow and Hall, 2013

Marginalized in Language Learning
在語言學習過程當中被邊緣化

Language learning in the context of the chapter is referred as a more general learning phenomena of global languages (e.g., International Standard English spoken in US and UK), or prestigious standard languages (e.g., Beijing-accented Chinese), or geographically and regionally hegemonic languages (e.g., Arabic, Chinese and Spanish). Language education/teaching can be seen as an unequally distributed resource which, simultaneously and subsequently, produces, re-produces and sustains both old and new inequalities, inherently connected to dominant ideologies, political structures and power relations (own fieldwork, 2007-2015). One cannot deny the fact that global-, prestigious-, standard-, foreign- and second language learning is in relation to one's upper social mobility (e.g., Gal, 1978; Lee, 2012, 2014a; Smith-Hefner, 2009). At any given time, native speakers of the world's 600 + local languages learn a small number of global-, prestigious-, standard- and regionally hegemonic languages. The reason why one is marginalized in his or her foreign/second language learning process is in relation to a multitude of political, economic and sociological factors and the chapter shall select three prominent ones (i.e., hierarchy and linguistic imperialism, difficulty in foreign/second language learning, and language education only for elites and mainstream/majority).

First, there is an issue of inequality in a 'symbolic' linguistic 'market,' language politics and 'linguistic imperialism' (see Bourdieu, 1991; Pennycook, 1994; Phillipson, 1992) -- hierarchy among languages -- in that one may not speak a prestige language as his or her native language and sees a need to learn globally or regionally powerful languages. Likewise, in a similar vein, Bourdieu (1991) developed his business metaphor to view linguistic-and-communicative market whereby languages are seen as symbolic capitals and powers. In such a symbolic marketplace metaphor, some languages and their native speakers have more capitals than others to gain profits, whereas other speakers are aware of their speech as inferior, thereby the native speakers of low 'capital' languages are marginalized. Thus, one is marginalized during the process to learn a more prestigious standard language which is not his or her native language (L1).

Second, there are difficulties (phonological-, vocabulary- and grammatical difficulties) facing learners in any foreign/second language learning, from a theoretical point of view of contrastive linguistics (see Aarts, 1982; Di Petro, 1978; James, 1992 for fuller accounts) and second language acquisition (see Ellis, 1997). That is to say, errors that have been made in a second language (L2) by L2 learners are often resulted from distinctly different structures of L1 and L2.

Third, the equal access to learn global-, prestigious-, standard- and regionally hegemonic languages is limited to elites and the mainstream, but is unfortunately not always accessible to the marginalized individuals and groups (own fieldwork, 2010-2015; Thumawongsa, 2011).

To tackle the aforementioned issues in language learning the minority is facing, the ELL campaign and field of study have evolved into its present form by pro-ELLers taking their leadership role and commitment in supporting the mission of ELL in Thailand and elsewhere.

Marginalized Language Users

被邊緣化的語言學習者

Marginalized language users are the case in point. Among marginalized population around the world, some are first language speakers of local and regional (aboriginal) minority languages. Moreover, this chapter refers to these non-national languages (stemming from abroad, some of which enjoy national state language status in foreign countries) as immigrant minority languages. The term of (new/recent) immigrant minority is borrowed from Extra and Yagmur (2011, p. 1173). In addition to all of this, the chapter refers to marginalized socio-economic minorities who speak dominant language variants as their first language labelled as dominant-language-speaking minorities.

TABLE 3.2: Classification of Language Users

附表 3.2: 語言使用者的類型

李育修製表

'Language user' individuals and groups (Five sub-groups)
1. Dominant-Language-Speaking Majority
2. Dominant-Language-Speaking Minority
3. Local/Indigenous (or Regional) Minority
4. (Century-old Immigrant) Ethnic Minority
5. (New/Recent) Immigrant Minority

Sources: Cook (2009); Extra and Yagmur (2011)

The Languages Quadrant
語言學習的象限

LANGUAGES or the LANGUAGES model (exemplified as a mnemonic) or the LANGUAGES quadrant is not a different set of conceptual and methodological toolkit, but a conceptual companion to the magnet of trend's model (Fig. 3.1). It is another attempt by pro-ELLers to articulate what it is meant to broaden one's repertoires by operating among and across numerous quadrants. In this model, a language user achieves more economic and social benefits if s/he is operating (learning and using languages) out of more number of quadrants. This framework is what pro-ELLers opt for a conceptual model, as well as an activity model for the LANGUAGES quadrant, constructed in the present chapter. It is also a device to facilitate the recognition and labeling of macro-level forces and ideologies that govern and operate language contact, language choice and language use (practice), among others. The acronym, L-A-N-G-U-A-GE-S, is developed with letters in each quadrant to represent (L for) localization [and indigenization], (A1 for) Americanization, (N for) nationalism [and standardization], (G1 for) globalization, (U for) urbanization [and cosmopolitanism], (A2 for) assimilation, (G2 for) geographically hegemonic (or powerful) languages, (E for) Englishlization, (S for) separatism [insurgency or terrorism]) under which language users are categorized within nine quadrants.

Different Quadrants, Different Language User Groups

Sociolinguistically, one may operate out of one or more quadrants simultaneously or sequentially. Rather than discussing every quadrant in great details, I instantiate the L-quadrant and A2-quadrant speakers in the following:

L-Quadrant & A1-Quadrant Speakers

A speaker who is under the influence of localization (see Fig. 1) and operates linguistic communications in the L (localization) quadrant and the A2 (assimilation/integration) (see Fig. 2) is tied to a relatively stable and resident speech community, in which they live relatively autonomous, un-mobilized and un-globalized lives. Despite the fact that they are the most, if not fully, assimilated and integrated language users defined by the host population and their local L1 speech communities, they have little or no access to global-, prestigious-, standard-, foreign- and second language languages to the pursuit of upper social mobility. A language user operating out of the L (localization) quadrant and the A2 (assimilation/integration) might be little aware of that s/he speaks some indigenized varieties of global languages by incorporating code-switch/mix and truncated words (Blommaert, 2010) in a relatively monolingual speech, emphasizing that these un-local words are subjected to local speech styles and pragmatic norms. There is another notion of localization of language: "Localization is a self-expression and, at the same time, a response to the macro-level sociopolitical forces" such as globalization and nationalism (Lee, 2015).

A common theoretical and methodological approach to localization (see L quadrant in Fig. 2) of language and linguistic assimilation (see A2 in Fig. 3.2) highlight geographical variations (local variants and local practices) and consider language spread as a flow of unified linguistic-and-communicative systems and styles adapting to a new neighborhood in spatial and temporal levels. Some related interest in regards to L-quadrant and A2-quadrant speakers, as defined in the present chapter, are works of Pennycook's (2010) Language as a Local Practice – language as a situated social act (see Pennycook and Makoni, 2006) and sociolinguists who principally deal with stratified language contact (Labov, 1972), static variation, local distributions of varieties, creoles and pidgins. The chapter favors the view proposed by Pennycook (2010) that language is seen as a situated social act, but contests against the view that languages are simultaneously operated in both macro (global) and micro (local) level. The chapter argues the view in favor of focus on language use (practice), at times, in micro (local) levels (local codes and rules prevail) without an involvement in macro (global) levels. In this view, languages, in spite of being 'mobile resources' (Blommaert, 2010), are likely distributed and spread in a micro (local) level within bounded speech communities where speakers enjoy higher degrees of autonomy. Let me instantiate a particular case in a rural village of Thailand where two central-Thai speaking interlocutors deploy local code, genre, register, and speech style, in the discussion of 'how to get a papaya out of a papaya tree by means of a locally invented tool' without a sense of operating out of the G1-quadrant (globalization of the English language) and U-quadrant (urbanization of city language) (own fieldwork, 2013).

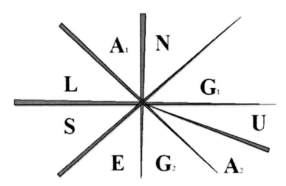

FIG. 3.2: The LANGUAGES quadrant

(L-A-N-G-U-A-G-E-S Mnemonic)

Informal (Language) Learning
非正式的語言學習

Besides sketching the two parallel models (Fig. 3.1 and 3.2) in the preceding sub-section and in what follows, the paper shall highlight another prominent (albeit often neglected) view of education/learning – informal (language) learning. The ELL campaign invites individual language learners to broaden their language repertoires from their situated quadrant (Fig. 3.2) to occupy more quadrants by creating target language exposure and learning resources. I intend to take my observations (of informal language learning where service-industry workers learned English from foreign customers in their workplace) further to account for possibilities of increasing the number of quadrants, illustrated in The LANGUAGES Quadrant (Fig. 3.2). The point of view in question is articulated below by Blommaert (Blommaert and Velghe, 2012, p.1, also cited in Velghe and Blommaert, 2014, p. 89):

Learning processes of languages develop in a variety of learning environments and through a variety of learning modes, ranging from regimented and uniform learning modes charactering schools and other formal learning environments, to fleeting and ephemeral encounters with language in informal learning environments.

As stated earlier at the outset of formulating the two correspondent theoretical frameworks (Fig. 3.1 and 3.2) that individuals' linguistic communication, language learning, language use (practice) and language contact revolve around one or more macro-level forces (Fig. 3.1), as well as operate out of one or more quadrants (Fig. 3.2), where their flows and movements do not occur in an arbitrary manner but are processed and organized metaphorically by magnets (Fig. 3.1) and quadrants (Fig. 3.2). One of the major contributions of informal (language) learning is to expand individuals' language repertoire by creating availability and accessibility for minorities who have little or no access to receive formal language education.

Methodology 研究方法

Qualitative methods were chosen for this study as a suitable method given a smaller number of individual case studies (not all 200 participants provided rich data) and the need for detailed descriptions from case studies.

PROJECT OBJECTIVES

Research Questions
探討的問題

Aligned with the ELL movement, there was a great temptation to search for answers to the research questions as I chose to position myself in the step 1 (capacity analysis) of the ELL steps.

RQ1: What approaches to language-learning-and-language-use were deployed by dominant-language-speaking minority language users to contribute to their foreign/second language learning, thus boarding their language repertoires (operating out of more quadrants)?

RQ2: What learning resources and learning process of global-, prestigious-, standard-, foreign- and second languages participants were engaged in formal or informal learning environments?

It should be noted that the second research question asked participants to reflect on the utilization of varied resources (on line or off line; receptive linguistic input or productive linguistic out; structured or unstructured learning activities) to foster language learning (both in- and out-of-class).

The Site & the Sample
資料蒐集地點和研究參與者

The study, reported in this chapter, considered how to achieve comparable language data and decides that participants recruited should not be excessively discrepant among themselves to ensure comparability with regard to their first and dominant language, and foreign/second language learning. With the comparability in mind, the study confirmed that all multiple sites under study were located within the Bangkok City and all participants were defined as the dominant-language-speaking language users and they shared fairly similar language repertoires (Standard Thai is their first/L1 and dominant language), except for the majority of bargirls who were native of Northeastern Thailand (type I minority) and a number of massage therapists who were native of Northern Thailand (type I minority).

The Bangkok City, home to more than 10 million dominant-language-speaking language users, provided a case study on the ELL. A number of journeys to Bangkok's four districts, one market, two monuments and three roads were made to locate, recruit and connect with participants. It should be noted that these sites were selected mainly because they were accessible to me as I regularly visited them in daily routines. Two different data-sets were created. The 65 participants (first data-set) of barbers, bargirls, hair salon stylists, massage therapists, street child/teen labors and street prostitutes were chosen on the basis of my personal networks. Second data-set were gathered from the rest of 135 participants (e.g., taxi drivers).

TABLE 3.3: The field and participants

Multiple Sites (Within Bangkok)	Sample	Number of Participants (N=200 from two different data-sets)
Asoke District Bangkabi District Huamak District Phayathai District Khaosan Road Ladprao Road Rachawa Road Tewet Market Democracy Monument Victory	Barbers (Minority 2 & 4)	(n=10)
	Hair Salon Stylists (Minority 2 & 4)	(n=10)
	(Issan) Bargirls (Minority1 & 2 & 4)	(n=20)
	Bus Fare Collectors (Minority 2 & 4)	(n=20)
	Massage Therapists (Minority1 & 2 & 4)	(n=20)
	Restaurant Waiters & Waitress (Minority 2 & 4)	(n=20)

Monument	Taxi Drivers (Minority 2 & 4)	(n=28)
	Three-wheel Motorcycle Drivers (Minority 2 & 4)	(n=5)
	Maids and Cleaners (Minority 2 & 4)	(n=2)
	Motorcycle Taxi Drivers & (Minority 2 & 4)	(n=20)
	Street Vendors (Minority 2 & 4)	(n=20)
	Street Child/ Teen Labors (Minority 2 & 3 & 4)	(n=5)
	Street (Adult) Prostitutes (Minority 2 & 4)	(n=20)

Note. Please see Table 3.1 for references of types of minority, defined in the present study context.

Data Collection & Analysis
資料採集和分析

Informed by the two parallel theoretical frames (Fig. 1 and 2), the study also adopted an approach to data which combined and coordinated field methods and perspectives derived from traditions of ethnography of communication, linguistic anthropology, sociolinguistics (e.g., Blommaert, 2010; Schilling, 2013), educational linguistics (e.g., Hornberger, 1989, 2002, 2003, 2004), language education/learning. More specifically, this research adopted the qualitative approach in data gathering and data analysis (Merriam, 2009), due to the fact that the study did not obtain a large sample size and it will not be statistically representative and the results will not be generalizable to the target population of millions of Thai working class in the service industry and in the labor market as a whole. Empirical data on language and linguistic communication in its social context were at the core of the study. Thus, interviews and observations of authentic conversations were documented and transcribed. The data were collected with the assistance of a field-site translator, a native speaker of Standard Thai and a fluent speaker of English (certified as an advanced English speaker by the Intensive English Program, Indiana University, in August 2005).

The primary data for this study was taken from in-depth and face-to-face interviews, complemented by field observations, with an emphasis on methods in spoken language research (not multimodal and literate research). Interview is by far one of the most common types of qualitative research method and it is most likely the primary measuring instrument for the present study. The study included face-to-face semi-structured interviews with about 200 participants. The participants interviewed were aged between 15 to 65 years old. Interviews were held in their respective workplaces and residences, and lasts between 20 minutes to 1 hour. Furthermore, the data for the pilot study had been collected during a number of ongoing fieldwork periods in multi-sited communities and districts (inaugurating in August 2014). Instead of asking participants to provide concise information on particular language-use (practice) and language learning questions, interview questions were kept brief, and interviewees (participants) were encouraged to talk at length about topics of interest to them (Schilling, 2013, p. 7).

Field observations were made for participants conversing in a foreign or second language (e.g., Chinese or English) with one or more interlocutors. Besides the collection of interview data and notes from field visits (observations), important bodies of applied linguistics, educational linguistics and sociolinguistics literature (with a focus on language education/learning) (e.g.,

Blommaert and Velghe, 2012; Velghe and Blommaert, 2014) were also consulted.

There were multiple ways to measure the vocabulary knowledge, oral language proficiency, grammar awareness and reading comprehension/skills in English of participants. They were the informal oral test administered by me (author has lived in the US for in-and-out 10 years), interactions with me that required them to produce English (e.g., send a text message to my mobile phone in English) and their self-report on English language proficiency.

Analyzing language-use patterns of the dominant-language-speaking language users in Thailand was a challenge, due to paucity of reliable data drawn upon representative samples by previous studies. As far as the data analysis was concerned, the interview questions elicited the following data to provide answers for the research questions: (a) demographic information (secondary interview question), (b) the first/L1 and dominant language of the participants (secondary interview question), and (c) what learning resources and learning process of global-, prestigious-, standard-, foreign- and second languages participants were engaged in formal or informal learning environments (primary interview question that aimed to elicit the desired data to answer the research questions).

Broad content analysis conventions were deployed to interpret interview data and field notes derived from observations, aimed at combining both emic and etic (interactional) data. Triangulation (of interview data, field-notes derived from observations and literature), member-checks with participants and peer (referee) review by colleagues were measures adopted to ensure the validity of the study.

PROJECT OUTCOMES

Findings 研究成果

Overview of Results

The first research question investigated what approaches deployed by the dominant-language-speaking language users that contributed to their learning of English (and other foreign/second languages). The results revealed that the globalization of English and the regionalization of East-Asian languages motivated participants to learn English and/or Chinese and/or Japanese.

Moreover, formal classroom language instruction and informal interactions with English-speaking customers were two language resources utilized by the dominant-language-speaking language users to develop their language abilities. As for what approaches deployed by the dominant-language-speaking language users to foster their language learning, some participants reported that their physical attractiveness (e.g., the makeup they put on their face and/or the costume and dress they were wearing) determined their opportunities for interactions with English-speaking foreign customers. They also actively greeted customers by speaking simple English words and/or phrases, aimed to increase the interactions with them. As for what strategies were adopted when communicating with English-speaking foreign customers, some reported that they spoke some keywords in English sentences during their conversations. However, some relied heavily on senior Thai workers to translate from English to Thai and from Thai to English when needed for the effective communication with customers.

The second research question investigated what learning resources and process were utilized when engaged in formal or informal language learning environments. The data revealed that language learning was more effective in informal learning environments whereby the English-speaking (and foreign/second language-speaking) customers played the role as informal tutors. On the one hand, informal tutors functioned as linguistic input providers – the dominant-language-speaking language users received exposure to English and/or Chinese and/or Japanese. On the other hand, it was commonplace for the dominant-language-speaking language users to repeat what their customers said and memorized the utterances of English and/or Chinese and/or Japanese from their customers.

Globalization of English
全球化經濟趨勢下促使英語使用日益頻繁

Not surprisingly, a recent movement in the acquisition, learning and development of the English language among participants (service-industry workers) studied had been to shift away from learning English in favor of an interest in how to best speak, read and write it towards an interest in how to utilize it as a mere additional language for workplace only. For most participants studied and defined as type IV minority (Table 1), the utilization of English as the language to operate out of the G-quadrant (Thailand's globalized tourism industry has been largely overlapping with its service industry) was a major obstacle. Thai bargirls and massage therapists were not alone in having informal tutoring from their foreign customers to improve their English oral proficiency. Likewise, taxi drivers, catered for expatriates and tourists, as well as restaurant waiters and waitress working in restaurants catered for foreign customers, were jumping on the same band wagon.

I shall return to this salient finding in the proceeding section. And yet, I distinguished among three dominant-language-speaking groups with respect to vocabulary knowledge, grammar awareness, oral proficiency and reading comprehension in English: (1) limited bilinguals (predominantly Thai with little English), (2) fluent bilinguals (despite speak Thai dominantly, English was fluent to function) and (3) Thai-dominant groups (predominantly Thai with nearly zero English). However, only fluent bilinguals among Thai service-industry workers contributed to fostering the acquisition, learning and development of English, gaining more economic and social benefits than their counterparts. In other words, limited bilinguals and Thai-dominant language users were not operating out of the G-quadrant (see Fig. 3. 2 for globalization of English quadrant), but were operating out of the L- (localization of vernaculars such as Isaan (Northeastern Thai) and Kammuan (Northern Thai)), N- (nationalism of state language such as Standard Thai) and A2- (assimilation in L1 speech community) quadrants simultaneously.

Localization of Dialects, Nationalism of State Language, Urbanization of City Language

In this chapter, the term first language (L1) was adopted to refer to the language dominant-language-speaking minority language users were exposed to from birth and was used continuously at home. They were viewed as to be successful in the L quadrant (localization of dialects and vernaculars) as master of local language. For participants who were trans-regional migrants from provincial Thailand to the Bangkok City, their L1 was their regional vernacular. However, the majority of these transregional dominant-language-speaking migrants experienced simultaneous acquisition and learning of L1 (regional vernaculars) and L2 (standard Thai) before learning the L3 (mostly, English). Thus, they achieved success in the A2- (assimilation in L1 speech community), L- (localization) and N- (nationalism of state language – Standard Thai) quadrants. By contrast, participants who have their origin in the Bangkok City or Central Thailand reported that they were monolingual Standard Thai speakers before learning English at schools and their second language (L2) was referred to English.

Regionalization of East-Asian Languages

A number of bargirls showed their growing interest to learn Japanese, because there was a growing number of Japanese business men and Japanese tourists to visit their bars. It was also because of that Japanese was a geopolitically powerful language (see regionalization in figure 1 for explanations) and Japan was the home country for a large number of expatriates in Thailand. Some bargirls and transgender bargirls also reported to learn Chinese as they worked in Hong Kong and/or

Singapore and/or Taiwan. However, Korean language was least favored by these dominant-language-speaking language users compared to Chinese and Japanese.

Two Themes
兩個研究發現的主題

Although there were differences in language-learning-and-language-use practices, two main categories of approaches were identified across 200 participants. We looked at three different case studies of informal (English) learning to illustrate the two themes.

For reasons of confidentiality and privacy, names for bargirls and street teen workers have been changed.

Theme 1
formal educational experiences

Fang's case – the massage therapist

案例研究：按摩師

In the first case study of the massage therapist Fang (pseudonym), a type I (Northern Thai native) and type II (lower socio-economic status) minority (see Table 3.1), we saw how educational background provided a good basis for her acquisition, learning and development of the English language in informal educational settings. Fang, a middle-age Northern Thai woman from Chiang Rai who spoke Kammuang as her L1 and Standard Thai as her L2, although she simultaneously acquired and learned both L1 and L2 at home and in school. English has become her L3 as a consequence of her formal education (she did well in her English subject at school and undergraduate program) and informal learning with foreign customers. Besides learning English in her formal educational settings, Fang also loved to practice English with foreign customers. She was considered a fluent bilingual (Thai-dominant with English to function). However, tens of thousands of Thai massage therapists were facing obstacles in their L2 and L3 learning as type IV minority defined in the present study (Table 1). Fluent English-speaking Thai massage therapists, like Fang, were very rare.

Fang worked at a Bangkok massage parlor where female massage therapists sit behind a glass partition to allow male customers to look at them before a selection was made. Fang's massage parlor was catered primarily for Thai-speaking male customers. Thus, she did not need to learn a L3 in her full-time workplace. However, her English-speaking ability enabled her to take part-time jobs as a freelancer to provide massage service in hotels for a number of foreign nationals including Japanese, Hong Kong, Taiwanese and Singaporean men.

Kaew's case – the waitress and bargirl in a bar-style restaurant
案例研究: 酒吧餐廳服務生

In a contrast, Kaew (pseudonym), a 24-year-old Issan L1 (type I minority as a Northeastern native) and Standard Thai L2-speaking bargirl of Bangkok (type II minority as in lower socio-economic status), was seen as a limited bilingual (Thai-dominant with little or no English speaking ability, but had become English-literate as a result of formal education), hereby she was also regarded as a type IV minority (facing obstacles in L2 and L3 learning). During her years of formal schooling (she was an undergraduate student who studied in a special weekend program at a community university), she had acquired English vocabulary knowledge and English reading comprehension (she was able to send a text message in English to my (author's) mobile phone), while her English speaking ability was surprisingly limited as a university student. According to Kaew, she learned how to read and write English from her schools, but cannot function in English oral communication. As a limited bilingual, she cannot access to the higher-end English-speaking service sector. Although she was English-literate (she was evidently being able to send a text message in acceptable English as well as non-standard English), Kaew only utilized her Thai L1 to work in a predominantly Thai-speaking bar, catered for Thai-speaking customers.

Also, when comparing Fang's case with Kaew's case, it was not difficult to see that fluent bilingual (Thai-dominant with good English oral proficiency to function) leaded to success to across from L and N quadrants (localization of vernacular and nationalism of state language) to G quadrant (globalization of English). However, reading comprehension in English made almost no difference in what quadrants (Fig. 2) these participants operated.

When comparing the quantity and quality of English instructions provided in Fang's and Kaew's undergraduate programs, Fang's relatively higher socio-economic status determined her access to more opportunities and resources than Kaew's. In other words, Fang's relatively higher financial standing was the underlying reason for her success in English. As a financially stable undergraduate student, Fang completed her studies within four years without interruption, during which she accessed to educational resources to learn English. Although they both were considered in lower social standing, Kaew's relatively lower income placed her in a disadvantaged position as she cannot continue to study from time to time. For instance, Kaew dropped out from her undergraduate program years ago and worked in Cambodia as a waitress in a casino before she took on the job as a waitress in the bar restaurant. Kaew was in need to work in the bar restaurant during weekdays, in order to pay for her undergraduate program in the weekend. As a result, Kaew did not concentrate on the learning of English because she focused on earning income.

Liang's case – the street teen labor & sex worker
案例研究：街頭性工作者

Liang, a L1 speaker of the Standard Thai and did not speak any regional vernaculars, was defined as a type II minority (lower socio-economic status) and type III minority (out-of-school teen) in the present study (see Table 3.1). Although she was also seen as a type IV minority, her inability to function in English was not seemed to be a major obstacle for her work as she claimed. I interviewed Liang (pseudonym) on the street where she worked as a street teen prostitute (she had changed her national identification cards multiple times and even the Thai police cannot verify if the information about her age in her national identification card was valid). When Liang wanted to speak English to foreign customers and did not know how to say English vocabulary, she claimed that it was because of the fact that she was never being able to complete any degrees in formal educational settings. She told me that she never completed her primary school and I doubt if she attended any classes at school. More than one occasion, Liang told me that she equated her failure in speaking English to her never-completed formal education. According to Liang, her prior schooling experiences were inseparable from her lower confidence to say a few words in English.

PHOTO 3.1: Liang

Photo Credit: Author

圖 3.1：作者替蓮（匿名）拍照

2015年

Liang also made a special case study. Although her operation was only out of A2-, L- and N- quadrants (assimilation in her L1 speech community, localization and nationalism of state language), she might have more interactions with foreign customers than other two aforementioned cases in the G quadrant (globalization of English). She explained that the overwhelming majority of her foreign customers were not sex tourists, but long-term residents (expatriates) and they acquired the Thai language, hereby they spoke Thai to her.

Theme 2
the pattern of English-for-customer and/or
English-as-an-additional-language-for-work

In the meantime, a large majority of participants revealed that their English-speaking interlocutors (customers and/or tourists) were functioned as their informal tutors (teachers). Although these English-speaking customers expected service provided by Thai service-industry workers (instead of teaching English), their speaking of English provided the needed linguistic inputs for these workers. As the study suggested that of all the components involved in one's learning of foreign/second languages, teachers played a crucial role on learner's success or failure. Data also demonstrated that informal tutors' qualification exerted a powerful influence on participants' learning of English and foreign/second languages. It should not be surprised that much data thus far have shown that informal (language) learning environments (e.g., streets and workplaces including bars and massage parlors) were more effective (to acquire spoken fluency) than (language) learning in formal educational settings, claimed by participants in the present study.

As observed from the current practices in Thailand, one of the most important features of the language-learning-and-language-use practices among Thailand's service industry workers was that English was seen as an additional language, termed English-as-and-additional-language-for-work. That is to say, English was primarily adopted in the workplace. The utilization of English did not go across a number of language domains such as family, government and public places. In other words, oral language proficiency in English was only required at the level of transmitting information by Thai service industry workers to communicate with their foreign customers. This phenomenon was termed English-for-customer in the present chapter. Nonetheless, it was also true that English as a foreign and second language learners generally saw a need to master more than 800 English vocabulary, in order to function in everyday conversation. This was not viewed as a serious problem facing participants in the present study, because they claimed that they rarely talked to foreign customers more than their job-related affairs. For instance, it was commonplace that Thai taxi drivers, catered for foreign tourists, needed to have knowledge of basic English vocabulary related to places their foreign passengers planned to go (e.g., hotels, department stores and sky train stations) and being able to say numbers in English (the underlying assumption was that these Thai taxi drivers were able to negotiate the price of the transportation fares).

Across 200 participants researched (regardless of their service sectors catered for Thais or foreigners or both), the majority of them was viewed as limited bilinguals (Thai-dominant speakers with little vocabulary knowledge, grammar awareness and oral proficiency in English, but some had reached a good level of reading comprehension) and Thai dominant (with nearly no English proficiency) groups as type IV minority (facing major obstacles in L2 and L3 learning). They were successful in the L and N quadrants (see Fig. 2), operating out of localization of vernacular and nationalism of the state language (Standard Thai). Only a few number of Thai bargirls were seen as fluent bilinguals (who can function in English lexical and syntactic levels although they demonstrated worse grammar awareness of Standard English). Many Thai bargirls were operating out of the A2-, L- and N-quadrants (see Fig. 3.2) because their bars were catered for Thai men. However, some Thai bargirls had changed their quadrants from A2, L and N to G (globalization of English) working in bars catered for foreign customers (see Fig. 3.2), because changing quadrants were a big boost of their income.

Conclusion 結論

The data gathered for this pilot study provided insights into the fact that, on the one hand, individuals' educational background provided a basis for him or her to further development in his or her L3 (English) as evidenced in the case of Fang. On the other hand, the optimistic perspective of the realization of the ELL movement was challenged by the pessimistic case such as Liang's story. That is, a failure in prior formal education also resulted in less confidence to learn a L2 or L3 (English) as seen in Liang's case.

As mentioned earlier, informal tutoring by interlocutors (foreign customers) in informal educational settings resulted in expansion of language repertoires and the increase of the number of quadrants (Fig. 2) among the dominant-language-speaking language users. Educational implications of these results were discussed herein. As noted above, we had seen evidence from participants that the English-speaking foreign customers were instrumental in their acquisition, learning and development of English as L3. Thus far I have not seen other studies that have questioned the advantageous effects of customers functioned as informal English tutors for service-industry workers in a developing country.

The informal learning from exposures to English-speaking foreign customers should not be the only available resource for English among Thai workers in the service industry. In the long term, formal educational experiences also played a key role for further development of English among a few number of fluent bilingual participants studied. Thus, better resources and possibilities were needed to fostering acquisition, learning and development of the English language for type I (those who were not seen as ethnic majority), type II (lower socio-economic status), type III (out-of-school street child/teen workers) and type IV (those who faced major obstacles in L2 and L3 learning) minorities (see Table 3.1) in Thailand and other developing countries.

Our research team, enacting as pro-ELLers, concluded this chapter with implications and suggestions for educational policy, planning and programing, corporate training courses for service industry employees and development agency. With regard to recommendations for the improvement of vocabulary knowledge, oral proficiency and literacy/reading comprehension in English among service-industry workers in the developing countries (where English is not the first language), the pro-Ellers of this chapter proposed that a combined effort of educational background, English-for-customer and English-as-an-additional-language-for-work should be at the core of development planning and implementation. Specially, this paper considered formal educational experiences to have a long-term impact on service-industry workers' vocabulary knowledge, oral language proficiency and literacy/reading comprehension in English, by which they were enabled to operate out of more quadrants (Fig. 3. 2) as a means to gain more economic and social benefits. Although many challenges were inherent, the educational sector and service-industry sector should envision and implement educational programs and corporate training courses with an emphasis on basic vocabulary knowledge, some levels of grammar awareness and oral proficiency in English needed to function as English-for-customer and English-as-an-additional-language-for-work for service-industry workers who spoke Thai as L1/dominant language. These educational policies, programming and corporate trainings, many of which aimed to realize ELL (particularly, equity in English language learning) for service-industry workers defined as type I and type II minority (Table 3.1), opened up new possibility for them to operate out of more quadrants (Fig. 3. 2) as a means of expanding language repertories.

（本文原稿於2016年4月發表在《語言研究的理論和實作期刊》第六卷第四期）

ENDNOTES

Service-industry workers in developing countries find it challenging and difficult to learn how to speak English in classrooms. However, after graduation from schools, this is how they learn to speak English (and other foreign languages) from their expatriate customers. Some of them have opportunities to become fluent English speakers, largely because they have extended exposures and opportunities to practice English by communicating, socializing and interacting with English-speaking customers in their workplace (e.g., bars and restaurants in the tourism destination). In other words, the workplace one way or another maximizes real-world English communication practices for workers in the service sector and at the same time maximizes their English fluency.

For further information about this chapter (if you want to discuss with the author), please contact:

Hugo Lee, Faculty Member

International College

National Institute of Development Administration

18th fl., Navamin Building, 118 Seri Thai Rd,

Khlong Chan, Bang Kapi, Bangkok 10240

Hugo Lee, Consultant Roster Member

United Nations

Economic & Social Commission for Asia & the Pacific

3rd fl., United Nations Conference Center, ESCAP HR

United Nations Building, 76 Rajadamnern Nok Ave

Bangkok 10200

T. 088-607-2560

E. hugoclubheart3@gmail.com ___ Li Y-h Hugo

W. https://indiana.academia.edu/YuHsiuLee

參考文獻 References

1. Aarts, F. (1982). The contrastive analysis debate:
   Problems and solutions. *Studia Anglica Posnaniensia*, 14, 47-68.
2. Abhakorn, J. (2013). Classroom interaction and thinking skills
   development through teachertalks.
   Kasetsart Journal of the Social Sciences, 34, 116-125.

Jan Blommaert
3. Blommaert, J. (2010). *The sociolinguistics of globalization.*
   Cambridge: Cambridge University Press.
4. Blommaert, J., & Velghe, F. (2012). Learning a supervernacular:
   Textspeak in a South African Township. *Tilburg Papers in
   Culture Studies, 22.*
   Tilburg: University of Tilburg
   http://www.tilburguniversity.edu/research/institutes- and-
   researchgroups/babylon/tpcs/
   (Accessed 17/12/2014).

Pierre Bourdieu
5. Bourdieu, P. (1991). *Language and symbolic power.*
   Cambridge: Polity.
6. Cohen, E. (1987). 'Phut Thai dai!': Acquisition of hosts' language
   among expatriates in Bangkok.
   International Journal of Sociology of Language, 1987, 5-20.

Serafin M. Coronel-Molina

7. Coronel-Molina, S. M., & Rodrı´guez-Mondon˜edo, Miguel. (2012). Introduction: Language contact in the Andes and universal grammar. *Lingua*, 122, 447-460.

8. Di Petro, R. J. (1978). *Language structures in contrast.* Rowley, MA: Newbury House.

John Draper

9. Draper, J., (2010). Inferring ethnolinguistic vitality in a community of Northeast Thailand. *Journal of Multilingual and Multicultural Development, 31* (2), 135-147.

10. Draper, J. (2012). Reconsidering compulsory English in developing countries in Asia: English in a community of Northeast Thailand, *TESOL Quarterly* 46.4, 777-811.

11. Ellis, R. (1997). *Second language acquisition.* New York: Oxford University Press.

12. Equity [Def. 1] (n.d.). In Oxford Dictionaries Online. http://www.oxforddictionaries.com/ (Accessed 18/12/2014).

13. Extra, G., & Yagmur, K. (2011). Urban multilingualism in Europe: Mapping linguistic diversity in multicultural cities. *Journal of Pragmatics*, 43, 1173–1184.

Joshua Fishman

14. Fishman, J. A. (ed.) (1991). *Reversing language shift: Theoretical and empirical foundations of assistance to threatened languages*. Clevedon: Multilingual Matters Ltd.
15. Fishman, J. A. (1988/1999). The new linguistic order. *Foreign Policy* 113, 26-40.
16. Fishman, J. A. (ed.) (2001). *Can threatened languages be saved: Reversing language shift revisited: A 21st century perspective*. Clevedon: Multilingual Matters Ltd.

Susan Gal

17. Gal, S. (1978). Men can't get wives: Language change and sex roles in a bilingual community. *Language in Society* 7.1, 1-16.
18. Hobsbawm, E. (2007). *Globalization, democracy and terrorism*. London: Little, Brown.

Nancy Hornberger

19. Hornberger, N. H. (1989). Continua of biliteracy. *Review of Educational Research*, 59 (3), 271-296.
20. Hornberger, N.H. (2002). Multilingual language policies and the continua of biliteracy: An ecological approach. *Language Policy*, 1, 27–51.
21. Hornberger, N. H. (eds.) (2003). *Continua of biliteracy: An ecological framework for educational policy, research, and practice in multilingual settings*. Tonawanda, NY: Multilingual Matters.

22. Hornberger, N. H. (2004). Continua of biliteracy and the bilingual educator: Educational linguistics in practice. *International Journal of Bilingual Education and Bilingualism*, 7 (2&3), 155-171.

23. "Inequality between the rich and the poor has reached its highest point in the past thirty years" [Video file] http://www.channelnewsasia.com/tv/live (Accessed 9/12/2014).

24. James, C. (1992). *Contrastive analysis: Applied linguistics and language study.* Singapore: Longman Singapore Publishers.

Michio Kaku

25. Kaku, M. (2012). *Physics of the future: The inventions that will transform our lives.* London, UK: Penguin Books.

Kimmo Kosonen

26. Kosonen, K. (2008). Literacy in local languages in Thailand: Language maintenance in a globalized world. *The International Journal of Bilingual Education and Bilingualism*, 11, 170-188.

William Labov

27. Labov, W. (1972). The social stratification of (r) in New York City Department Stores. In Labov, W. *Sociolinguistic patterns.* Philadelphia, PA: University of Pennsylvania Press, 43-54.

Hugo Yu-Hsiu Lee (李育修)

28. Lee, H, Y.-H. (2015). Theorizing globalization and minorities in Asian cities: Viewed from the language contact zone of Thailand in the making of languages and minorities. *Journal of Applied Sciences*, *15* (2), 329-342.

29. Lee, H, Y.-H. (2010). Exploring biliteracy developments among Asian women in diasporas:
The case of Taiwan. Ph.D. dissertation, Indiana University.

30. Lee, H, Y.-H. (2012). English for the purpose of reducing the poverty of orphans with disabilities in Thailand, *Journal of Education and Practice*, *3* (6), 87- 99.

31. Lee, H, Y.-H. (2013). Bargirl style of language choice and shift: A tale from the land of smile. *Theory and Practice in Language Studies*, *3* (3), 411-422.

32. Lee, H, Y.-H. (2014a). Losing Chinese as the first language in Thailand, *Asian Social Science*, *10* (6), 176-193.

33. Lee, H, Y.-H. (2014b). Speaking like a love entrepreneur: Language choices and ideologies of social mobility among daughters of peasants in Thailand's tourist sites. *Language, Discourse and Society*, *3* (1), 110 -143.

Aree Manosuthikit

34. Manosuthikit, A. (2013). Language ideologies and practices of a Burmese community in the US: A critical perspective on multilingualism. Ph.D. Dissertation, University of Wisconsin, Madison.

35. Merriam, S.B. (2009). *Qualitative research: A guide to design and implementation.* San Francisco, CA: Jossey-Bass/John Wiley & Sons, Inc.

Morita Liang

36. Morita, L. (2007). Discussing assimilation and language shift among the Chinese in Thailand. *International Journal of Sociology of Language*, 186, 43-58.

Dipika Mukherjee

37. Mukherjee, D., & David, M, K. (2011) (eds.). *National language planning and language shifts in Malaysian minority communities.* Leiden: International Institute of Asian Studies/Amsterdam: Amsterdam University Press, 59-70.

Alastair Pennycook

38. Pennycook, A. (1994). *The cultural politics of English as an international language.* London, Longman.

39. Pennycook, A., & Makoni, S. (Eds). (2006). *Disinventing and reconstituting languages.* Clevedon, UK: Multilingual Matters.

40. Pennycook, A. (2010). *Language as a local practice.* London and New York: Routledge.

Chapter 4

Speaking like a Love Entrepreneur among Peasants' Daughters

```
love entrepreneurs

bargirls
```

第四章

從農夫的女兒變身成都市愛情企業家的語言轉換模式

THIS CHAPTER ADDRESSES an important set of issues: how language choices between dominant, standard and international codes are conditioned by increasingly globalized industries and social models that accompany them and are created by them. Particularly it examines how gender ideologies related to languages and social actions shape love industry workers' orientations toward foreign/second language learning and societal language uses. All of these aforementioned issues and data have the potential to make a contribution to the literature (published research materials) on language, discourse and society.

This chapter examines the social meanings of language choices, shifts and the ideologies of differentiation that emerged from the migration of young peasant women and men from Isaan to central Thailand, where they were engaged in the love industry, whose loci were the seaside city of Pattaya and the metropolis of Bangkok. Attention in this article is thus paid to language uses and code choices in Thailand's love industry discourse, through a young Isaan women's bar-based counter-public subculture, in addition to an analysis of the social meanings of their language choices and linguistic shifts.

摘要（四、五章）

超過90%的「泰國愛情企業家」（尤其是酒吧舞女和阻街女郎）都是來自泰國東北農村的女孩，離鄉來到曼谷和泰國濱海城市（主要集中在芭達雅）的酒吧和夜店上班，真的能改變家境由貧轉富嗎？在學校從來沒有好好學過英語，要如何在滿口英語的FARANG（歐美白人男性）顧客的酒吧坐檯？本章和下一章（第五章）就像一次曼谷市中心的深度旅遊和探險，載您闖入go-go酒吧的紅燈區，處處充滿驚奇和驚豔。然而曼谷首都和海邊觀光景區大肆興建的酒吧，立即成就兩件事情：一、它讓泰國東北農村的女孩學會說英語。二、它讓泰國東北ISSAN方言在曼谷市中心和泰國海濱都市傳承和擴散。

ACKNOWLEDGMENTS

The original study reported in chapter 4 was edited and proof reading by Jack Clontz (PhD, University of California, San Diego, USA), Emeritus Professor, Maebashi Kyoai Gakuen International College, Japan（日本前橋共愛學園國際大學）. It was peer-reviewed by editorial board members (editorial office in London) in the *International Sociological Association's Language, Discourse and Society* (ISSN 2239-4192).

"As a child growing up in an Isaan village, my mom always reminded me that it was my responsibility to provide financial support for her, my dad, my grandpa, my grandma, and my brothers and sisters. By this she meant, or she believed that I understood what she meant, that, as the first-born daughter in my family, I was the source of income for my whole family even at the expense of my own life."

"Being a second-class citizen in an Isaan village due to my gender by birth and a third-class citizen since discriminated against by the rest of my country due to the Northeastern region of my origin brought distinct burdens."

[These two verbalized vignettes are derived from a set of interviews in which Isaan bargirls orally narrated their life stories to the author in 2012]

Introduction 導論

THIS CHAPTER REPORTS a study that investigates the lesser-studied bar multilingualism. It deals with linguistic code choices and language shifts amongst love industry workers in Thailand's tourist sites. This includes an analysis of the correlation between sociological variables and linguistic strategies (language choices and linguistic shifts) used by young Thai men and women employed in the Thai love industry. Findings show that, on the one hand, English, the informal official language of the love industry, is seen as the language of social upward mobility for both Isaan and non-Isaan young women. On the other hand, Isaan Thai, the language of the majority of the bargirls, is viewed as the language of socializing for non-Isaan young women engaged in this domain of work. This study confirms previous research by suggesting that young women's choices and shifts vis-à-vis language can be best understood in the context of the strategies they adopt in regard to life chances and life style choices.

Background and Rationale

研究背景

Bar multilingualism, or the use of a number of languages or dialects, in addition to choosing one medium of linguistic exchange over another, and the common shifting from one linguistic means of expression to another, are veiled expressions of aspiration by these Thai love industry workers and emblematic of their desire for upward social and economic mobility. As such, this phenomenon also provides the ways whereby these workers associate willy-nilly with a cosmopolitan counter public, showing resistance to traditional Isaan family values, particularly regarding appropriate gender roles and the subculture of young Isaan women.

Viewed from the sociolinguistic aspects of mobility, the migration of daughters of peasant families from Northeastern rural Thailand or Isaan to urban-cosmopolitan tourist sites in Central Thailand is explored within the context of potential social and economic opportunities, and the new Thai entrepreneur class, which particularly appeals to young Isaan women. The aim of this article is also to address the question of how language choice – the choice to speak English by Isaan young woman and other young women in the love industry – is both perceived as a mechanism whereby poverty is reduced, and is complementary to the phenomenon of converging ethnolects (non-Isaan young women working in the love industry speak Isaan Thai to their compatriots); How language shifts (away from the habitual change from Thai to English) is employed as a mean of upgrading one's life style. The researcher is next concerned with showing how changes in linguistic indexical systems are correlated with community boundary configurations, and to non-Isaan young women's participation in the discursive practices and convergent speech styles when speaking with older Isaan women. The researcher also focuses attention on gendered discrepancies in linguistic strategies: the role the love industry plays in men's and women's disparate progress towards being able to converse in the English language is taken into consideration.

No other modern ethno linguistic minority and young women's subculture in Thailand receives as much media attention, and produces as much mainstream anxiety, as does the young women known as Isaan bargirls. For many years, young females, from the Northeastern region of Thailand in particular, have strategically engaged in foreign language learning and language shift as a mean of socio-economic upward mobility. In light of this phenomenon, the researcher is concerned to address the question of the precise nature of the social meaning of language choices and shifts by the members of young Isaan women's speech communities in the discourse used by these women, who are involved in Thailand's love industry. The researcher also examines the disparity between Isaan and non-Isaan women's speech, and between men's and women's speech, as used by love industry workers in Thailand.

Albeit the social science literature has well documented both the love industry in Thailand (Brown, 2000; Manzanares & Kent, 2006; Lee, 2013) and the ethno linguistic vitality of Isaan Thai vis-à-vis language choice among members of the Isaan speech community (Draper, 2010), the connections between these superficially desperate phenomena have not been examined at length; Little is understood of this significant socio-linguistic phenomenon. For this reason, the researcher further investigates the effects of the love industry on young Isaan women's strategic linguistic behaviors as contrasted to non-Isaan women and men engaged in the same activity. Accordingly, the lacunae in the literature warrant the contribution that can be made by this study. In this contribution, the researcher attempts to integrate the approaches of linguistic anthropologists and sociolinguists by examining the following three groups of love industry workers: Isaan women, non-Isaan women and Thai men. A particular focus is made on social factors leading to disparities in language choices and shifts.

It is a commonplace in sociolinguistics, in sociology of language, in linguistic anthropology and in dialectology, that social factors, or sociological variables, play a major role in foreign and second language learning, bi- and multilingual development, language maintenance and shifts. The question of what influences one's linguistic behavior has enormous social relevance and, at the same time, there is little doubt that previous studies about the relationship between language and social variables (e.g., class, gender, and social network) are plentiful. In the past few decades, sociolinguists and linguistic anthropologists have attempted to establish a set of sociolinguistic norms that could adequately account for the obvious fact that social phenomena are reflected in individual and group linguistic behaviors (Fishman, 1964, 1965, 1989, and 1991; Gal, 1978, and 1979; Gumperz, 1964; Labov, 1966, 1972, and 1980; Lee, 2013). There is little doubt that their well-grounded findings are applicable and relevant to complementary studies carried out in disparate contexts.

Initially, sociolinguists, linguistic anthropologists and dialectologists have surveyed language contacts, choices, maintenance and shifts in relatively isolated and immobile communities (e.g., generational immigrant communities and long-established ethno linguistic communities). Nowadays, the researchers in the same fields that use conventional sociolinguistic norms to account for the practices of their target research populations (such as the one studied by the author of this article) encounter difficulties. Thus, linguistic anthropologists and sociolinguists need to examine individuals and groups who are unprecedentedly mobile at geographic, social and occupational levels. As an example, my principal interest for the present study lies in surveying the language choices of love industry workers/migrants from rural Isaan to the urban metropolis and tourist areas of Thailand in their interactions with tourists/interlocutors on a global scale. An exploration of the dynamics of socially patterned linguistic behaviors among love industry workers may produce fresh perspectives through illuminating new mechanisms to account for multifaceted human sociolinguistic behaviors in regard to this understudied sociolinguistic phenomenon.

The two following sections review the background, the literature and the context, first, in regard to the Thai love entrepreneur class and, second, in respect to the linguistic and communicative repertoire in Thailand. Accordingly, this study should shed light on the linguistic hierarchy in Thailand vis-à-vis the ethno linguistic vitality of Isaan oral communication. Then, the researcher is concerned to illuminate the concepts of language choice and shift insofar as they bear upon closely related inquiries in the areas of language and gender, of ethnolect convergence, and of discursive practice.

Setting the Scene:
Thailand's Love Industry
泰國的愛情企業

This section presents the macro-level context of the love industry as the creation of a new entrepreneur class, admittance to which appeals to young peasant women from Thailand's impoverished Isaan area. In respect to technical terms used in the study of the love industry in Thailand (albeit these terms do, however, raise issues of their own), the author of the present article uses the terms "love industry workers" or "love entrepreneurs" as catch-all phrases, which are convenient umbrella terms and mutually exchangeable. Workers in the love industry, or so-called "love entrepreneurs", are defined as freelancers, who sell their companionship (and more) to foreign tourists in entertainment venues. Some, who are between the ages of thirteen and thirty, are referred to as bar girls (i.e., those who wait in bars to meet foreign male tourists) and "go-go" girls (i.e., dancers or strippers in clubs, or in discos), (see more detailed treatment of these terms in Manzanares & Kent, 2006). Others are tour guides for foreign male tourists. Being qualified as a female love industry worker means that the relationships with foreign male tourists are a career: these relationships are a primary source of income to support herself and her family (Nicks, 2010: 187). Female love industry workers' career is short-term (e.g., weekend) or long-term (e.g., being a girlfriend). Conversely, Thai male "love industry workers" are referred to as beach boys (dek goh in the Thai language) and are often around the age of thirty (Nicks, 2010; For a discussion of the language of sex in Thailand, see Boonmongkon & Jackson, 2012).

It should be noted that neither all love industry workers bar girls, nor all the other love industry workers, are involved in the commercial sex trade. Moreover, it should be clear that the love industry in Thailand (in Pattaya, Chiang Mai, Phuket, and the red-light districts in Bangkok) is far from being a true representation of Thailand's culture as a whole.

From the Rural Peasant to the Urban Entrepreneur Class

從農村的佃農搖身一變成都市企業家階級

Tired of the degrading, harsh, and humiliating poverty of rural Isaan or of working as laborers in the construction of buildings (approximately 150 baht/5 USD per day) and of electronics manufacturing plants (approximately 200 Baht/6 USD per day), other social and economic possibilities promised in urban areas are appealing to these young peasant women. Contrasted to relatively low income earned by Thai men working in the love industry, Thai bar girls earn their reputation as "love entrepreneurs". Some top earners receive monthly allowances from disparate foreign boyfriends. Table 1 presents the monthly allowance received by a young Thai bar girl from her clients.

TABLE 4.1:
A Young Thai Bar Girl's Monthly Allowance

Countries of origin for disparate boyfriends	Amount/month (Thai Baht)
Sweden	50,000
U.K. (#1)	40,000
Venezuela	35,000
U.K. (#2)	30,000
Germany	20,000
Total	175,000 THB/month = 5,000 USD/month

Source: Ken Klein's book, *Building a House in Thailand*, cited by Nicks, 2010

Moving from the definitions of terms and returning to the main thread, the present and later sub-sections provide a selective review of the market of the love industry in Thailand with a focus on the commodity and the customer. The commodities in the love industry of Thailand are known as bargirls and freelancers of many kinds. "The love industry [in Thailand] is a multi-billion dollar economy" (Nicks, 2005). These include younger and older Northeastern Isaan women, Northern Thai women, Thai men, Burmese, Cambodian/Khmer, Laotian, Yunan/Chinese women and others from a variety of ethnic backgrounds. Among Thai women from disparate ethnic backgrounds, the Northeast Isaan region (e.g., Buri Ram, Korat, Udon, Ubon, Si Saket and Roi Et), supplies nearly 80 percent of female workers in the sex industry (Manzanares and Ken, 2006). The reasons why Northeastern Thailand is the biggest supplier of women engaged in the love industry is rooted in a number of principal factors. The reasons for this phenomenon are manifold.

FIG. 4.1: Northeastern Isaan Region of Thailand

Left Photograph, Map of Isaan in Thailand.
Source: <http://siam-longings.com/wp-content/uploads/map%20of%20thailand%20isaan.jpg> with permission.

Right Photograph, Provinces of Isaan.
Source: <http://thethailandlife.com/wp-content/uploads/2012/03/isaan-map-.gif> with permission.

First, poverty is largely responsible for Isaan women's engagement in the love industry. "Isaan girls are poor; tourists are rich; I bridged the gap!" (comment by a former Isaan love entrepreneur, cited in Manzanares and Kent, 2006). Some Isaan people live under desperately impoverished conditions. Within their relatively primitive villages, insufficient schooling systems produce uneducated and unskilled Isaan youth (Manzanares and Ken, 2006).

Second, investment in face-making instead of a better standard-of-life is a chief factor accounting for Isaan women selling their companionship (and more) to foreign male tourists. In some Isaan villages, face-making for Isaan parents is far more important than the welfare of their daughters and their sense of well-being. How much money an Isaan daughter sends to her parents determines the status of her face and her family's status, albeit at the extreme expense of her involvement in the love industry. It is not uncommon that some Isaan mothers' biggest dream is to bear and raise a daughter who can constantly send money home to make face by means of buying cars and electronic appliances (e.g., televisions and air conditioners) to exhibit to fellow villagers by employing the technique of invidious comparison (Manzanares and Ken, 2006).

Third, a principal cause of the phenomenon also lies in gender ideologies stemming from traditional Isaan family values: "My [Isaan] culture holds all women to be not only inferior but expendable," a comment made by Lon, a former love industry worker in Thailand (Manzanares and Kent, 2006). In some Isaan villages, "daughters are cast in the role of caretakers of the family" instead of sons (Brown, 2000). These family values are grounded in Isaan religious beliefs. In Theravada Buddhism, sons earn merit for their parents by simply becoming a monk and staying in a temple for three months to fulfill family duty. However, daughters, particularly first-born daughters, are expected to become the primary income earners and must take care of the needs and welfare of the whole family (Manzanares and Ken, 2006). Therefore, a strong sense of obligation to care for parents is essential to caring members of an Isaan community. Nevertheless, for some Isaan families, at times driven by poverty and at other times driven by greed, there is no limit to the perceived duty to parents of daughters. In the Northeastern regions of Thailand, it is small wonder that the love industry and the sex trade have been well-established, inasmuch as Isaan parents may well expect their young daughters to become prostitutes (Brown, 2000).

TABLE 4.2:
Selected Quotations
regarding Gender Ideologies vis-à-vis Isaan Women

Selected quotations	Sources
"Women are pawns in times of need."	Thai Proverb
"Men are gold; women are cloth. Men look like gold; when gold falls in the mud, we can clean it. Women look like white clothes; when they fall in the mud, we can never clean them so that they will be white again."	Khmer Proverb, cited in Manzanares and Ken, 2006
"A family owed money to a dirty and repulsive beggar. In lieu of repaying the debt, the parents sent their daughters to live with the beggar to share his bed until the debt was repaid."	Isaan Moral Story, cited in Manzanares and Ken, 2006

Fourth, although this view is widely contested, numerous Western tourists and participants in love industry sectors in Thailand insist that the dark-complexioned Isaan women are more attractive than light-complexioned women (e.g., their Chinese-Thai counterparts) to male Western tourists (Bangkok Diaries, 2009). It is no less obvious that the love industry sectors are at pains to provide light-complexioned female workers to Eastern tourists, while concerned to provide dark-complexioned Isaan girls to Western tourists.

In sum, gender discrimination against Isaan women in addition to rural poverty and a limited educational background (uneducated), fewer job opportunities (unskilled) in Isaan and their dark complexion as a commodity (it should be acknowledged that the dark-complexioned belief is widely debated) give rise to correlations between the workings of the love industry and Isaan women, that is, the love industry is one of the fast-track ways to earn money by young Isaan women.

In combination with the present discussion of the commodity bought and sold in the love industry in Thailand, the customer partly accounts for the sustainability of this industry. Throughout its modern history, Thailand has been receiving tourists from the East (e.g., Japan, South Korea, Taiwan, Hong Kong, India, and Middle Eastern countries), the West (e.g., France, Germany, Sweden, Switzerland, the U.S.A., and the U.K.), Africa and most of the world. After the U.S.A. pulled out of Vietnam, tourists were soon to replace American military personnel as customers in Thailand's love industry as planned in an unofficial partnership by the love industry and the tourism industry (Brown, 2000). Western tourists, as opposed to Eastern tourists, are particularly attracted to younger, pretty, sexy, and, most importantly, submissive Thai women. At the same time, Thai love entrepreneurs advertise and cater to "meet[ing] the unfulfilled needs" of Western men who want "better treatment than [what they receive from] their aggressive, demanding and unfeminine Western women"

(Brown, 2000). As it turns out, every year millions of Western and Eastern male tourists (along with smaller number of foreign women) visit Thailand in "seeking for fulfillment" (Nick, 2005). "Many are survivors of traumatic marital break-ups and believe that Thailand is a good place to make a new start" (Nick, 2005).

TABLE 4.3:
Selected Quotations in respect to the Match
between Western Male Tourists and Isaan Women

Selected quotations	Sources
"In the year of 2004, my hometown in America registered 49 marriages and 32 divorces. Is the modern relationship of the Western world on the deathbed? An owner of a Bangkok matchmaking agency claims that oriental-style marriages have a much higher success rate than conventional Western legal marriages."....... "For me, being the provider [financial contributor to Thai wife's family] is a far better option than constant fights with a 'liberated' [Western] woman. And long-term, it's a cheaper option too."	Thaivisa.com Web Site, cited in Nicks, 2005: 14
"Many of these men come to Thailand because their wives have left them; they do not communicate with their families; or they cannot find a girlfriend back home. Sometimes they are here for company or 'companionship' which may not even be sexual that they can't find in their own countries."	Manzanares and Ken, 2006

"One girl from Patpong [a major red light district in Bangkok] marries a foreigner every week.	Manzanares and Ken, 2006

After a selective review focusing on the commodity and the customer in Thailand's love industry, an analysis of the linguistic and communicative repertoire in Thailand and social factors leading to disparities in language choice is needed so as to provide a framework of descriptive data for the present chapter.

Thailand's Linguistic Repertoire
泰國的語言生態

A comparatively small number of studies have explored the interplay of socially engendered dialects constitutive of the multifaceted diglossia, regimes of language, styles of speaking and the complex linguistic and communicative repertoire in Thailand. In such a high-stakes setting of linguistic contact, Thailand is a locus wherein the issue of language maintenance and shift is inescapably prominent (e.g., see Howard, 2010 for Muang speakers' language maintenance and shift in Northern Thailand; see Draper, 2010 for Isaan Thai speakers' language maintenance and shift in Northeastern Thailand; also see Lee, 2011a, 2011b, 2012, for language-related issues vis-à-vis minorities such as urban refugees and orphans with disabilities in Thailand), among minorities (e.g., Isaan Thai in Northeastern Thailand, Khmer in Eastern Thailand, Karen in Northern and Western Thailand, and Malay in Southern Thailand [LePoer, 1987]).

Thailand is simultaneously subject to convergence and divergence both linguistically and culturally. To better understand the relationship between love industry workers and their language choices in Thailand, it is imperative to start with the effects of urbanization and globalization. On the one hand, previous research reveals that one of the effects attributed to urbanization (e.g., see Batibo, 2009 for the effects of urbanization on language maintenance and shift; see Smith-Hefner, 2009 for the effects of urbanization on language shift in Indonesia; see Cheshire *et al.* 2011, for 'multicultural London English' in London) is language contact, shift, and loss. Internal diversity is a salient feature of the ethnolinguistic and cultural landscape of the Kingdom of Thailand, particularly with respect to the mass cross-regional migration from rural villages to the urban areas of Bangkok, Chiang Mai, and Pattaya. For instance, there is a huge flow of rural Isaan-peasant women to Bangkok and Pattaya, one of the two urban centers of Thailand, for the sake of better social and economic opportunities. On the other hand, some of the many effects attributed to globalization, in this case, global tourism, is language contact, linguistic convergence, and code switching.

Multilingual communities in Thailand's tourist sites provide a salient case allowing the examination of linguistic heterogeneity, societal multilingualism, indexicality and the sociolinguistics of mobility. In urban Thailand's tourist sites, varieties of language contacts, code-switching/mixing and alternating, multi-dialects, language maintenance and shift have been emerging, notwithstanding the fact that the English language has exerted a dominating presence and influence on all the other languages. The linguistic alternatives/repertoire available to speakers in these communities to be described includes three distinguishable speech patterns (i.e., Isaan Thai, Standard Thai, and English) among others (e.g., Western languages such as German, Russian, Polish, Serbian, Dutch, Danish, Norwegian, Finnish, Spanish, Italian and French; East Asian languages such as Mandarin, Mongolian, Japanese and Korean; Mid-Eastern languages including Iranian, Hebrew and Arabic; West-Asian language including Hindi, Tamil, Punjabi, Urdu and Bengali; West African languages (especially several distinct Nigerian languages) and even Central Asian languages (e.g., Uzbek). It is observed that the regional Laotian vernacular spoken in Northeastern Thailand, known as Thai Isaan, intermingles with the official, national and standard variety of the Thai language, termed Standard Thai, and is intertwined with more global-oriented languages (especially, English).

A perspective that is useful in the analysis of Thailand's diglossia and linguistic repertoire and, at the same time, frames this study stems from 'ethnolinguistic vitality' theory (formulated by Giles et al., 1977; Landry and Bourhis, 1997: 32). It is defined as what 'makes a group likely to behave as a distinctive and active collective entity in intergroup situations.' In this vein, the political status of languages recognized by the state (e.g., institutional support), demographics, economic considerations (e.g., medium of communication in commerce) and cultural capital are means of 'objectively' measuring the continued linguistic existence of an ethnic group's mother tongues, native languages and inherited languages within a linguistically heterogeneous society. By contrast, members of an ethnic group are asked to subjectively rate and predict the present and inferred future vitality of their languages as 'subjective' measures to account for the degree of ethnolinguistic vitality of their languages (e.g., see Draper, 2010 for an assessment of the ethnolinguistic vitality of Isaan Thai).

In a similar vein, it is desirable to examine more closely Thailand's diglossia and speech varieties in a perceived ranked order, inasmuch as linguistic hierarchy can be seen as a measure accounting for ethnolinguistic vitality. By means of linguistic normalization (Vallverdú, 1985: 90)—defined as a process through which normative views and acts vis-a vis a language, or a dialect, are established—and, at the same time, when the use of language at disparate social levels becomes differentially extended, languages and dialects accordingly become stratified and ranked in a linguistic hierarchy. As is known from surveys based on theoretical and empirical studies of language attitudes, language ideology and ethnolinguistic vitality in Thailand (e.g., Chanyam, 2002, Draper, 2010: 135-136), Standard Thai is seen as the most "prestigious variant" and accent (ranked No. 1), followed by Northern (ranked No. 2) and Southern [variants and] accents (ranked No. 3), and then Northeastern Isaan (ranked No. 4). This ranking, or linguistic hierarchy, is in agreement with the typical sociolinguistic explanation that languages spoken by dominant groups are perceived as more prestigious than languages spoken by minority groups (Labov, 1972, cited by Draper, 2010: 136).

Among less powerful Thai varieties, the regional vernacular termed Isaan is a branch of the Tai-Kadai language family (Lee, 2011c), and is linguistically close to the Laotian language. Isaan Thai is spoken in nearly the entire Northeastern region of Thailand. Isaan Thai is also the ethnic name of the largest minority group of Thailand (Draper, 2010: 135). In 1983, it was estimated that there were approximately 15-23 million Isaan Thai speakers in Thailand, including the 88 percent who converse in Isaan Thai with family members in the home with 11 percent communicating in code-mixing discourse combining Isaan Thai and Standard Thai with 1 percent speaking exclusively in Standard Thai (Lewis, 2009; cited by Draper, 2010: 135).

Nonetheless, a more recent examination of the Isaan vernacular has reported an ongoing intergenerational shift away from a stable bilingualism combining Isaan and Standard Thai towards the exclusive use of the Standard Thai variety, due largely to the influence of mass media (e.g., newspapers, television and radio) and schooling systems (i.e., Isaan children in the course of schooling underwent rapid language shift so that they spoke the Standard Thai variety according to their parents, reported by Draper, 2004, 2010). The fact that some Isaan lexical items, or lexis, suffering loss (Jantao, 2002, cited in Draper, 2010: 136), e.g., some Isaan person references have been replaced and mixed with the Standard Thai variety. This appears to be consistent with the stages of language shift toward language death identified by Fishman's Graded Intergenerational Disruption Scale (GIDS) (1964, 1991) to the field of language maintenance and shift (Draper, 2010: 136).

TABLE 4.4:

Perceived Language Hierarchy and Prestige in Thailand

Ethno-national Languages and Varieties of Spoken Languages	Ranking #
English	1
European languages	2
Eastern-Asian languages	2
Standard Thai	3
Northern Thai	4
Southern Thai	4
Northeastern Thai (Isaan)	5
No. of categorization of languages compared = 7	

Source: Chanyam, 2002

Echoing the language shift away from the Isaan variety toward the Standard Thailand variety, Isaan people are often discriminated against in their workplaces (e.g., jobs in urban areas as being only maids, construction workers, gardeners and taxi drivers) (see Draper, 2010: 140). A comprehensive treatment of the language maintenance and shift of the Isaan Thai language can be found in Draper, 2004, 2010.

PROJECT OBJECTIVES

Theorizing the Sociolinguistics of the Mobility of Young Women in Thailand's Love Industry

In view of the panoramic review addressing the love industry and the linguistic repertoire in Thailand just outlined in the preceding sections, understanding the nexus between sociological factors and language choices in respect to love industry workers in Thailand is a major challenge. Social factors leading to discrepancies between language choices and shifts have been a central preoccupation and is well documented in the literature of sociolinguistics as broadly defined (e.g., Fishman, 1964, 1989, 1991; Giles *et al.*, 1977), as well as developing sociolinguistic norms that account for the extent of language use, choice, maintenance and shift.

Attempts to define the terms 'language choice,' 'maintenance and shift' have been shaped by, or in turn have shaped, well-known sociolinguists in our time (e.g., Fishman 1991; Gal 1978, 1979). In the light of a variety of perspectives, the author of this chapter presents definitions as follows. First, as extrapolated from the concept of 'linguistic competence' as evinced by an ideal speaker-listener in a homogeneous speech community (Chomsky, 1965) formulated the notion of 'linguistic repertoire' in which a speaker of a language has at his or her disposal a wide range of linguistic variants and develops a register of speech sufficient to undertake a wide range of communicative tasks. Furthermore, Hymes (1974) developed the notion of 'communicative competence,' and initiated research in the fields of the 'ethnography of communication' and 'interactional sociolinguistics'. In Hymes' framework, language choice is referred to as a speaker's linguistic and communicative competence enabling the choice of style and variants with a speaker thereby drawing on his or her linguistic and communicative repertoire as suiting a particular purpose or function. The choice of a speech variety, nonetheless, is by no means a random phenomenon. Rather, the code choice made has to be deliberately selected by the speaker in the light of her or his social and interactional perspective so as to reach a level of satisfactory accommodation to the perceived linguistic situation in the language domain in which current discourse is being undertaken.

A second approach or perspective that guides this chapter is the distinction between languages in themselves (objective assessment) and attitudes, beliefs, stereotypes and social implications which individuals hold in respect to languages (subjective assessment). Drawing on this distinction in order to frame this research investigation largely stems from the fact that in a class-conscious society, Thais, to a varying degree, are hypersensitive to the socio-economical implications of accents, varieties (standard versus non-standard), dialects and speech styles as a means of symbolizing the stratification of class, status and prestige. In this vein, we must take into account that dictum that "our language embraces us long before we are defined by any other medium of identity" (Delpit and Dowdy, 2002: xvii). Thus, to a degree, language choice becomes a matter of ideology. The concept of 'language ideologies' is defined as beliefs concerning languages held 'by their users as a rationalization, or justification, of perceived language structure and use' (Silverstein, 1979: 193). In this light, the notion of 'language ideologies' is useful in accounting for why minority languages are maintained when their users are oppressed by users of dominant and hegemonic languages (see Woodlard, 1985 for Catalan speakers in Spain). For a crucial introduction to the field of language ideology, see Woolard, 1998.

Regarding the discussion of language choices, 'language shift' is another key concept. Gal (1978, 1979: 1) describes 'language shift' as a process through which "the habitual use of

one language is being replaced by the habitual use of another"
at disparate times.

In addition to approaching language choice largely by drawing
on the aforementioned concepts, the researcher is concerned to
examine the intertwined roles of gender, language choice and
shift in the light of work conducted in anthropological
linguistics, sociolinguistics and in a number of other fields. It
must be acknowledged that the interconnection between gender
and language choice has long been recognized and has reached
a high level of understanding (see Gal, 1978; Mukherjee, 2003;
Smith-Hefner, 2009; Lee, 2013). Thus, there is abundant
evidence to show that language choice is often gendered.

On the one hand, a number of previous studies have shown
women were more likely to have no or limited proficiency in
majority languages in view of lesser access to resources and
power (e.g., education) than men in an agricultural (or working
class) community. The socioeconomically disadvantaged
situation of indigenous women in Latin America has been
illustrated by Hill (1987). In these cases in Latin America,
women had less access to education and so spoke limited
Spanish (a good command of Spanish was essential for these
indigenous women in order to be able to access educational and
employment opportunities, and would thus enable them to
participate in the paid labor force), a state of affairs in contrast

to the situation of men. In a similar example, the male elite of the Nugunu or Cameroon villagers in Ombessa, Africa exhibited greater competence in the French language and achieved higher levels of educational attainments than did their female counterparts (Robinson, 1996: 212-213).

On the other hand, previous studies also found that women were constantly searching for a medium that would grant them access to valuable economic and social benefits, opportunities, resources, prestige and symbolic capitals. For instance, in Gal's pioneering work on the Hungarian-German bilingual town of Oberwart in Austria (Gal, 1978), a shift away from Hungarian speech to the use of the German language was found to be occurring among peasant women in view of the symbolic linkage between German speech and industrial work that was available to both Hungarian-speaking men and women, albeit being more appealing to the latter than to the former. It appeared that German-speaking factory jobs represented socio-economic advancement, whereas Hungarian-speaking agricultural work was linked to hard-work, low-income, rural, and peasant life. For a fuller treatment of gender and sociolinguistics, see Eckert, (1997) in Coates (1997) and Coates (2004).

An area of related interest to this strand of research on young women's social and economic opportunities is studying the effects of urbanization on gendered language choices. Urban centers, by and large, draw poverty-stricken populations from rural areas, due largely to social and economic inducements, such as more job opportunities, better basic infrastructure, and a modern lifestyle (Batibo, 2009: 26). In developing countries, it is estimated that 70 million migrants flow annually from rural areas into cities in the search for a better life (Seabrook, 2007). One of the many effects attributed to urbanization is language shift. In her well-regarded article, Smith-Hefner (2009) discussed the phenomenon of language shift from the Javanese (indigenous) language toward the national language of Indonesian emerging in Javanese youth in the nation-state of Indonesia. She went on to argue that in contrast to young men, young women were more likely to shift from Javanese toward the use of Indonesian, which was seen as a means of acquiring the symbolic capital necessary to accommodate their roles in forming part of the new working class.

In connection with this exploration of language choice by young Thai women vis-à-vis relevant concepts, it is to be observed that sociolinguists and linguistic anthropologists refer to the distinctive language usages and uses by speakers of an ethnic group as 'ethnolects' (see definitions of ethnolects in Clyne (2000); see problems with ethnolects in Jaspers (2008)). An ethnolect approach can better account for the fact that some non-group or out-group members adopt elements of another group's ethnolect in an attempt to bond with members of a different ethnic group, thereby forming cross-ethnic and multi-ethnic friendship groups. In view of what we know of language contact, it would be only expected that speakers from different ethnic groups would 'converge' in speech by virtue of borrowing linguistic forms typical of members of another ethnic group (see Coronel-Molina and Rodrı́guez-Mondoñedo, 2012 for examples of linguistic convergence in Andes). It can also be argued that the phenomenon of linguistic 'convergence' involves attempts to be understood by others through "symbolic references" to an extent adequate for undertaking communicative acts through utterances and speech acts (e.g., Clark, 1996, cited in Enfield, 2009: 91). At the same time, this phenomenon is "micro-political" and "coalitional" since designed to ensure that desirable interpersonal relationships are fostered by means of common or shared experiences, including code-switching/mixing with the speech and adopting linguistic features of the discourse of interlocutors from another ethnic group (Enfield, 2009: 91).

To continue in this vein, discursive practice (Young, 2009; Hall, 2011: 255-273) with respect to the study of language choice and shift is another key perspective and approach to the women's speech communities studied by the researcher. An approach through discursive practice is useful in accounting for face-to-face language use, or language-in-interaction, inasmuch as it captures the social and interactional realities of speech events and recurring communicative episodes. Such a practice is "conventionalized" (Hall, 2011: 256), whereby participants develop their competence by means of "repeated experiences" "with more experienced participants" (Hall, 2011: 256; Vygotsky, 1978). The discursive practice of communication between Isaan and non-Isaan women at work (in this case, in bars) can be better understood as the practice of being socialized into elder sibling-junior sibling relationship, or as extending "family relations" into a "social hierarchy" (for discussion of elder sibling-junior sibling relation in Thailand, see Howard (2007: 206-208). These aforementioned concepts are taken as the point of departure and account for patterns of language choices and shifts among the studied target populations.

Data Collection & Analysis
資料採集和分析

The researcher (author of the chapter) borrows techniques from ethnographical studies of communication (Hymes, 1974) and combines these techniques with approaches involving case studies, questionnaires, exploratory interviews, and field observations in order to conduct a survey research investigation. The data collection and the analysis are undertaken simultaneously. The researcher takes an eclectic approach and asks the research question of what sociological factors (social meanings) enable the emergence of bar multilingualism, i.e. language choices and shifts in this particular context.

Data were primarily collected on the basis of an exploratory questionnaire, which was going through the following topics: demographic characteristics, estimates of the participation in love industry activities, assessments of the respondents' daily uses of languages, and assessments of the language-use patterns and perceptions (language ideology) of the ethno linguistic vitality of Isaan. The later were measured using a 9 points Likert scale (from 0 i.e. "strongly disagree" to 8 i.e. "strongly agree". Then semi-structured interviews were realized to probe explanations from informants. On the overall basis, a shorthand observation list was developed; it was used for both participative and non-participative observations of naturalistically occurring speech acts. The questionnaire, the interview protocol and the observation list employed were tailored to suit the research setting. As it turns out, the triangulation among questionnaire responses, interview data, and observation data yields significant data. The findings are validated by questionnaire data, interview data and the extant literature.

The macro-concepts of language choice, language ideology, language shift, ethnolect convergence and discursive practice provide the theoretical and analytical concepts used to analyze the data. The analysis consists of dissembling and reassembling the elements of these data of in order to identify theme to answer to the research question by transforming them into findings that can be investigated by statistics, theoretical descriptions and interpretive explanations.

Sites and Samples: The Place of Bangkok and Pattaya in Thailand's Multilingual Tourist Sites and Societal Multilingualism

資料蒐集地點和研究參與者

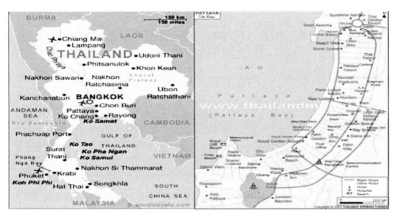

FIG. 4.2: Two Survey Sites: Bangkok Metropolis and Pattaya
Coastal Town in Thailand
Source: Left Photograph, Map of Thailand. Taken from
<www.wordtravels.com>, with permission.
Source: Right Photograph, Map of Pattaya. Taken from
>www.thailandmapxl.com/pattaya-map.html>, with permission.

TABLE 4.5:
Cross-Tabulation of Multi-Ethnicity
& Genders of Participants

Isaan woman sample	Non-Isaan woman sample	Thai men sample	Total
n=100	*n*=50	*n*=50	*N*=200

TABLE 4.6:
Characteristics of the Participants
研究參與者的個資

Love Entrepreneurs	N	% of sample
Gender		
Female	150	75
Male	50	25
No response		
Ethnicity		
Isaan	100	50
Non-Isaan	100	50
Educational Attainments		
K-6	160	80
Middle School	40	20
High School		
Undergraduate		
No response		
Employment Status		
Freelancers	200	100
Debt-Bondage		
No response		
Multiage	*M*=27	*SD*=6

The three target populations (Isaan women's, non-Isaan women's and Thai men's speech communities) and the two survey sites (Bangkok and Pattaya) investigated are unique, similar to and differ from previous studies in numerous respects. Although there are six respects listed in the following sub-sections, it should be said that there are more unique than the six stated here.

First, although one of the most vigorous arenas of previous studies in language maintenance and shift is found within cross-bordered and transnational immigrant communities (see Mukherjee, 2003, for migrated Indian brides and their role in the language maintenance of the Bengali community in Malaysia; see Kim and Starks, 2010, for the bilingualism among Korean immigrants in New Zealand) and the segregation of disparate ethnic communities (see Labov, 1972 for a classical Philadelphia study of the black and white ethnic communities), this article still arguably presents a clear-cut case of a domestically trans-local and cross-regional migrant community, consisting of the majority of Isaan girls who have moved from Northeastern Thailand to resettle in the seaside resort city (Pattaya) and the capital city (Bangkok) of Central Thailand. Compared to relatively smaller numbers of women (Lanna speakers) from Chiang Mai (Northern Thailand) and a few Bangkokians/Standard Thai speakers (although they come from respectable families, they participate in the love industry, so as to supplement their income and improve their standard of life), Isaan women nonetheless constitute the majority of workers in the love industry. It is estimated that approximately 100,000's Isaan women participate in the love industry in Pattaya (<pattaya-funtown.com> online). This figure makes Pattaya the location of the largest Isaan speech community outside Northeastern Thailand. This accounts for the nickname of Pattaya as 'Little Isaan' (Phuket has the second largest Isaan speech community outside Northeastern Thailand, followed by red-light districts in Bangkok). The Isaan women studied are largely responsible for language maintenance and shift among love-industry workers in this seaside tourist site (Pattaya), due largely to the role they play in this community (The author comments further on this later in the proceeding results section).

Second, 50 bars (out of approximately 500, 10%) are surveyed in the two survey sites, *viz.,* the Pattaya beach town and Bangkok Metropolis. It must also be acknowledged that it is problematic to ascertain a definite total number of bars in Pattaya and Bangkok, given that the total number is growing. If not bars, meeting places in malls, massage parlors, karaoke restaurants, night clubs (e.g., go go bars), and other entertainment venues are alternative sites to be investigated. Some bar-owners in Bangkok tend to hire bargirls who are Khmer or Lao-Khmer, thus the *lingua franca* in these bars, albeit code-mixed with Khmer and Laotian/Isaan vocabulary, phrases and syntax, is of the Standard Thai variety instead of the Isaan variety. In the present article which is narrowly focused on the discrepancy between Isaan and non-Isaan speech communities, the consideration of other bars, particularly in respect to those located in the Bangkok Metropolitan Area which mainly employ Standard-Thai-speaking bargirls, are beyond the scope of this inquiry.

Third, besides the multi-sited approach, to be included in the sample of the present study is young women (multi-age M=27, SD=6), as well as men, participants have to be freelancers. By the same token, it is imperative that participants cannot be in debt-bondage to traffickers. This entails that their job description is to willingly sell their companionship (or more) to foreign tourists in a variety of ways (e.g., pay-as-you-go love). During data collection, the members of the sample population, as divided into three sub-groups (see Table 5), give consent to participate in this study. The sample represents approximately 1 percent of the total target population, given that "a general consensus appears to be that at any time there are between 300,000 and one million women" participating in the love industry in Thailand (Leather, 2005: 14). It must also be acknowledged that the total target population (i.e., Thais, regardless of whether Isaan or non-Isaan, engaging in the love industry) is fluctuating, largely due to the fact they are geographically dispersed and mobile by means of a loose-knit and, relatively speaking, weakly-tied Isaan community in this beach resort and the urban metropolis concomitant with maintaining stronger ties with their home villages. Moreover, it is no less obvious that the Isaan ethnic group likely forms numerous close-knit networks by means of their workplaces (e.g., bars, shopping malls, and so forth), while at the same time develops differing levels of resistance and integration into cosmopolitan, modern and non-Isaan domains of urban life styles. For a more detailed treatment with respect to the profiles of the sample, please refer to Table 6.

Fourth, within the multiple-sited research setting, the distinction between a majority group and a minority group, as well as a higher-status language and a lower-status vernacular, or dialect, assessed by normative sociolinguistic measures, turns out to be invalid and reversed when compared to urban centers outside the survey sites. This is consistent with the notion of an alternative linguistic market (Woodlard, 1985) in which the investigated sites are primarily bars in this coastal town (Pattaya) and the urban metropolis (Bangkok), thereby excluding a few places (e.g., Phuket and some districts in Bangkok) in the metropolitan areas of Thailand wherein Isaan enjoys *lingua franca* status, while at the same time Standard Thai is more dominant than Isaan outside of these bars. As such, young Isaan women are the most active and visible members and core groups in the communities studied. Non-Isaan women participating in the love industry find it more difficult to take on an active role, largely as a result of the fact that the Isaan language dominates in the social-networks of bars and is the marker of in-group and out-group members employed in the bars (The author comments further on this later in the results section).

Fifth, these two survey sites are subject to considerable language contact with Western and Eastern tourists due largely to the constant influx of foreign tourists. In 2008, it was estimated that nearly 5.8 million foreign tourists paid a visit to Pattaya (<pattaya-funtown.com> online).

PROJECT OUTCOMES

Summary of Analysis of the Social Meanings of Language Choices and Shifts
語言選擇和語言轉換背後的社會意義

Previous studies of the use of language by women often showed that their language choice and shift were notably associated with potentially bettering the conditions of life and life chances, such as poverty reduction, social and economic mobility (from the margins of society to the new middle class) (Gal, 1978; Smith-Hefner, 2009; Lee, 2013), resistance against public ideologies (Gagné, 2008) and improved lifestyles. The present findings extend the results of these previous investigations by indicating that women of disparate ethnic groups (Isaan and non-Isaan) engaged in the same activity in the same industry had different degrees of association with the same languages (in this case, English and Isaan), while discrepancies in associations led to different social and economical outcomes.

Data analysis suggests that correlations between language-use patterns and several social factors are small but statistically significant for the women and men studied here. Findings indicate that differences in the roles (e.g., majority-minority, dominant-subordinate, and empowered-disempowered) played by these social actors in the love industry are reflected in linguistic behaviors. First, social factors leading to the maintenance of Isaan speech in the work domains of the two sites and Isaan women's shift away from Isaan speech toward English speech is explored. Second, social factors leading to non-Isaan women's progressive shift toward the Isaan vernacular and ethnolect convergence with Isaan is examined. Thirdly, the researcher comments on social factors linked with the love industry leading to relatively monolingual the Thai men examined being relatively monolingual (less striking shift).

Isaan Women's Speech Community: Language Choice as a Means of Poverty Reduction and Social and Economic Mobility, and Language Shift as a Means of Resistance against Gender Ideologies and Lifestyle Enhancement

First, the love industry has created the largest Isaan speech community outside home villages in Northeastern Thailand (It should be also noted that Phuket, another tourist site in

Thailand, is the second largest Isaan speech community outside the Isaan home region), has tremendously contributed to the language maintenance of the Isaan speech. Consistent with Woolard's (1985) observation of an alternative linguistic market that challenges a single linguistic hierarchy, it is argued that while the Isaan vernacular in its home region suffers language shift away from the Isaan variety toward Standard Thai speech (Draper 2004, 2010), the ethnolinguistic vitality of Isaan is relatively strong and symbolically opposes the dominant and legitimized Standard Thai code in the seaside town (Pattaya) and work domains (bars) in Bangkok Metropolis, largely due to the fact that Isaan women constitute the vast majority of bargirls. By the same token, while the Isaan young women's speech communities studied are not only subject to the constant lose of population (e.g., some married Western tourists and others moved or returned to Isaan villages to invest in small business), they are still also subject to the constant influx of novice Isaan women coming to work in the love industry, as well as increasingly fellow non-Isaan co-workers' adoption of Isaan ethnolects. (The researcher further comments on this at length.)

TABLE 4.7:
A minimal evaluation of the Ethnolinguistic Vitality of the Isaan
speech in home villages vs. love-industry work domains

EV of Isaan	Home Villages (Northeastern Thailand)	Work Domains (Bars)
	Getting Weaker (Gradual shift to Standard Thai use in the younger generations)	Getting Stronger (Maintained)

Note. EV=Ethnolinguistic Vitality

Second, numerous avenues of investigation converge on the fact that the maintenance and ethnolinguistic vitality of Isaan vernacular is relatively strong in the two tourist sites studied. Among these are the linguistic normalization theory (Vallverdú, 1985), the ethnolinguistic vitality theory (Giles *et al.*, 1977), the ethnolect theory (Clyne, 2000) and the discursive practice theory (Young, 2009; Hall, 2009). By means of the establishment of normative usages and uses in work domains and elsewhere, along with the extension of its multifaceted utility in socio-economical and socio-cultural life, the notion of linguistic normalization propounded by Vallverdú (1985) largely accounts for the fact that Isaan vernacular has been continually gaining ground in the battle with the Standard Thai variety and English speech for fuller normalization in the seaside resort of Pattaya and work domains (bars) in Bangkok Metropolis studied by the researcher. In the same vein, the formation of demographic (given the vast majority of love industry workers are Isaan) and economical (the language adopted in commercial activities on streets and in the love industry) capital (Giles *et al.*, 1977) largely account for the strong ethnolinguistic vitality of Isaan vernacular in this seaside town. The Isaan vernacular, albeit discriminated against, oppressed, stigmatized and stereotyped in official domains (e.g., workplaces, educational institutions and the mass media) (Draper, 2010: 135), is warmly welcomed and embraced in the seaside town (Pattaya) studied, given that locals and tourism-oriented business sectors rely heavily on Isaan women to attract foreign male tourists. This confirms Mandanares and Kent's (2006: 46) observation that since Isaan is the *lingua franca* in bars non-Isaan women see a need to learn the Isaan vernacular to understand what the majority of Isaan women in the bars are discussing at any one time (Manzanares and Ken, 2006: 46). Moreover, for some non-Isaan women part of becoming love-industry workers involved a shift in language choice and use away from Northern, Central and Standard Thai varieties to the adoption of Isaan ethnolects in their work domains. Illuminating in this connection is the fact that novice non-Isaan intakes were instructed by their seniors with respect to acquirable skills and manners (e.g., Western-style make-up) deemed to attract male Western tourists. In the light of the discursive practice approach pursued by Hall (2011) and Young (2009), the researcher also addresses how members of the non-Isaan women's groups learn and develop the competences needed in the love industry, while honing their newly acquired linguistic and behavioral capacities under the guidance of more experienced Isaan participants in the love industry (Vygotsky, 1978) through being socialized into an Isaan-style elder sibling/younger sibling hierarchy (see Howard, 2007: 206-208).

Third, among the three groups studied, the Isaan women's group as a whole exhibits a higher attainment of English speech. Although the Isaan variety is maintained in the work domains of the two sites studied, the Isaan women's group is more likely to embrace English speech, thereby explaining the fact that a relatively small number of Isaan women shift toward English speech away from Isaan speech. However, at the same time, the non-Isaan women's group as a whole exhibits a habitual use of the Isaan vernacular in their work domains, accounting for their slow but steady shift toward Isaan speech away from their Thai varieties. In addition, the Isaan women's group markedly exhibits a gradual shift in progress toward English speech. The same progress, nevertheless, does not appear to be occurring among most members in the non-Isaan women's group and almost never does it occur in the Thai men's group (the researcher comments further on this with fuller treatment in the following sub-sections).

In the view of some of the Isaan women studied, their shift away from the Isaan vernacular to the habitual use of English speech is a means of coping with class struggle (this is not the Marxist notion of "class struggle") (they are considered third class citizens by the rest of Thailand, due largely to the region of their birth), gendered discrimination (they are second class in their villages, due largely to their gender by birth) and are impoverished. Thus, the shift is inextricably connected with enhancing face and life chances (capability of conversing in English with Western tourists is a means of increasing income).

Thus far, this study confirms the findings of numerous previous studies. Consistent with Smith-Hefner (2009: 72) (Indonesian women's shift away from the indigenous-Javanese speech to the national language of Indonesian is seen as contesting conventional gendered roles imposed to them), some Isaan women's gradual shift away from the Isaan vernacular to the habitual use of the English speech is a means whereby the gender ideology stemming from traditional Isaan family values can be resisted. Furthermore, in the just mentioned article (ibid.), young women in Java were particularly drawn into urban centers (e.g., Yogyakarta) because of enhanced possibilities for social mobility. Their shift away from the formal styles of Javanese to the less formal Indonesian, the national language, was linked to their newly acquired middle-class status (ibid.). It is argued that there are similar dynamics at work vis-à-vis the target population studied in this article. Possibilities of social mobility (from rural lower-class backgrounds to urban middle-class 'entrepreneurs') draw young Isaan peasant women to urban centers. Their shift away from the Isaan vernacular to English speech is linked to their socio-economic mobility, given English is the medium of communication used in their concomitant shift to love entrepreneurship.

Data also suggest that a gradual shift toward English speech is seen as a strategic plan pertaining to possibilities of life-style enhancement (e.g., "secret dreams of moving to Europe [or North America or Australia], having a prosperous new life" by marrying one of the Western male tourists was revealed by Lon, a former love entrepreneur in Thailand, cited in Manzanares and Kent, 2006: 105). Consistent with Gal's classic study undertaken in Oberwart, Austria, in 1978, data in her article suggest that "women's speech choices must be explained within the context of their social position, their strategic life choices" (Gal, 1978: 15).

In short, the view that women tend to have more to gain than men in the love industry of Thailand is suggested by the data in this study. Amongst the informants, Isaan women, contrasted to non-Isaan women, are the single greatest group of beneficiaries in the love industry of Thailand. The Isaan women studied choose to learn English, meet with male Western tourists and become love entrepreneurs to financially support themselves and their families. For some, they want a better quality of life and a brighter future after saving enough money to invest a small business in their home villages. At the same time, being fluent in English also means that they may be able to move to America, Europe or other western or first-world countries for an enhanced lifestyle.

Non-Isaan Women's Speech Community: Ethnolect Convergence and Language Choice as a Means of Participation in Discursive Practice

As is evidenced by the empirical data that certain changes (convergence with Isaan speech styles and shifts away from the native speech to the habitual use of the Isaan vernacular) in progress emerged in the non-Isaan women's group are not in progress in the Thai men's group. It is striking to see that the non-Isaan women's group studied as a whole demonstrates a greater use of the Isaan vernacular. This is a surprising result, given Standard (Central) Thai is considered the most prestigious variant (ranked No. 1) and a standard speech of the pan-Thai language family spoken in Thailand, followed by Northern (ranked No. 2) and Southern accents (ranked No. 3), and then Northeastern Isaan (ranked No. 4)   (see Chanyam, 2002; Draper, 2010: 135-136).

Talking Like a Beach Boy: Men's Speech in Thailand's Love Industry

The less favored role Thai men (contrasted to women engaged in the same activity) play in the love industry largely account for their relatively monolingual Thai speech and lower English proficiency.

Conclusion 結論

Limitations and Recommendations for Future Research

Albeit the aforementioned contributions to the literature of language, discourse and society, there are several issues that are under-addressed in the current form of this article. First, the present article is insufficiently contextualized in the literature on language and globalization, particularly language choices and globalized industries. A number of the references to the literature on language choices, language shifts and genders need to be brought up to date. The author of the present article will undertake another research to address the aforementioned issues.

Concluding Remarks

Overall, this article examines the essential components constitutive of a love entrepreneur linguistically and communicatively by discussing and analyzing how language choices, linguistics shifts, ideologies and gender influence the language use of love industry workers in Bangkok Metropolis and the seaside resort town of Pattaya. It draws upon arguments used to conceptualize the relationship between young women's linguistic strategies (language choices and shifts) and their life strategies (social upward mobility). One crucial feature of the association between women's language use and concomitant social and economical mobility that emerged in this study is the fact that women's language choice and shift is an enterprising activity and enabling strategic life choices. Two results from this linkage may have important pedagogical implications. One is the finding suggesting that English is the language of upward social mobility for both Isaan and Non-Isaan women. The other is the result indicating that Isaan is the language of sociability for non-Isaan women in their work domains (This is a relatively new [forty years ago was the beginning] linguistic convergence in the young non-Isaan women's speech community.) If this is the case, it may be imperative to provide human resource development opportunities to these women and men engaged in the activities of the love industry with training that can foster their learning of English speech and the Isaan vernacular.

TABLE 4.8:
Ethnolect Convergence
among Isaan and non-Isaan women studied

Media	Participants	Interlocutors	Domains	Sites	Converging w/
Speaking	Isaan	Co-workers and Customers	Work	B	ST/E
				P	E
		Others	Non-Work	B	ST
				P	I
	Non-Isaan	Co-workers and Customers	Work	B	I/ST/E
				P	I/E
		Others	Non-Work	B	ST
				P	I/E

Note. B=Bangkok, P=Pattaya, E=English, ST=Standard (Central) Thai
Variety, I=Isaan Thai Variety

The present investigation focuses only on the social meanings
that emerged from three relatively smaller speech communities
(100 Isaan women, 50 non-Isaan women and 50 Thai men). In
this study, social meanings that account for the language
choices and shifts investigated only represent some aspects of
the possible sociological variables/factors that contribute to
women's linguistic strategies. Future studies should examine a
more comprehensive population selection and explore a wider
range of social, economical, political and other correlations that
may exist between women's language choices and shifts and
their life choices and possibilities. Perhaps using the current
study as the foundation, future studies could well also examine

the associations with other speech communities in highly mobile, contact, and multi-ethnolect settings. In carrying out future investigations, it would be of quite some interest and considerable theoretical import to determine whether if the use of the English language and Isaan speech in the communities studied in this article continue to thrive or decline at different intervals in the future, perhaps up to a quarter century from the present time. As such, a longitudinal investigation ranging to-and-fro along a temporal continuum may even provide a means whereby predictive extrapolations could be framed if suitable independent variables could be isolated and projected.

This chapter has highlighted that young women do not merely simply choose, or shift to or from, a language out of their linguistic and communicative repertories; rather their linguistic strategies are better understood by taking into consideration their life strategies and possible life chances (Gal, 1978: 15; Smith-Hefner, 2009; Lee, 2013). This article demonstrates that the choice and shift of languages have a much wider-spread attraction for young Isaan and non-Isaan women than Thai men engaged in the activities of the love industry, as they seek to become members of a new entrepreneur class in urban centers in contradistinction to their former stigmatized peasant status in rural areas. Further, Isaan women take fuller advantage of these new social and economic opportunities than non-Isaan women and Thai men involved in the same industry. It is hoped that this article will prove useful in countering the ignorant and pernicious stereotyping and stigmatization of love industry workers. In addition, the researcher is concerned to indicate how engaging in meaningful language choice and linguistic shift can be a means whereby hope and a sense of future possibilities can be engendered in the young women involved in this unfairly maligned industry. It is also argued that the changes in orders of indexicalities pertaining to the continued reconfiguration of community boundaries (the work domains (bars)), as well as the neighborhoods of bars, in the two urban centers of Bangkok and Pattaya) reflect a restructuring of sociolinguistic and ideological hierarchy. Such a process in its core is one that engenders the formation of new varieties of speech, as well as stimulating social change, within the rapidly growing and incessantly changing nation of Thailand.

(本文原稿於2014年3月發表在國際社會學協會的《語言、談話和社會》期刊第三卷第一期)

For further information about this chapter (if you want to discuss with the author), please contact:

Hugo Lee, Faculty Member

International College

National Institute of Development Administration

18th fl., Navamin Building, 118 Seri Thai Rd,

Khlong Chan, Bang Kapi, Bangkok 10240

Hugo Lee, Consultant Roster Member

United Nations

Economic & Social Commission for Asia & the Pacific

3rd fl., United Nations Conference Center, ESCAP HR

United Nations Building, 76 Rajadamnern Nok Ave

Bangkok 10200

T. 088-607-2560

E. hugoclubheart3@gmail.com   Li Y-h Hugo

W. https://indiana.academia.edu/YuHsiuLee

參考文獻　References

1. Bangkok Diaries (2009): Thai Spec vs. Farang Spec, http://www.bangkokdiaries.com/2009/12/12/thai-spec-vs-farang-spec/ (Accessed August 13, 2012)

2. Batibo, H. M. (2009): Poverty as a Crucial Factor in Language Maintenance and Language Death: Case Studies from Africa. In Harbert, W., McConnell-Ginet, S., Miller, A., and Whitman, J., eds. *Language and Poverty*: 23-36. Bristol: Multilingual Matters.

3. Boonmongkon, P., & Jackson, P. A., (2012) (eds.): *Thai Sex Talk: The Language of Sex and　Sexuality in Thailand.* Chiang Mai: Silkworm Books.

4. Brown, L. (2000): *Sex Slaves: The Trafficking of Women in Asia.* London, UK: Virago Press.

5. Chanyam, N. (2002): *A Study of Language Attitude toward Thai Dialects and their Speakers: A Case Study of Four Campuses of Rajamangala Institute of Technology.* M.A. Thesis, The Faculty of Graduate Studies, Mahidol University, Thailand.

6. Cheshire, J., Kerswill, P., Fox, S., & Torgersen, E. (2011): Contact, the Feature Pool and the　Speech Community: The Emergence of Multicultural London English. *Journal of Sociolinguistics, 15* (2): 151-196.

Noam Chomsky

7. Chomsky, N. (1965): *Aspects of the Theory of Syntax.* Cambridge, MA: MIT Press.

8. Clark, H. H. (1966): *Using Language.* Cambridge: Cambridge University Press.

9. Clyne, M. (2000): Lingua Franca and Ethnolects in Europe and Beyond. *Sociolinguistica,* 14, 83-89.

10. Coates, J. (2004): *Women, Men and Language: A Sociolinguistic Account of Gender Differences in Language,* 3rd ed. Harlow, England; New York: Pearson Longman.

Serafin, Coronel-Molina

11. Coronel-Molina, Serafin. M., & Rodríguez-Mondoñedo, M. (2012): Introduction: Language Contact in the Andes and Universal Grammar. *Lingua,* 122, 447-460.

Lisa Delpit

12. Delpit, L. (2002): Introduction. In Delpit, L., & Dowdy, J. K. (eds.): *The Skin that We Speak: Thoughts on Language and Culture in the Classroom,* p. xvii. New York: The New Press.

John Draper

13. Draper, J. C. (2004): Isan: The Planning Context for Language Maintenance and Revitalization. *Second Language Learning and Teaching* 4, Electronic document, http://www.usq.edu.au/users/sonjb/sllt/4/Draper04.html, accessed August 14th, 2012.

14. Draper, J. C. (2010): Inferring Ethnolinguistic Vitality in a Community of Northeast Thailand. *Journal of Multilingual and Multicultural Development, 31* (2), 135-147.

15. Eckert, P. (1997): Gender and Sociolinguistic Variation. In J. Coates (ed.): *Language and Gender: A Reader*, 64–75. Malden MA, & Oxford, UK: Wiley-Blackwell.

16. Enfield, N. J. (2009): Language and Culture. In L. Wei., & V. Cook, (eds.): *Contemporary Applied Linguistics 2 (Linguistics for the Real World),* 83-97. London: Continuum.

Joshua Fishman

17. Fishman, J. (1964): Language Maintenance and Language Shift as a Field of Enquiry. *Linguistics*, 9, 32-70.

18. Fishman, J. (1965): Who Speaks What Language to Whom and When? *La Linguistique*, 2, 67-88.
    Fishman, J. (1989): The Spread of English as a New Perspective for the Study of Language Maintenance and Language Shift. In J. A. Fishman (ed.): *Language and Ethnicity in Minority: Sociolinguistic Perspective*, 32-263. Clevedon: Multilingual Matters.

19. Fishman, J. (1991): *Reversing Language Shift: Theoretical and Empirical Foundations of Assistance to Threatened Languages.* Clevedon: Multilingual Matters.

20. Gagné, I. (2008): Urban Princesses: Performance and "Women's Language" in Japan's Gothic/Lolita Subculture. *Journal of Linguistic Anthropology, 18* (1), 130-150.

Susan Gal

21. Gal, S. (1978): Peasant Men Don't Get Wives: Language and Sex roles in a Bilingual Community. *Language in Society*, *7* (1), 1-16.

22. Gal, S. (1979): *Language Shift: Social Determinants of Linguistic Change in Bilingual Austria*. New York: Academic Press.

23. Giles, H., Taylor, D. M., & Bourhis, R. Y. (1977): Towards a Theory of Language in Ethnic Group Relations. In H. Giles (ed.): *Language, Ethnicity and Intergroup Relations*, 307-348. London, Academic Press.

John Gumperz

24. Gumperz, J. (1964). Linguistic and Social Interaction in Two Communities. *American Anthropologist*, 66,137-154.

25. Hall, J. K. (2009): Language Learning as Discursive Practice. In L. Wei., & V. Cook, (eds.): *Contemporary Applied Linguistics 1* (Language Teaching and Learning). 255-274. London: Continuum.

26. Hill, J. (1987): Women's Speech in Modern Mexicano. In Philips, S. U., Steele, S., & Tanz, C (eds.): *Language, Gender, and Sex in Comparative Perspective*, 121-160. Cambridge: Cambridge University Press.

27. Howard, K. M. (2007): Kinterm Usage and Hierarchy in Thai Children's Peer Groups. *Journal of Linguistic Anthropology*, *17* (2), 204-230.

28. Howard, K. M. (2010): Social Relationships and Shifting Languages in Northern Thailand. *Journal of Sociolinguistics*, *14* (3), 313-340.

Dell Hymes

29. Hymes, D. (1974): *Foundations in Sociolinguistics: An Ethnographic Approach*. Philadelphia: University of Pennsylvania Press.

30. Jantao, R. (2002): *Code-Mixing between Central Thai and Northeastern Thai of the Students in Khon Kaen Province*. MA Thesis, The Faculty of Graduate Studies, Mahidol University, Thailand.

31. Jaspers, J. (2008): Problematizing Ethnolects: Naming Linguistic Practices in an Antwerp Secondary School. *International Journal of Bilingualism*, *12* (1&2): 85–103.

32. Kim, S. H. O., & Starks, D. (2010): The Role of Fathers in Language Maintenance and Language Attrition: The Case of Korean-English Late Bilinguals in New Zealand. *International Journal of Bilingual Education and Bilingualism*, *13* (3), 285-301.

William Labov

33. Labov, W. (1996): *The Social Stratification of English in New York City*. Washington DC: Center for Applied Linguistics.

34. Labov, W. (1972): *Sociolinguistic Patterns*. Philadelphia, PA: University of Pennsylvania Press.

35. Labov, W. (1980): *Locating Language in Time and Space*. New York: Academic Press.

36. Landry, R., & Bourhis, R. Y. (1997): Linguistic Landscape and Ethnolinguistic Vitality: An Empirical Study. *Journal of Language and Social Psychology*, 16, 23-49.

37. Leather, S. (2005): *Private Dancer*. Mediapolis, Singapore: Monsoon Books.

Hugo Yu-Hsiu Lee (李育修)

38. Lee, H, Y.-H. (2013): Bargirl Style of Language Choice and Shift: A Tale from the Land of Smile. *Theory and Practice in Language Studies*, *3* (3), 411- 422.

39. Lee, H, Y.-H. (2012): English for the Purpose of Reducing the Poverty of Orphans with Disabilities in Thailand. *Journal of Education and Practice*, 3 (6): 87-99.

40. Lee, H, Y.-H. (2011a): English for Communication Purposes among Non-Native Speaking Heterogeneous Urban Refugees in Thailand: Discouragement in Bilingual and Biliteracy Development. *Modern Journal of Applied Linguistics*, *3* (2), 237-253.

41. Lee, H, Y.-H. (2011b): English Language Teaching at Expenses of Thai Language Teaching for Urban Refugee Language Learners in Thailand: Social Inequalities Related to What Languages to Teach. *Journal of Language Teaching and Research*, *2* (4), 810 - 815.

42. Lee, H, Y-H. (2011c): Some Remarks on Reconstructing the Prehistoric Linguistic Relationships of the Tai-Kadai Language Family and its Putative Linguistic Affiliations with other Language Families. *International Review of Social Sciences and Humanities*, 2 (1), 163-175.

43. LePoer, B. L. (1987): *Thailand: A Country Study*. Washington: GPO for the Library of Congress.

44. Lewis, P. M. (2009) (ed.): *Ethnologue: Languages of the World* (Sixteenth Ed.). Dallas, Texas: SIL International.

45. Manzanares, J., & Kent, D. (2006): *Only 13: The True Story of Lon*. Bangkok, Thailand: Bamboo Sinfonia Publications.

46. Map of Isaan in Thailand (2012): Electronic image, http://siam-longings.com/wp content/uploads/map%20of%20thailand%20isaan.jpg, (Accessed August 13th, 2012)

Dipika Mukherjee

47. Mukherjee, D. (2003): Role of Women in Language Maintenance and Language Shift: Focus on the Bengali Community in Malaysia. *International Journal of the Sociology of Language*, 161, 103-120.

48. Nicks, P. (2010): *Love Entrepreneurs: Cross-Culture Relationship Deals in Thailand*. Bangkok, Thailand: Fast Track Publishing.

49. Provinces of Isaan (2012): Electronic image, http://thethailandlife.com/wpcontent/uploads/2012/03/isaan-map-.gif (Accessed August 13th, 2012)

50. Robinson, C. D. W. (1996): *Language Use in Rural Development: An African Perspective (Contributions to the Sociology of Language)*. Berlin: Mouton de Gruyter.

51. Seabrook, J. (2007): *Cities*. London: Pluto Press.

52. Silverstein, M (1979): Language Structure and Linguistic Ideology. In C. Paul., F. H. William., & L. H. Carol (eds.): *The Elements: A Parasession on Linguistic Units and   Levels*, 193-247. Chicago: Chicago Linguistic Society.

Nancy J. Smith-Hefner

53. Smith-Hefner, N. J. (2009): Language Shift, Gender and Ideologies of Modernity in Central Java, Indonesia. *Journal of Linguistic Anthropology, 19* (1), 57-77.

54. Vallverdú, F. (1985): *El fet lingüística com a fet social* (6th Ed). Barcelona: Edicions 62.

Lev Vygotsky

55. Vygotsky, L. (1978): *Mind in Society: The Development of Higher Psychological Processes*. Cambridge: Cambridge University Press.

56. Woolard, K. A. (1982): The Problem of Linguistic Prestige: Evidence from Catalonia. *Penn Review of Linguistics*, 6, 82-90.

57. Woolard, K. A. (1985): Language Variation and Cultural Hegemony: Toward an Integration of Linguistic and Sociolinguistic Theory. *American Ethnologist*, 12, 738-48.

58. Woolard, K. A. (1998): Language Ideology as a Field of Inquiry. In B. B. Schieffelin, K. A. Woolard., & P. V. Kroskrity (eds.): *Language Ideologies: Practice and Theory*, 3-49. New York: Oxford University Press.

59. Young, R. (2009): *Discursive Practice in Language Learning and Teaching*. Malden MA, & Oxford, UK: Wiley-Blackwell.

Chapter 5

Bargirl Style of Language Use

bargirls

love entrepreneurs

domestic migrants

第五章

酒吧女郎風格的語言選擇

TRADITIONAL RESEARCH FRAMEWORKS in education and learning have given little regard to informal (language) learning in non-educational settings. It is widely recognized that gender has been identified as a crucial component to understand (language) education/learning, yet relatively few studies have undertaken an analysis of gender and informal (language) learning in the workplace. The chapter examines informal (language) learning that emerged from the internal migration of 50 young peasant women, known in Thailand's love industry as 'bargirls' (who work in bars). It focuses on differences of physical (sexual) attractiveness in informal (language) learning. In this inquiry I draw mainly upon informal learning theory and sociolinguistics of mobility, and it is within these two key theoretical frameworks that I position my ongoing ethnographic work. Findings show that (workplace-based) bargirl style of (language) learning does not occur in vacuum and should not be separated from social, cultural and economic factors, and the love-industry discourse. It is likely that their physical (sexual) attractiveness determines the large extent of their choices of informal (language) learning (e.g., some are more attractive to Japanese male customers (than American counterparts) and they consequently learn the Japanese language with private tutors (not in formal educational settings) and frequently use the Japanese language in the bar). Research results also show that Thai bargirls' possibilities for upper social and status mobility in the contemporary Thai society are linked to their gender (e.g., being a girlfriend or a spouse of an American man or a Japanese man) and informal (language) learning (e.g., they informally learn to speak fluent English or Japanese).

IT IS widely recognized that language use, choice and shift have been identified as crucial components to understand the sociolinguistics of mobility, yet relatively few studies have undertaken an analysis of the effects of strategic linguistic change in the workplace, such as bars. In the present study as reported in the chapter 5, the author surveyed the language choices and shifts of bar girls and beach boys in the capital of Thailand, Bangkok, and the seaside tourist attraction, Pattaya, with a focus on bar English and bar bilingualism or multilingualism. The author applied sociolinguistics of mobility to analyze how social meanings are reflected in language changes. The author confirmed his findings with previous studies and argued that young women's choices and shifts vis-à-vis language can be best understood in the context of the strategies they adopt in regard to life chances and life style choices.

ACKNOWLEDGMENTS

The original study reported in chapter 5 was edited and proof reading by Jack Clontz (PhD, University of California, San Diego, USA), Emeritus Professor, Maebashi Kyoai Gakuen International College, Japan（日本前橋共愛學園國際大學）. It was peer-reviewed by the editorial board of the Theory and Practice in Language Studies (print ISSN 1799-2591; online ISSN 2053-0692). The photo credit for the FIG 1 should go to the photographer who took the front cover picture for the *Time Magazine* (June 21st, 1993 edition).

Background 背景

STRATEGIC LANGUAGE CHOICE and shift do not occur in a vacuum and should not be separated from cultural, economic, financial, social and other contextual factors, which are often focused in analyses. In spite of this, language use, choice and shift of young peasant women of Northeastern (Isaan) Thailand, as well as non-Isaan women from Northern, Central and Southern Thailand, employed in bars associated with life-style choices have received limited empirical attention in Thailand's sociolinguistic literature. The author in this study as reported in this chapter examined joint effects of mass foreign (sex) tourism and local love (prostitution) industry on behaviors of language changes, with data drawn from bar girls and beach boys in Thailand. Taken together, findings highlighted young women's and men's language choices and shifts associated with their life opportunities in the love industry.

FIG 5.1: Get rich quick English for bar girls

Reference: As of use by the conference presentation titled Learning like a (female) love entrepreneur: The secret of how daughters of peasants learn to speak like bargirls in Thailand, written by Hugo Yu-Hsiu Lee（李育修）, "International Conference on Gender and Education: Critical Issues, Policy and Practice". 28-30 May 2015 – Bloomington, IN, United States. ICGE 2015 Conference Committee

Source: http://teakdoor.com/pattaya-forum/38360-pattaya-bar-girls-survival-guide-now-3.html
http://teakdoor.com/the-teakdoor-lounge/87746-get-rich-quick-english-bar-girls.html

In Thailand, no other modern ethnolinguistic minority and young women's subculture receives as much international media attention as does the young women known as Isaan bargirls. For many years, young females from the Northeastern Thailand have strategically engaged in foreign language learning (e.g., English, Western languages and Japanese) and language shift as a means of socio-economic upper mobility. In light of this phenomenon, the author of this chapter is concerned to address the question of the precise nature of the social meaning of language choice and shift by the members of young Isaan women's speech communities in the discourse used by these women who are involved in Thailand's love industry. The author also examines the disparity between Isaan and non-Isaan women's speech and between men's and women's speech as adopted by love industry workers in Thailand.

Thailand's Heterosexual Love Industry
泰國的愛情企業

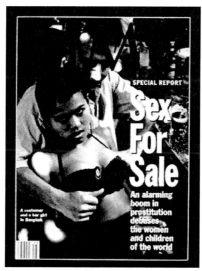

FIG 5.2: Front cover picture of the Time Magazine
published in June 21, 1993

(Reporting on world prostitution, a Bangkok bargirl sat in the lap of
a Western male tourist)

Source:
http://content.time.com/time/covers/0,16641,19930621,00.html

Service industries are one of the largest commercial sectors of economics in the developed world (Wilson, 2008). 'Service' is seen as a key concept in Thai society (ibid). High qualities of personal and individual services (due largely to hospitality management of hotels, resorts, restaurants and massage parlors) have made Thailand successful in the competition of global tourism. However, it is strongly believed that the same key concept of 'service' presumably contributes to the success of Thailand's love industry (Stearn, 2004), as the following quote illustrates (A middle-aged American tourist commented on the high quality of service provided by love-industry workers in Thailand in the following words):

I don't really k\think of them as prostitutes. It's not like that. They are more like a girlfriend—GFE or "girlfriend experience" as it's called. Because it's not just about sex. These girls know how to take care of you and make you feel special. You wake up in the morning, and they're already making your breakfast or ironing your clothes. It is unbelievable!

--Field notes by Pack (2011) on July 7th, 2007

It is evidenced that Thailand's high quality of service industry is one of the key elements that attracts mass tourism, "a phenomenon of large-scale packaging of standardized leisure services at fixed prices for sale to mass clients" (Poon, 1993). Motivated by values and interests, tourists seek 'authenticity' and first-hand experiences from what local people have to offer in a foreign country (Przeclawski, 1993).

In this light (high quality of service industry in Thailand), sex is an ever-growing industry in Thailand, which was worth USD $4 billion in the mid-1990s (Bishop and Robinson, 2002) and worth USD $15,866,797 from 13.8 million international tourists in 2006 (Woywode, 2007). It is unfortunate but true that poverty has driven young women and men into the love industry (prostitution) in Thailand, particularly with regard to the Bangkok metropolis and the Pattaya seaside city, standing out as global centers of the love (sex) industry for international tourists. Another illustration of Bangkok's image as a global leader of love industries was impressed upon the western world when some stories concerning young Thai girls sold by impoverished parents and rescued by charity workers published in newspapers and magazines with headlines, e.g., 'Voyage to a life of shattered dreams,' 'Disneyland for pedophiles,' and 'Pedophiles find paradise on a white beach in Thailand.' The reputation of Bangkok as a hub for sex tourism is also supported by the lyrics of Murray Head's 1984 dance hit "One Night in Bangkok"

> *One night in Bangkok makes a hard man humble*
> *Not much between despair and ecstasy*
> *One night in Bangkok and the tough guys tumble*
> *Can't be too careful with your company*
> *I can feel the Devil walking next to me*
> *… …*
> *One night in Bangkok and the world's your oyster*
> *The bars are temples but the pearls ain't free*
> *You'll find a God in every golden cloister*
> *And if you're lucky then the God's a she*
> *I can feel an angel sliding up to me*

It is widely recognized that no official documentation, accurate statistics and hard empirical data exist on populations of workers involved in the heterosexual love (sex) market in Thailand, due largely to topic sensitivity for Thai academics, the difficulty of definition (e.g., what constitute a love-industry/sex worker), status of young girls and women (Wilson, 2008) and other contextual factors. Although substantial (both academic and non-academic) literature exists on bar girls and 'farang' (Thais refer to Westerners as 'farang'), its range and quality are varied from case to case.

Western tourists' perspectives are presented on websites as personal diaries and self/life stories by independent writers (e.g., Hutchison, 2002; Stearn, 2004). However, scholarly academic studies can be found in Cohen's (2011) research of *Thai tourism: Hill tribes, islands and open-ended prostitution.* Parallel to this, Walker and Erlich (1992) reported the relationship between 'Farang' and bar girls in Thailand (also see Lake & Schirbel, 2000; Perve & Robinson, 2007). For a fuller discussion of Thailand's love industry as a 'customized professional services market,' please see Wilson (2008).

As noted above, poverty is largely responsible for Isaan women's engagement in the love industry. *"Isaan girls are poor; tourists are rich; I bridged the gap!"* (Comment by a former Isaan love entrepreneur, cited in Manzanares and Kent, 2006). A principal cause of the phenomenon also lies in gender ideologies stemming from traditional Isaan family values: *"My [Isaan] culture holds all women to be not only inferior but expendable,"* a comment made by Lon, a former love industry worker in Thailand (Manzanares and Kent, 2006). In some Isaan villages, *"daughters are cast in the role of caretakers of the family"* instead of sons (Brown, 2000). These family values are grounded in Isaan religious beliefs. In Theravada Buddhism, sons earn merit for their parents by simply becoming a monk and staying in a temple for three months to fulfill family duty. However, daughters, particularly first-born daughters, are expected to become the primary income earners and must take care of the needs and welfare of the whole family (Manzanares and Ken, 2006). Therefore, a strong sense of obligation to care for parents is essential to caring members of an Isaan community. Nevertheless, for some Isaan families, at times driven by poverty and at other times driven by greed, there is no limit to the perceived duty to parents of daughters.

Thailand's Linguistic Ecology
泰國的語言生態

Thailand is an ethnically and linguistically diverse State with an estimated 74 languages spoken (Ethnologue, 2005) (For an examination of literacy/orthographies in local languages of Thailand, please see Kosonen, 2008). In respective regions, Northern Thai (Kammeuang), Northeastern Thai (Isaan or Lao), Central Thai (Standard Thai) and Southern Thai (Pak Thai) play key roles as regional languages of wider communication (localization) (Smalley, 1994). However, the Royal Thai government has exalted Central or Standard Thai variety as the national and official language for the use in public domains (e.g., educational institutes and government offices), aimed at strengthening Thailand's national unity (nationalism). Standard Thai is thus the most prestigious language. However, the use of Standard Thai has become a major obstacle in educational achievements and other sectors for not only speakers of other Thai varieties, but also speakers of other ethnolinguistic minorities whose native languages are not related to Thai (Kosonen, 2008). Moreover, increasing globalization has triggered increasing interest in the use of the English language (globalization). This can be seen among love-industry workers. A selective view of theoretical issues and empirical findings relating to the use of the English language can be found in the finding report in this present article. For a more comprehensive treatment of the facts and issues of linguistic diversity and language ecology in Thailand, please see Smalley (1994).

Key Concepts:
Language Choice, Language Shift and Language Vitality
本章重要概念：語言選擇、語言轉換和語言活力

Gendered language-use-and-choice research has a long history in the field of sociolinguistics/sociology of language/language in society commencing from Gal's (1978) pioneering work in a bilingual town in Austria. There is also a long-standing tradition of language-shift research in the same fields of study. This present section is a selective review of facts and theoretical issues concerning language choice and language shift.

Social factors leading to discrepancies between language choices and shifts have been a central preoccupation and is well documented in sociolinguistic literature as broadly defined (e.g., Fishman, 1964, 1965, 1989, 1991; Giles *et al.*, 1977), as well as developing sociolinguistic norms that account for the extent of language use, choice, maintenance and shift.

In the present chapter, the researcher (author) uses the term 'language choice' in its most general sense to refer to the daily uses and code choices available in one's repertoire. Attempts to define the terms 'language choice,' 'maintenance and shift' have been shaped by, or in turn have shaped, well-known sociolinguists in our time (e.g., Fishman, 1991; Gal, 1978, 1979). In the light of a variety of perspectives, the author of this article presents their definitions as follows.

First, as extrapolated from the concept of 'linguistic competence' as evinced by an ideal speaker-listener in a homogeneous speech community (Chomsky, 1965) formulated the notion of 'linguistic repertoire' in which a speaker of a language has at his or her disposal a wide range of linguistic variants and develops a register of speech sufficient to undertake a wide range of communicative tasks. Furthermore,

Hymes (1974) developed the notion of 'communicative competence,' and initiated research in the fields of the 'ethnography of communication' and 'interactional sociolinguistics'. In Hymes' framework, language choice is referred to as a speaker's linguistic and communicative competence enabling the choice of style and variants with a speaker thereby drawing on his or her linguistic and communicative repertoire as suiting a particular purpose or function. The choice of a speech variety, nonetheless, is by no means a random phenomenon. Rather, the code choice made has to be deliberately selected by the speaker in the light of his or her social and interactional perspective so as to reach a level of satisfactory accommodation to the perceived linguistic situation in the language domain in which current discourse is being undertaken.

A second approach or perspective that guides this chapter is the distinction between languages in themselves (objective assessment) and attitudes, beliefs, stereotypes and social implications which individuals hold in respect to languages (subjective assessment). Drawing on this distinction in order to frame this research investigation largely stems from the fact that in a class-conscious society, Thais, to a varying degree, are hypersensitive to the socio-economical implications of accents, varieties (standard versus non-standard), dialects and speech styles as a means of symbolizing the stratification of class, status and prestige. In this vein, we must take into account that dictum that "our language embraces us long before we are defined by any other medium of identity" (Delpit and Dowdy, 2002, xvii). Thus, to a degree, language choice becomes a matter of ideology. The concept of 'language ideologies' is defined as beliefs concerning languages held "by their users as a rationalization, or justification, of perceived language structure and use" (Silverstein, 1979, p.193). In this light, the notion of 'language ideologies' is useful in accounting for why minority languages are maintained when their users are oppressed by users of dominant and hegemonic languages (see Woodlard, 1985 for Catalan speakers in Spain). For a crucial introduction to the field of language ideology, see Woodlard, 1998. Since integral to the discussion of language choices, 'language shift' is another key concept. Gal (1978, 1979, p.1) describes 'language shift' as a process through which "the habitual use of one language is being replaced by the habitual use of another" at disparate times.

In addition to approaching language choice largely by drawing on the aforementioned concepts, the author of this chapter is concerned to examine the intertwined roles of gender, language choice and shift in the light of work conducted in anthropological linguistics, sociolinguistics and in a number of other fields. It must be acknowledged that the interconnection between gender and language choice has long been recognized and has reached a high level of understanding (see Gal, 1978; Mukherjee, 2003; Smith-Hefner, 2009). Thus, there is abundant evidence to show that language choice is often gendered.

On the one hand, a number of previous studies have shown women were more likely to have no or limited proficiency in majority languages in view of lesser access to resources and power (e.g., education) than men in an agricultural (or working class) community. The socioeconomically disadvantaged situation of indigenous women in Latin America has been illustrated by Hill (1987). In these cases in Latin America, women had less access to education and so spoke limited Spanish (a good command of Spanish was essential for these indigenous women in order to be able to access educational and employment opportunities, and would thus enable them to participate in the paid labor force), a state of affairs in contrast to the situation of men. In a similar example, the male elite of the Nugunu or Cameroon villagers in Ombessa, Africa exhibited greater competence in the French language and achieved higher levels of educational attainments than did their female counterparts (Robinson, 1996, pp. 212-213).

On the other hand, previous studies also found that women were constantly searching for a medium that would grant them access to valuable economic and social benefits, opportunities, resources, prestige and symbolic capitals. For instance, in Gal's (1978) pioneering work on the Hungarian-German bilingual town of Oberwart in Austria, a shift away from Hungarian speech to the use of the German language was found to be occurring among peasant women in view of the symbolic linkage between German speech and industrial work that was available to both Hungarian-speaking men and women, albeit being more appealing to the latter than to the former. It appeared that German-speaking factory jobs represented socio-economic advancement, whereas Hungarian-speaking agricultural work was linked to hard-work, low-income, rural, and peasant life. For a fuller treatment of gender and sociolinguistics, see Eckert, 1997 in Coates, 1997 and Coates, 2004.

An area of related interest to this strand of research on young women's social and economic opportunities is studying the effects of urbanization on gendered language choices. Urban centers, by and large, draw poverty-stricken populations from rural areas, due largely to social and economic inducements, such as more job opportunities, better basic infrastructure, and a modern lifestyle (Batibo, 2009, p.26). In developing countries, it is estimated that 70 million migrants flow annually from rural areas into cities in the search for a better life (Seabrook, 2007). One of the many effects attributed to urbanization is language shift. In her well-regarded article,

Smith-Hefner (2009) discussed the phenomenon of language shift from the Javanese (indigenous) language toward the national language of Indonesian emerging in Javanese youth in the nation-state of Indonesia. She went on to argue that in contrast to young men, young women were more likely to shift from Javanese toward the use of Indonesian, which was seen as a means of acquiring the symbolic capital necessary to accommodate their roles in forming part of the new working class.

In connection with this exploration of language choice by young Thai women vis-à-vis relevant concepts, it is to be observed that sociolinguists and linguistic anthropologists refer to the distinctive language usages and uses by speakers of an ethnic group as 'ethnolects' (see definitions of ethnolects in Clyne, 2000; see problems with ethnolects in Jaspers, 2008). An ethnolect approach can better account for the fact that some non-group or out-group members adopt elements of another group's ethnolect in an attempt to bond with members of a different ethnic group, thereby forming cross-ethnic and multi-ethnic friendship groups. In view of what we know of language contact, it would be only expected that speakers from different ethnic groups would 'converge' in speech by virtue of borrowing linguistic forms typical of members of another ethnic group (see Coronel-Molina and Rodrı´guez-Mondon˜edo, 2012 for examples of linguistic convergence in

Andes). It can also be argued that the phenomenon of linguistic 'convergence' involves attempts to be understood by others through "symbolic references" to an extent adequate for undertaking communicative acts through utterances and speech acts (e.g., Clark, 1996, cited in Enfield 2009, p. 91). At the same time, this phenomenon is "micro-political" and "coalitional" since designed to ensure that desirable interpersonal relationships are fostered by means of common or shared experiences, including code-switching/mixing with the speech and adopting linguistic features of the discourse of interlocutors from another ethnic group (Enfield, 2009. p. 91).

Across many studies that examine gendered language choice and shift of all the above-mentioned concepts and constructs, it has emerged that a perspective that is useful in the analysis of Thailand's diglossia and linguistic repertoire and, at the same time, frames this study stems from 'ethnolinguistic vitality' theory (formulated by Giles *et al.*, 1977; Landry and Bourhis, 1997, p. 32). It is defined as what 'makes a group likely to behave as a distinctive and active collective entity in intergroup situations.' In this vein, the political status of languages recognized by the state (e.g., institutional support), demographics, economic considerations (e.g., medium of communication in commerce) and cultural capital are means of 'objectively' measuring the continued linguistic existence of an ethnic group's mother tongue/s, native languages and inherited languages within a linguistically heterogeneous society. By contrast, members of an ethnic group are asked to subjectively rate and predict the present and inferred future vitality of their languages as 'subjective' measures to account for the degree of ethnolinguistic vitality of their languages (e.g., see Draper 2004, 2010 for an assessment of the ethnolinguistic vitality of Isaan Thai).

Methods and Survey Sites
(Bangkok and Pattaya)
研究方法和研究地點（曼谷和芭達雅）

Below, the author of this chapter gives a brief summer of research questions, sites, participants, measuring instruments, procedures and analysis. The researcher employed multiple methods of data collection and analysis over the period of field-site investigation.

The relationship between language use, language choice and language shift has been of increasing interest over the past half quarter century, whereas the role of workplace or life choice in these fields of sociolinguistic literature (particularly in Thailand) remains significantly under-explored. Thus, the research questions pursued are as follows:

PROJECT OBJECTIVES

(i) What is the extent to which the ethnolinguistic vitality of the Isaan speech variety can be maintained in Thailand's love industry?

(ii) How can we describe the language-use-and-choice patterns observed in bars of Thai love-industry workers?

(iii) How does the love industry appear to contribute to its workers' English language learning?

(iv) What are social meanings behind language use, choice and shift of Thai love-industry workers?

The study reported in this chapter investigated language-choice-and-shift behaviors of love-industry (sex) workers in Bangkok, the capital of Thailand, and Pattaya. Bangkok is the largest city in the country, whereby more than a quarter of the population resides. Moreover, the majority of the population is monolingual, with an estimate of 90 % of the Standard Thai speakers. Pattaya has similarities to major metropolitan tourist cities in Thailand, with a growing economy and as a regional tourist center has a great amount of tourists from North America, Western Europe, Middle East and Eastern Asia.

In the study as reported in this chapter, a criterion-sampling is adopted. Thai love-industry workers can generally be considered to be one of three main types (Thai bar (sex) workers fall into three main categories, defined in this study):

(a) Sample 1 (Female, N=200): Northeastern (Isaan) bar girls
(b) Sample 2 (Female, N=50): Non-Isaan bar girls from
    Northern, Central and Southern regions of Thailand
(c) Sample 3 (Male, N=50): Thai men/beach boys
    The average (mean) of participants was 25 years.

Building on an analysis of existing attempts to measure language-choice-and-shift behaviors, the author of the study adopted a triangulation with data stemming from three disparate sources: questionnaire surveys, interviews and observations. With regard to instruments, participants were measured by 5-point scale Likert-type questionnaire items. Individual preliminary interviews, focus-group interviews and retrospective interviews were accompanied by non-participant observations and were carried out at the beginning-point and mid-point of the course of research, prior to triangulation of data at the end of the course of the research. To draw findings from data, a constant comparison method was applied. Results were taken concurrently (by means of triangulation) from questionnaire, observation or interviews.

PROJECT OUTCOMES

Findings研究成果

(Please consult with Endnote1.)

Isaan Woman Sample

Answers to Research Question (i): What is the extent to which the ethnolinguistic vitality of the Isaan speech variety can be maintained in Thailand's love industry?

TABLE 5.1:
A minimal evaluation of the ethnolinguistic vitality of the Isaan language in home villages versus love-industry workplace settings, 2011-2013

[2]Ethnolinguistic Vitality of Isaan Language	*Home Villages (Northeastern Thailand)*	*Work Domains (Bars in Bangkok & Pattaya)*
	Getting Weaker (Gradual shift to Standard Thai language among younger generations)	Getting Stronger (Maintained)

---

[2] Note that data gathered between 2011-2015 show the sign of stronger Isaan and weaker standard Thai in bars, whereas data obtained in recent years from 2015-2018 show otherwise where standard Thai is increasingly getting stronger

The love industry has created the largest Isaan speech community outside home villages in Northeastern Thailand (It should be also noted that Phuket, another tourist site in Thailand, is the second largest Isaan speech community outside the Isaan home region), has tremendously contributed to the language maintenance of the Isaan speech. Consistent with Woolard's (1985) observation of an alternative linguistic market that challenges a single linguistic hierarchy, it is argued that while the Isaan vernacular in its home region suffers language shift away from the Isaan variety toward Standard Thai speech (Draper, 2004, 2010), the ethnolinguistic vitality of Isaan is relatively strong and symbolically opposes the dominant and legitimized Standard Thai code in the seaside town (Pattaya) and work domains (bars) in Bangkok Metropolis, largely due to the fact that Isaan women constitute the vast majority of bargirls. By the same token, while the Isaan young women's speech communities studied are not only subject to the constant lose of population (e.g., some married Western tourists and others moved or returned to Isaan villages to invest in small business), they are still also subject to the constant influx of novice Isaan women coming to work in the love industry, as well as increasingly fellow non-Isaan co-workers' adoption of Isaan ethnolects (The author further comments on this at length.).

Moreover, numerous avenues of investigation converge on the fact that the maintenance and ethnolinguistic vitality of Isaan vernacular is relatively strong in the two tourist sites studied. Among these are the linguistic normalization theory (Vallverdú, 1985), the ethnolinguistic vitality theory (Giles et al., 1977), the ethnolect theory (Clyne, 2000) and the discursive practice theory (Young, 2009; Hall, 2009). By means of the establishment of normative usages and uses in work domains and elsewhere, along with the extension of its multifaceted utility in socio-economical and sociocultural life, the notion of linguistic normalization propounded by Vallverdú (1985) largely accounts for the fact that Isaan vernacular has been continually gaining ground in the battle with the Standard Thai variety and the English speech for fuller normalization in the seaside resort of Pattaya and work domains (bars) in Bangkok Metropolis studied by the researcher. In the same vein, the formation of demographic (given the vast majority of love industry workers are Isaan) and economical (the language adopted in commercial activities on streets and in the love industry) capital (Giles *et al.*, 1977) largely account for the strong ethnolinguistic vitality of Isaan vernacular in this seaside town. The Isaan vernacular, albeit discriminated against, oppressed, stigmatized and stereotyped in official domains (e.g., workplaces, educational institutions and the mass media) (Draper, 2010, p. 135), is warmly welcomed and embraced in the seaside town (Pattaya) studied, given that locals and tourism-oriented business sectors rely heavily on Isaan women to attract foreign male tourists. This confirms Mandanares and Kent's (2006, P. 46) observation that since Isaan is the *lingua franca* in bars non-Isaan women see a need to learn the Isaan vernacular to understand what the majority of Isaan women in the bars are discussing at any one time (Manzanares and Ken, 2006, p. 46). Moreover, for some non-Isaan women part of becoming love-industry workers involved a shift in language choice and use away from Northern, Central and Standard Thai varieties to the adoption of Isaan ethnolects in their work domains. Illuminating in this connection is the fact that novice non-Isaan intakes were instructed by their seniors with respect to acquirable skills and manners (e.g., Western-style make-up) deemed to attract male Western tourists. In the light of the discursive practice approach pursued by Hall (2011) and Young (2009), the researcher also addresses how members of the non-Isaan women's groups learn and develop the competences needed in the love industry, while honing their newly acquired linguistic and behavioral capacities under the guidance of more experienced Isaan participants in the love industry (Vygotsky, 1978) through being socialized into an Isaan-style elder sibling/younger sibling hierarchy (see Howard 2007, pp. 206-208).

Answers to Research Question (ii): How can we describe the language-use-and-choice patterns observed in bars of Thai love-industry workers?

TABLE 5.2:
Language-use patterns of Isaan women studied,
2011-2013

Representative Informants (n= 15)	Interlocutors (Domain: Work - Bars)			
	Western Tourists (e.g., American, British, German and French)	Eastern Tourists Including those from Gulf States (e.g., Japanese, Chinese, Taiwanese, Hong Kong-nese, Singaporean, Indians)	Colleagues (from Thailand)	Friends (from Thailand and abroad)
1	English	English	Isaan	Isaan
2	English	English	Isaan	Standard Thai
3	English	English	Isaan	Isaan
4	English	English	Isaan	Standard Thai
5	English	No Data	Both Standard	Isaan

			Thai & Isaan	
6	English	English	Isaan	Isaan
7	English	English	Isaan	Isaan
8	English	English	Isaan	Isaan
9	English	English	Isaan	Isaan
10	English	No Data	Both Standard Thai & Isaan	Isaan
11	English	English	Isaan	Isaan
12	English	English	Isaan	Isaan
13	English	English	Isaan	Isaan
14	English	English	Isaan	Isaan
15	English	No Data	Isaan	Isaan

TABLE 5.3:
Percentage of language-use patterns
of Isaan women studied, 2011-2013

Interlocutors (Domain: Work - Bars)	Percentages
Language use with western customers	English: 100
Language use with eastern customers	English: 85 Others (e.g., Chinese and Japanese): 15
Language use with colleagues	Isaan: some 98 but others nearly 0 Standard Thai: some only 2 but others 100

Among the three groups studied, the Isaan women's group as a whole exhibits a higher attainment of English speech. Although the Isaan variety is maintained in the work domains (bars) of the two sites studied, the Isaan women's group is more likely to embrace English speech, thereby explaining the fact that a relatively very small number of Isaan women shift toward English speech away from the Isaan speech and the Standard Thai. However, at the same time, some members of the non-Isaan women's group (not as a whole) exhibits a habitual use of the Isaan vernacular in their work domains (this language-use pattern was very apparent in 1990s), accounting for their slow but steady shift toward the Isaan speech away from their Standard Thai and other Thai varieties. In addition, a significant number of members from Isaan women's group markedly exhibits a gradual shift in progress toward the English speech. The same progress, nevertheless, does not appear to be occurring among most members in the non-Isaan women's group and almost never does it occur in the Thai men's group (the author comments further on this with fuller treatment in the following sub-sections).

Answers to Research Question (iii): How does the love industry appear to contribute to its workers' English language learning?

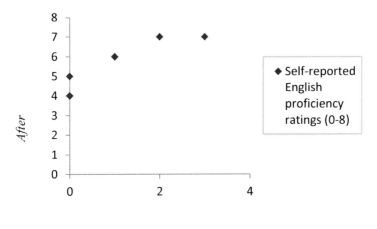

Before

Representative Isaan women	Before entering the love industry	After entering the love industry
1	0	4
2	0	5
3	1	6
4	1	6
5	2	7
6	2	7
7	3	7
8	3	7

Note. Key to numbers indicating language proficiency 0=no proficiency, 1=begin to understand and grasp some words and phrases, 2=beginning level, 3=beginning-intermediate level, 4= intermediate level, 5=intermediate-advanced level, 6=advanced level/good command, 7= fluent/native-like, 8=native proficiency

FIG 5.3:
Self-reported English Proficiency Ratings
Claimed by Isaan Women's Group studied

In the view of some of the Isaan women studied, their shift away from the Isaan vernacular to the habitual use of the English speech is a means of coping with class struggle (this is not the Marxist notion of "class struggle") (they are considered third class citizens by the rest of Thailand, due largely to the region of their birth), gendered discrimination (they are second class in their villages, due largely to their gender by birth) and are impoverished. Thus, the shift is inextricably connected with enhancing face and life chances (capability of conversing in English with Western tourists is a means of increasing income).

Thus far, this chapter confirms the findings of numerous previous studies. Consistent with Smith-Hefner (2009, P. 72) (Indonesian women's shift away from the indigenous-Javanese speech to the national language of Indonesian is seen as contesting conventional gendered roles imposed to them), some Isaan women's gradual shift away from the Isaan vernacular to the habitual use of the English speech is a means whereby the gender ideology stemming from traditional Isaan family values can be resisted. Furthermore, in the just mentioned article (ibid.), young women in Java were particularly drawn into urban centers (e.g., Yogyakarta) because of enhanced possibilities for social mobility. Their shift away from the formal styles of Javanese to the less formal Indonesian, the national language, was linked to their newly acquired middle-class status (ibid.). It is argued that there are similar dynamics at work vis-à-vis the target population studied in this article. Possibilities of social mobility (from rural lower-class backgrounds to urban middle-class 'entrepreneurs') draw young Isaan peasant women to urban centers. Their shift away from the Isaan vernacular to the English speech is linked to their socio-economic mobility, given English is the medium of communication used in their concomitant shift to love entrepreneurship.

Data also suggest that a gradual shift toward the English speech is seen as a strategic plan pertaining to possibilities of life-style enhancement (e.g., "secret dreams of moving to Europe [or North America or Australia], having a prosperous new life" by marrying one of the Western male tourists was revealed by Lon, a former love-industry workers in Thailand, cited in Manzanares and Kent, 2006, P. 105). Consistent with Gal's classic study undertaken in Oberwart, Austria, in 1978, data in her article suggest that "women's speech choices must be explained within the context of their social position, their strategic life choices" (Gal, 1978, P. 15).

In short, the view that women tend to have more to gain than men in the love industry of Thailand is suggested by the data in this study. Among the informants, Isaan women, contrasted to non-Isaan women, are the single greatest group of beneficiaries in the love industry of Thailand. The Isaan women studied choose to learn English, meet with male Western tourists and become love entrepreneurs to financially support themselves and their families. For some, they want a better quality of life and a brighter future after saving enough money to invest a small business in their home villages. At the same time, being fluent in English also means that they may be able to move to America, Europe or other western or first-world countries for an enhanced lifestyle.

Answers to Research Question (iv): What are social meanings behind language use, choice and shift of Thai love-industry workers?

With respect to Isaan women's speech community under consideration, their language choice is a means of poverty reduction and social and economic mobility, and language shift is a means of resistance against gender ideologies and lifestyle enhancement.

Non-Isaan Woman Sample

Answers to Research Question (i): What is the extent to which the ethnolinguistic vitality of the Isaan speech variety can be maintained in Thailand's love industry?

As is evidenced by the empirical data that certain changes (convergence with Isaan speech styles and shifts away from the native speech to the habitual use of the Isaan vernacular) in progress emerged in the non-Isaan women's group are not in progress in the Thai men's group. It is striking to see that the non-Isaan women's group studied as a whole demonstrates a greater use of the Isaan vernacular. This is a surprising result, given Standard (Central) Thai is considered the most prestigious variant (ranked No. 1) and a standard speech of the pan-Thai language family spoken in Thailand, followed by Northern (ranked No. 2) and Southern accents (ranked No. 3), and then Northeastern Isaan (ranked No. 4) (see Chanyam, 2002; Draper, 2010, pp. 135-136).

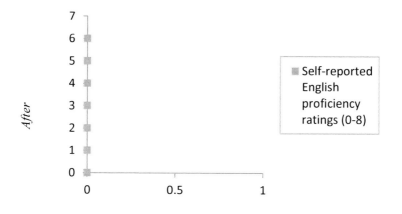

	7			
	6			
	5			

After

0   0.5   1

Before

■ Self-reported
English
proficiency
ratings (0-8)

Representative Non-Isaan women	Before entering the love industry	After entering the love industry
1	0	0
2	0	1
3	0	2
4	0	3
5	0	3
6	0	4
7	0	5
8	0	6

Note. Key to numbers indicating language proficiency 0=no proficiency, 1=begin to understand and grasp some words and phrases, 2=beginning level, 3=beginning-intermediate level, 4= intermediate level, 5=intermediate-advanced level, 6=advanced level/good command, 7= fluent/native-like, 8=native proficiency

FIG 5.4:
Self-reported Isaan Proficiency by Ratings
Claimed by non-Isaan Women studied

Answers to Research Question (ii): How can we describe the language-use-and-choice patterns observed in bars of Thai love-industry workers?

Not surprisingly, the use of the English language, the Isaan vernacular and the Standard Thai variety are alternated (code-switch) in bars by non-Isaan female workers.

TABLE 5.4:
Language-use Patterns of non-Isaan Women studied

Representative Informants (No. of representative informants=15)		Interlocutors (Domain: Work)			
		WT	ET	CW	F
1		E	--	I	STI
2		E	E	I	ST
3		E	--	I	STI
4		--	E	I	ST
5		E	--	STI	I
6		--	E	STI	ST
7		E	E	I	I
8		E	E	I	I
9		E	E	STI	I
10		--	--	STI	I
11		E	E	I	I
12		E	E	STI	STI
13		E	E	I	I

14		--	--	STI	I
15		E	--	STI	I

Note. WT=Western Tourists, ET=Eastern Tourists, CW=Co-Workers, F=Friends, E=English, ST=Standard (Central) Thai, I=Isaan, and STI=both Standard Thai and Isaan

TABLE 5.5:
Percentage of Language-use Patterns of non-Isaan Women studied

Interlocutors (Domain: Work)	Percentages
Language use with Western customers	English: 95
Language use with Eastern customers	English: 60 Others (e.g., Japanese): 40
Language use with co-workers	Isaan: 95 Standard (Central) Thai: 5

Answers to Research Question (iii): How does the love industry appear to contribute to its workers' English language learning?

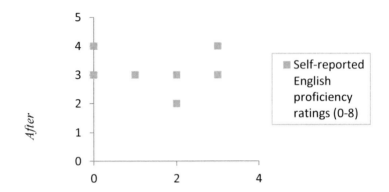

Before

Representative non-Isaan women	Before entering the love industry	After entering the love industry
1	0	4
2	0	3
3	1	3
4	1	3
5	2	2
6	2	3
7	3	3
8	3	4

Note. Key to numbers indicating language proficiency 0=no proficiency, 1=begin to understand and grasp some words and phrases, 2=beginning level, 3=beginning-intermediate level, 4= intermediate level, 5=intermediate-advanced level, 6=advanced level/good command, 7= fluent/native-like, 8=native proficiency

FIG 5.5:
Self-reported English proficiency Ratings
Claimed by non-Isaan women's group studied

Answers to Research Question (iv): What are social meanings behind language use, choice and shift of Thai love-industry workers?

In regard to the non-Isaan women employed in bars, ethnolect convergence and language choice are means of participation in discursive practice (with the majority of Isaan-speaking co-workers) in their workplace (bar language domains).

Thai Man Sample

The less favored role Thai men (contrasted to women engaged in the same activity) play in the love industry largely account for their relatively monolingual Thai speech and lower English proficiency.

Answers to Research Question (ii): How can we describe the language-use-and-choice patterns observed in bars of Thai love-industry workers?

The pattern of results seen in the Thai man sample is also not surprising to find that they are relatively monolingual Thai speakers, despite some can converse in the basic English language with Western tourists.

TABLE 5.6:
Language-use Patterns among Thai men studied

Representative Informants (No. of representative informants=15)		Interlocutors (Domain: Work)			
		WT	ET	CW	F
1		--	--	--	ST
2		--	--	ST	ST
3		--	--	ST	ST
4		--	E	ST	ST
5		--	--	ST	ST
6		--	E	ST	ST
7		E	E	I	I
8		E	--	I	I
9		--	--	I	I
10		--	--	ST	ST
11		E	E	--	ST
12		E	--	--	ST
13		E	--	--	ST
14		--	--	--	ST
15		--	--	--	ST

Note. WT=Western Tourists, ET=Eastern Tourists, CW=Co-Workers, F=Friends, E=English, ST=Standard (Central) Thai, I=Isaan, and STI=both Standard Thai and Isaan

TABLE 5.7:
Percentage of Language-use Patterns among Thai men studied

Interlocutors (Domain: Work)	Percentages
Language use with Western customers	English: 60 No active communication: 40
Language use with Eastern customers	English: 40 Others (e.g., Japanese): 10
Language use with co-workers	Isaan: 30 Standard (Central) Thai: 70

Answers to Research Question (iii): How does the love industry appear to contribute to its workers' English language learning?

It seems that Thai men employed in the love industry are less able to learn the English language than their female counterparts.

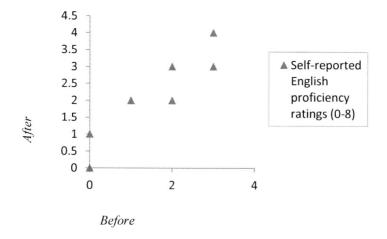

Representative male love entrepreneurs	Before entering the love industry	After entering the love industry
1	0	0
2	0	1
3	1	2
4	1	2
5	2	2
6	2	3
7	3	3
8	3	4

Note. Key to numbers indicating language proficiency 0=no proficiency, 1=begin to understand and grasp some words and phrases, 2=beginning level, 3=beginning-intermediate level, 4= intermediate level, 5=intermediate-advanced level, 6=advanced level/good command, 7= fluent/native-like, 8=native proficiency

FIG 5.6:
Self-reported English proficiency ratings
claimed by Thai men studied

Discussion and Concluding Remarks
討論和結論

As discussed earlier, previous research of the use of language by women often showed that their language choice and shift were notably associated with potentially bettering the conditions of life and life chances, such as poverty reduction, social and economic mobility (from the margins of society to the new middle class) (Gal, 1978; Smith-Hefner 2009), resistance against public ideologies (Gagné, 2008) and improved lifestyles. The present findings extend the results of these previous investigations by indicating that women of disparate ethnic groups (Isaan and non-Isaan) engaged in the same activity in the same industry had different degrees of association with the same languages (in this case, English and Isaan), while discrepancies in associations led to different social and economical outcomes.

Summary of Answers to Research Question (ii): How can we describe the language-use-and-choice patterns observed in bars of Thai love-industry workers?

There exists hard evidence that the Isaan speech is well-maintained in bars of Bangkok and Pattaya. Further, illustrations of the disparate results of language-use-and–choice patterns among Isaan women, non-Isaan women and Thai men studied can be seen in the comparison among afore-mentioned Tables and Figures.

TABLE 5.8: Ethnolect Convergence
among Isaan and non-Isaan Women studied

Media	Participants	Interlocutors	Domains	Sites	Converging with
Speaking	Isaan	Co-workers and Customers	Work	B	ST/E
				P	E
		Others	Non-Work	B	ST
				P	I
	Non-Isaan	Co-workers and Customers	Work	B	I/ST/E
				P	I/E
		Others	Non-Work	B	ST
				P	I/E

Note. B=Bangkok, P=Pattaya, E=English, ST=Standard (Central) Thai Variety, I=Isaan Thai Variety

TABLE 5.9: Mean Language-use Scores

M	Isaan women (n=100)	Non-Isaan women (n=50)	Men (n=50)
English	93	78	50
Isaan	98	95	30
Standard Thai	2	5	70

FIG 5.7: Percentages of Language Use

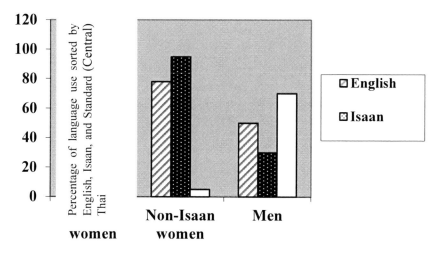

Taken together, the study reported in this chapter has reexamined that young women do not merely simply choose, or shift to or from, a language out of their linguistic and communicative repertoires; rather their linguistic strategies are better understood by taking into consideration their life strategies and possible life chances (Gal 1978: 15; Smith-Hefner 2009). This chapter demonstrates that the choice and shift of languages have a much wider-spread attraction for young Isaan and non-Isaan women than Thai men engaged in the activities of the love industry, as they seek to become members of a new entrepreneur class in urban centers in contradistinction to their former stigmatized peasant status in rural areas. Further, Isaan women take fuller advantage of these new social and economic opportunities than non-Isaan women and Thai men involved in the same industry.

（本文原稿於2013 年3月發表在《語言研究的理論和實作期刊》
第三卷第三期）

For further information about this chapter (if you want to discuss with the author), please contact:

Hugo Lee, Faculty Member

International College

National Institute of Development Administration

18th fl., Navamin Building, 118 Seri Thai Rd,

Khlong Chan, Bang Kapi, Bangkok 10240

Hugo Lee, Consultant Roster Member

United Nations

Economic & Social Commission for Asia & the Pacific

3rd fl., United Nations Conference Center, ESCAP HR

United Nations Building, 76 Rajadamnern Nok Ave

Bangkok 10200

T. 088-607-2560

E. hugoclubheart3@gmail.com   f Li Y-h Hugo

W. https://indiana.academia.edu/YuHsiuLee

ENDNOTES

Despite the substantial number of bargirls (sample size is more than 200) studied in the project (two sites: Bangkok and Pattaya) reported in this chapter, findings derived from this 2012-2013 dataset should be regarded only as an introduction to the ever-increasing literature that concern with bargirls in Thailand and Southeast Asia. Much of the research result (project outcomes) reported in this chapter focuses on one-year data gathered in 2012-2013, thereby should be contributing to a limited extent to the growing number of articles and books written about Thai bargirls and love entrepreneurs.

參考文獻　References

1. Batibo, H. M. (2009). Poverty as a crucial factor in language maintenance and language death: Case studies from Africa. In Harbert, W., McConnell-Ginet, S., Miller, A., & Whitman, J. P. (eds.). *Language and Poverty*, p. 23-36. Bristol: Multilingual Matters.

2. Bishop, R., & L.S. Robinson. (2002). Travellers' tails: Sex diaries of tourists returning fromThailand. In S. Thorbek and B. Pattanaik (eds.). *Transnational Prostitution*, pp. 13–23. London: Zed Books.

3. Brown, L. (2000). *Sex Slaves: The Trafficking of Women in Asia.* London, UK: Virago Press.

4. Chanyam, N. (2002). A study of language attitude toward Thai dialects and their speakers: A case study of four campuses of Rajamangala Institute of Technology. M.A. Thesis, The Faculty of Graduate Studies, Mahidol University, Thailand.

Noam Chomsky

5. Chomsky, N. (1965). *Aspects of the Theory of Syntax.* Cambridge, MA: MIT Press.

6. Clark, H. H. (1996). *Using Language.* Cambridge: Cambridge University Press.

7. Clyne, M. (2000). Lingua franca and ethnolects in Europe and beyond. *Sociolinguistica, 14*, 83-89.

8. Coates, J. (2004). *Women, Men and Language: A Sociolinguistic Account of Gender Differences in Language* (3rd ed.). Harlow, England; New York: Pearson Longman.

9. Cohen, E.. (2001). *Thai tourism: Hill tribes, islands and open-ended prostitution (2nd ed.).* Bangkok: White Lotus Co. Ltd.

Serafin M. Coronel-Molina

10. Coronel-Molina, S. M., & Rodríguez-Mondoñedo, M. (2012). Introduction: Language contact in the Andes and Universal Grammar. *Lingua, 122*, 447-460.

Lisa Delpit

11. Delpit, L. (2002). Introduction. In Lisa, D., & Joanne, K. D. (eds.). *The Sking that We Speak: Thoughts on Language and Culture in the Classroom*, p. xvii. New York: The New Press.

John Draper

12. Draper, J. C. (2004). Isan: The planning context for language maintenance and revitalization. *Second Language Learning and Teaching, 4.* Available online at http://www.usq.edu.au/users/sonjb/sllt/4/Draper04.html, (Accessed August 14th, 2012).

13. Draper, J. C. (2010). Inferring ethnolinguistic vitality in a community of Northeast Thailand. *Journal of Multilingual and Multicultural Development, 31* (2), 135-147.

14. Eckert, P. (1997). Gender and sociolinguistic variation. In Coates, J (ed.). *Language and Gender: A Reader*. pp. 64-75. Malden MA, & Oxford, UK: Wiley-Blackwell.

15. Enfield, N. J. (2009). Language and culture. In Li Wei., & Vivian, C (eds.). *Contemporary Applied Linguistics 2. (Linguistics for the Real World)*. pp. 83-97. London: Continuum.

16. Ethnologue (2005). *Ethnologue: Languages of the World* (15th ed). Dallas: SIL International.Retrieved on November 30th 2012 from the Web Site: http://www.ethnologue.com/web.asp.

Joshua Fishman

17. Fishman, J. (1964). Language maintenance and language shift as a field of enquiry. *Linguistics, 9*, 32-70.

18. Fishman, J. (1965). Who speaks what language to whom and when? *La Linguistique, 2*, 67-88.

19. Fishman, J. (1989). The spread of English as a new perspective for the study of language maintenance and language shift. In J. A. Fishman (ed.), *Language and Ethnicity in Minority Sociolinguistic Perspective*, 32-263. Clevedon: Multilingual Matters.

20. Fishman, J. (1991). *Reversing Language Shift: Theoretical and Empirical Foundations of Assistance to Threatened Languages*. Clevedon: Multilingual Matters.

21. Gagné, I. (2008). Urban princesses: Performance and "women's language" in Japan's Gothic/Lolita subculture. *Journal of Linguistic Anthropology, 18* (1), 130-150.

Susan Gal

22. Gal, S. (1978). Peasant men don't get wives: Language and sex roles in a bilingual community. *Language in Society, 7* (1), 1-16.

23. Gal, S. (1979). *Language Shift: Social Determinants of Linguistic Change in Bilingual Austria.* New York: Academic Press.

24. Giles, H., Taylor, D. M., & Bourhis, R. Y. (1977). Towards a theory of language in ethnic group relations.
    In Howard, G (ed.), *Language, Ethnicity and Intergroup Relations*, pp. 307-348. London, Academic Press.

25. Hall, J. K. (2009). Language learning as discursive practice. In Li Wei., & Vivian, C (eds.). *Contemporary Applied Linguistics 1 (Language Teaching and Learning)*, pp. 255-274. London: Continuum.

26. Hill, J. (1987). Women's speech in modern Mexicano. In Philips, S. U., Steele, S., & Tanz, C (eds.). *Language, Gender, and Sex in Comparative Perspective*, pp. 121-160. Cambridge: Cambridge University Press.

27. Howard, K. M. (2007). Kinterm usage and hierarchy in Thai children's peer groups. *Journal of Linguistic Anthropology, 17* (2), 204-230.

28. Hutchison, N. (2002). *A fool in paradise.* Tumbi Umbi, NSW: Mitraphab Centre Pty Ltd.

Dell Hymes

29. Hymes, D. (1974). *Foundations in Sociolinguistics: An Ethnographic Approach.* Philadelphia: University of Pennsylvania Press.

30. Jaspers, J. (2008). Problematizing ethnolects: Naming linguistic practices in an Antwerp secondary school. *International Journal of Bilingualism, 12* (1&2), 85–103.

Kimmo Kosonen

31. Kosonen, K. (2008). Literacy in local languages in Thailand: Language maintenance in a globalized world. *International Journal of Bilingual Education and Bilingualism, 11* (2), 170-188.

32. Lake, M., & K. Schirbel. (2000). *Love, Sex and Trust: Romantic Adventures in Thailand.* Phuket: Meteve Phuket Co. Ltd.

33. Landry, R., & Bourhis, R. Y. (1997). Linguistic landscape and ethnolinguistic vitality: An empirical study. *Journal of Language and Social Psychology, 16,* 23-49.

34. Manzanares, J., & Kent, D. (2006). *Only 13: The true story of Lon.* Bangkok, Thailand: Bamboo Sinfonia Publications.

35. Pack, S. (2011). "Where men can be men": Resituating Thai masculinity. *Asian Social Science, 7* (9), 3-8.

36. Perve, E., & C. Robinson. (2007). *Love in the Land of Smiles.* Chiang Mai: Alligator Service Co., Ltd.

37. Poon, A. (1993). *Tourism, Technology and Competitive Strategies.* Wallingford: CAB International.

38. Przeclawski, K. (1993). Tourism as the subject of interdisciplinary research. In D.G. Pearce & R.W. Butler (eds.). *Tourism Research*, pp. 9–19. London: Routledge.

39. Seabrook, J. (2007). *Cities.* London: Pluto Press.

40. Silverstein, M. (1979). Language structure and linguistic ideology. In Paul C., William F. H., & Carol L. H (eds.). *The Elements: A Parasession on Linguistic Units and Levels*, pp. 193-247. Chicago: Chicago Linguistic Society.

William Smalley

41. Smalley,W. A. (1994). *Linguistic Diversity and National Unity: Language Ecology in Thailand.* Chicago: The University of Chicago Press.

Nancy J. Smith-Hefner

42. Smith-Hefner, N. J. (2009). Language shift, gender and ideologies of modernity in Central Java, Indonesia. *Journal of Linguistic Anthropology, 19* (1), 57-77.

43. Stearn, D. (2004). *Pattaya: Patpong on steroids.* Kincumber, NSW: Mitraphab Centre Pty Ltd.

44. Vallverdú, F. (1985). *El fet lingüística com a fet social* (6th Ed). Barcelona: Edicions 62.

Lev Vygotsky

45. Vygotsky, L. (1978). *Mind in Society: The Development of Higher Psychological Processes.* Cambridge: Cambridge University Press.

46. Walker, D., & R.S. Erlich. (1992). *'Hello my big big honey!'.* Bangkok: Dragon Dance Publications.

47. Wilson, J. D. (2008). Thai bar girls and farang: a customized inter-cultural professional services market. *Human Resource Development International, 11* (4), 401-415.

48. Woolard, K. A. (1985). Language variation and cultural hegemony: Toward an integration of linguistic and sociolinguistic theory. *American Ethnologist, 12,* 738-48.

49. Woolard, K. A. (1998). Language ideology as a field of inquiry. In Schieffelin, B. B., Woolard, K., & Kroskrity, P. (eds.). *Language Ideologies: Practice and Theory,* pp. 3-49. New York: Oxford University Press.

50. Woywode, M. (2007). *The Intercultural Environment in Thailand.* Google search: 'Intercultural environment Thailand' (Accessed November 25, 2007).

51. Young, R. (2009). *Discursive Practice in Language Learning and Teaching.* Malden MA, & Oxford, UK: Wiley-Blackwell.

第四部　尋求政治庇護者、都市難民的語言議題

Part 4.
Issues in Language Education, Language Use
(Communication) for Asylum Seekers and Urban Refugees

Chapter 6

Issues in Language Education for Urban Refugee Children and Youth

> urban refugees
>
> refugee children
>
> refugee youth

第六章

難民孩童的語言教育議題

THIS INQUIRY ON young refugee language learners presents findings that have been yielded from an empirical study and conducted over a period of 8 months in Thailand. This study took an angle in multidisciplinary fields of language teaching by examining socio-economic inequalities occurred to urban refugee children and adolescents resulted from their formal schooling interruption as closely in relation to what languages are taught in their humanitarian based language learning programs. A central argument throughout this chapter has been balancing languages to teach for these young language learners by refocusing attentions on teaching needed Thai language that helps formal schooling interrupted refugee children and adolescents to resume their study in local Thai schools, accompanied by teaching globally-oriented English language. By the same token, while the promise of English language teaching and learning might empower young urban refugee students, English language teaching cannot be at expenses of Thai language teaching because the latter is urgently needed for these young urban refugees to continue their formal schooling and decreases inequalities.

摘要（六、七章）

　　多數難民來到泰國曼谷的聯合國難民署UNHCR申難，卻不會講國際語言（英語）和申難泰國當地的語言（泰語），所以

難民兒童	難民中心職員	幫助難民
在難民中心	是泰國人	學會使用
上英語課	難民不是泰國人	英語和泰語
同時也需要	只好彼此用非母語	刻不容緩
學習泰語	的英語溝通	
	造成溝通上	
	很多障礙	

ACKNOWLEDGMENTS

The original study reported in chapter 6 was peer-reviewed by the editorial board of the Journal of Language Teaching and Research (ISSN 1798-4769).

Introduction 導論

IN DISCUSSING RELATIONSHIP between foreign/second language teaching and inequalities in societies resulted from formal schooling interruption, the needs of what languages to teach for marginalized minority groups such as young urban refugee students are frequently overlooked. A real example is given as follows: Teaching English language is commonly seen as a crucial resource for English as foreign/second language learners to access power, prestige, status, and socio-economic mobility. However, challenging traditional notions of teaching a powerful language such as English to decrease social inequalities, data obtained from urban refugee language learners in Thailand show otherwise. On condition that these young refugee language learners continue to study in English language programs provided by refugee shelters, they are in a disadvantaged position to not acquire needed Thai language competencies from their heterogeneous and linguistically diverse refugee peers and refugee English teachers, and are therefore unable to enroll in local Thai schools. Receiving English language education among these young urban refugees is at expenses of learning immediately needed Thai language to terminate their formal schooling interruption.

One of the causes of inequalities is access to schooling. As evidenced by data in this study, acknowledged factors that impact socio-economic inequality include formal schooling interruption among urban refugee children and adolescents. Often socio-economic inequalities between mainstream groups and minority refugee communities can partially be caused by continuation of formal schooling with the former and continuation of formal schooling interruption with the latter. Ideally, formal schooling interrupted refugee children and adolescents should be entitled with Thai language courses as preparation to enroll in local Thai schools. Humanitarian based language programs designed for urban refugee children and adolescents organized by nongovernment groups, nonetheless, fail to offer regular Thai language courses in preparing young refugee students with Thai language proficiencies needed to continue their formal schooling in Thailand. When English language teaching and Thai language teaching as two competing orientations in language teaching markets, English language teaching often foregrounds Thai language teaching in humanitarian based language learning programs, resulted from administrative decisions as well as urban refugee language learners' choices. Prioritizing English language teaching accompanied with discouraging Thai language teaching increases socio-economic inequalities for urban refugee children and adolescents from their Thai counterparts. To close this gap, this study suggests that beliefs and/or ideologies that promote English language teaching only should be contested. Moreover, Thai as a second language courses are recommended for formal schooling interrupted urban refugee students to enable them in resuming formal schooling in Thailand, ultimately shortening their socio-economic inequalities from their Thai counterparts.

Background 研究背景

Refugees and Asylum Seekers Resettle in Urban Areas of Thailand

In the world we are living today approximately eleven million people are displaced at a domestic level and transnational level (UNHCR, 2006).   Suffering, hardship, misery, torment and adverse economy resulted from internal political unrest such as civil wars are evident especially when their victims come to live in our neighborhoods as refugees.   More often than not wars generate enormous death tolls, disrupt accumulation of physical capitals and properties, and erode freedom in civil levels.   Transnational migration occurs when these horrors displace population from their home countries to resettle in a new country.   For the reason that civil conflicts, political, and religious persecutions by and large go on for many years, these forced migrants have been frequent and on the rise in numerous countries of the world.   Those seeking asylum hope for refugee status being granted and individuals "owing to a well-founded fear of being persecuted for reasons of race, religion, nationality, membership of a particular social group or political opinion, is outside the country of his/her nationality and is unable or, owing to such fear is unwilling, to avail himself of the protection of that country" are categorized as refugees by the United Nations (Huguet & Punpuing, 2005).

Many countries have acknowledged an ethical responsibility to admit refugees and rendered humanitarian assistance to these extremely vulnerable persons. The Kingdom of Thailand is one of the largest shelters in the world for displaced people, refugees and asylum seekers. Millions of displaced people flee their homelands to escape war, long-term economic struggle, political or religious persecution, and violence by military to settle in Thailand (Huguet & Punpuing, 2005). Some asylum seekers from different countries come to Thailand and take residence in urban areas, because it has comparatively easy-to-meet visa requirements than other countries (Jesuit Refugee Service, n.d, online). Most of them come from countries of Afghanistan, Congo, Mainland China, Nepal, North Korea, Pakistan, Sri Lanka and Vietnam. Sociolinguistically transnational refugee resettlements should be seen as a life-long process. Exploring needs in language teaching and learning among urban refugees is essentially a moral imperative to help them resettle in Thailand.

Issues of Language Teaching in Humanitarian based Language Learning Programs in Thailand

Despite Thailand is a prominent receiving country for refugees and asylum seekers in almost worldwide migration and resettlement, yet there is increasingly a huge gap between humanitarian based language learning programs in Thailand and actual language needs among refugees. Data in this study show that these language learning programs at urban refugee shelters are at risk to create enormously large social inequality for urban refugee children and adolescents from their Thai counterparts, because of languages they do not offer to teach. On the one hand, formal schooling interrupted refugee children and adolescents do not receive regular Thai language assistance, but they are entitled to enroll in a local Thai school nearby their residence. As a result, they continue their formal schooling interruption and are thus not ready to enroll in local Thai schools. On the other hand, the extreme focus on English language teaching in a number of urban refugee language learning programs skips the immediate need for young refugee students to learn Thai language. To make the matter worse, English language teaching focused programs designed for young urban refugee students fail to provide a comprehensive curriculum with balanced developments in different subject matters suited for refugee children and adolescents in primary and secondary levels. In any case teaching English language alone cannot possibly make up refugee children' and adolescents' needs in learning other subjects, i.e., mathematics, science and social studies.

PROJECT OBJECTIVES

The Call to Teach Thai Language Regularly for Urban Refugee Children and Adolescents in Thailand (during the early 2000s)

Despite the fact that learning English language has become a critical resource of gaining power, prestige, status, and socio-economic mobility in this age of globalization, we cannot rule out the need to teach a local language for urban refugees in countries where they resettle. Only when refugees become functionally communicative in Thai language do they begin to enjoy the rewards of living in this beautiful kingdom of Thailand. Data from this present inquiry show that learning Thai language can surely help urban refugees satisfy their fundamental needs and empower their self-esteem. Mastery of Thai language can help individual and communal refugees to successfully integrate into the mainstream Thai society while waiting for a third country to adopt them. There is emerging evidence from data in this current study to show that the attainment of any medium of wider communication, a nature language acquisition to its native speakers, turns out to be a huge task for transnational refugees if they do not receive any language education to learn common media of communication in their resettled countries. The lack of mastery over a common language is widely perceived as a frustrating limitation faced by cross-national refugees trying to adapt to a new environment. Learning a second language as medium of wider communication in a host country added life difficulties to these urban refugees. Ideally, language teaching programs provided for unwilling migrants should cater to meet their different needs in language and communication. These needs of language and communication might vary significantly from those other immigrants who are willing to move to Thailand. Despite occasional Thai language training courses are provided, in Thailand rarely do humanitarian based language learning programs consider urban refugee children's needs to learn Thai language in a regular Thai language program for 1-2 years before they are competent to enroll in nearby Thai schools.

Exploring research perspectives that frame the issue of language teaching for formal schooling interrupted refugee children and adolescents in Thailand, literature evidently show a positive effect on transnational refugees who receive second language education before they are placed in mainstream classrooms in a host country. Australia (Settlement English, n.d.), Canada (Adelman, 1990) and USA (Ellis, 2010), for example, prepare refugee children and adolescents with needed English as second language courses in enabling them to continue their formal schooling in their resettled English speaking countries. Nevertheless, data from this inquiry show that Thailand has produced little evidence of improvement in these humanitarian based language learning programs to help urban refugee children and adolescents learn Thai language regularly.

Methodology 研究方法

To develop an understanding regarding contextualized factors that lead to the emergence of English language teaching at costs of Thai language teaching for formal schooling interrupted refugee children and adolescents in urban areas of Thailand, this study pursues the following research question in this contribution: what are contextualized factors that shape and influence foreign/second language learning among formal schooling interrupted urban refugee children and adolescents in Thailand and how can we do to meet their needs of different languages through language teaching.

Urban Refugee Sites and Young Refugee Language Learners in Thailand

Two main types of refugees and asylum seekers currently resettle in Thailand—urban refugees and camp-based refugees. The scope of this inquiry has been limited to understand urban refugee children and adolescents particularly in regard to their language learning experiences at humanitarian based language learning programs and what languages taught in these programs are in relation to social inequalities created by extension of their formal schooling interruption.

Multiple urban refugee research sites across Thailand are characterized that in English language courses, young children focused English programs seem to coexist comfortably with adult refugee English teachers and some American volunteers. This study delved into 80 young refugee students' encounters with language needs to resume their formal schooling and what languages are taught in their humanitarian based language learning programs. Informants' age are ranged from 6-7 years old to 18-19 years old. Nuanced understanding of language teaching and learning have been expanded and modified by interview and questionnaire responses, and observation notes from these young refugee language learners in urban shelters. Adult urban refugees volunteer to teach young students in their language learning centers. Their language learning classrooms are where linguistically and culturally diverse urban refugee children and adolescents are taught in English language isolated from daily activities of neighboring Thai speaking residents. These English language education for urban refugee children and adolescents are also instructional settings where young refugee students learn to be competent members to please refugee English teachers. These urban refugee children' and adolescents' learning takes place in classroom language domains that are in particular socio-cultural and linguistic groups.

Data Collection & Analysis
資料採集和分析

Through interviews, observations and questionnaires, this paper disclosed what languages to teach and what languages are needed for urban refugee children and adolescents to end their formal schooling interruption in Thailand. The researcher carefully triangulates data collected from individual interviews, group interviews, follow-up interviews, participant observations, non-participant observations, and responses from questionnaires.

PROJECT OUTCOMES

Results and Discussion
(Please see Endnote 1.)
研究成果和討論

Three main contextualized factors that depicted a young urban refugee population characterized by a multifaceted set of English language teaching and learning are examined in details. First, data indicate a strong desire to learn English among young refugee students. Not surprisingly, data reveal that almost all urban refugee children and adolescents (98%, N=80) see a need to learn English language over Thai language. The powerful role of English language is influencing and shaping what are possibilities remained for languages other than English to teach in urban refugee settings in Thailand. Data point out that some urban refugee children and adolescents (60%, N=80) do not see a need to learn Thai language, because they do not want to enroll in a local Thai school but wait for a third country to adopt them. However, this paper argues that lack of Thai language speaking proficiencies among these refugee children and adolescents might put them in a disadvantaged position to prolong their length of formal schooling interruption. Data report estimated 3-4 years in average of formal schooling interruption for English language learning focused participants. By marked contrast, urban refugee children and adolescents (30%, N=80) who intend to enroll in local Thai schools see a need to learn Thai language. Data report estimated 1.5-2 years in average of formal schooling interruption for Thai language learning focused refugee children and adolescents. However, there are unfortunately no regular Tha i language teaching programs provided for these urban refugee children and adolescents who need to enroll in local Thai schools and terminate their formal schooling interruption, because Thai language learning programs are only provided periodically or occasionally as non-formal language education for adult learners.

Note that different language learning programs at urban refugee shelters across Thailand are differing in their size of student body and teaching staffs, geographical locations in the Kingdom of Thailand, and available language teaching and learning resources. Thus, data gathered in this present inquiry reported in this paper cannot be generalized and/or applicable to every language learning programs at urban refugee shelters across Thailand. Data presented below in table 1 and figure1 are merely estimated numbers on the basis of accessibility of limited data.

TABLE 6.1:
Responses of informants when asked what affects them to learn foreign/second languages

Contextualized factors	# of responses from 80 informants	% of responses from 80 informants
Seeing a need to learn English language	78	>90%
Heterogeneous and linguistically diverse refugees see a need to use English language as a common medium of communication	60	75%
Thai friends and Thai neighbors live close to refugee's residence	20	25%
Media: Newspapers, magazines, TV, and radio		
No opinion/unclear/neutrality		

Note: informants can choose more than one contextualized factors.

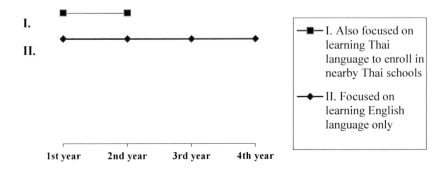

I. Young urban refugee language learners see a need to learn Thai language and intend to enroll in Thai schools nearby their residence: Estimated 1.5-2 years of formal schooling interruption

II. Young urban refugee language learners keep staying in English language learning programs and do not see a need to learn Thai language: Estimated 3-4 years of formal schooling interruption

FIGURE 6.1:

Relations between foreign/second language learning choices and time length of formal schooling interruption Continued finding reports in this study, secondly, data show a need to use English language as a common medium of communication among heterogeneous and linguistically diverse refugees from

Pakistan, Sri Lankan, Congo, and other countries. Even if urban refugees settle in a predominantly Thai language environment, their shelters and service centers except household language domains may not reflect the fact that the medium of communication is in Thai oral discourse. The data speak to the fact that heterogeneous and linguistically diverse urban refugees converse to each other in English language as a common medium of communication and as a medium of instruction in language learning programs. This contrast is dramatically lost in rural refugee camps, especially those who live with homogenous Burmese peers. In contrast to rural refugees who maintain their native languages within their homogeneous camps, urban refugees stated that heterogeneous and linguistically diverse peers have more effect on their increasingly use of English language as a common medium of communication when they cannot understand each others' native languages. Furthermore, data from this study contribute to current understandings of foreign/second language teaching in the context of transnational urban refugee communities by arguing that urban refugee children' and adolescents' desires to learn English language over Thai language are partially resulted from English language learning programs available and free to them. Data speak to a fact that learning English language or Thai language could be highly specific to refugee's language learning programs accessible to them. However, this study cannot go beyond its data to infer what expected outcomes are when Thai language learning programs are regular, available and free to urban refugee children and adolescents.

Third, the analysis shows that an immediate language contact with a predominant Thai language domain in Thailand has little effect or almost no effect on shaping everyday practices of English language among urban refugee communities. The Royal Thai Government did not sign 1951 Refugee Convention, so it does not have laws and permanent systems to decide whether a person is a refugee (see legal services in Bangkok Refugee Center, online). Moreover, the 1979 Immigration Act states that illegal immigrants, i.e., those without a passport, a valid visa to stay, and a work permit to get employed in Thailand, are subject to arrest, detention and deportation. Thus, urban refugees are struggling and in desperate need, seeking out a life in a hostile environment as they are not recognized as refugees by the Royal Thai government. As illegal aliens, they confront abuse, exploitation, hostility, language difficulties, prejudice, threats, and confusing legal status, and hence are subject to arrest, detention, deportation and human warehousing. Limited or no speaking proficiency in Thai language is dependent on the frequency of language contacts with linguistically diverse refugee peers as well as outside speakers of the predominant Thai language. Within a predominantly Thai language environment, informants assert that their less frequent language contacts with Thai language speakers outside their refugee shelters may have, nonetheless, negative effect on their Thai language learning. Note that Thai administrators and Thai social workers communicate with urban refugees in English language. For security reasons, the data reported here are evident that most urban refugees have less language contacts with outside Thai native speakers unless absolutely necessary. Although Thai government allows non-government religious organizations in collaboration with United Nations High Commissioner for Refugees (UNHCR) to provide shelters for illegal immigrants such as refugees and asylum seekers, Thai polices can arbitrarily arrest them and ask for bribes. Because some urban refugees rely on non-profit organizations and humanitarian assistance for their food supply, they might not see a need to learn Thai language to make a living in Thailand. However, other urban refugees who need to make a living in Thailand have fairly more frequencies of language contacts with Thai language speakers. It is very unfortunate but true that relatively isolated language socialization within diverse linguistic refugee communities greatly hinder urban refugee children and adolescents from acquiring needed Thai language proficiencies to continue their formal schooling in local Thai schools. To assume that young urban refugee children can be placed into mainstream Thai speaking schools without preparations in their Thai language competencies and proficiencies is beyond the scope of this current inquiry.

In combination with above three contextualized factors that affect teaching and learning of foreign/second languages among urban refugees in Thailand—a strong desire to learn English among young refugee students, a need to use English language as a common medium of communication among heterogeneous and linguistically diverse refugees, and an immediate language contact with a predominant Thai language domain in Thailand has little effect or almost no effect on shaping everyday practices of English language among urban refugee communities, now this paper shifts its attention to emphasize some findings. Challenging traditional notions of acquiring a foreign/second language of immediate medium of wider communication in a host country, the data from this current study prove that the predominantly Thai language domain plays a minimal role having little effect on the most dominant English language learning occurred among urban refugee children and adolescents in Thailand. In other words, most informants assert that they do not see an immediate need to acquire Thai language despite its demands, but data speak directly to the fact that they see a desperate need to learn English oral and written discourse. Data from this study propose to shift our perspective from viewing foreign/second language teaching as a focus on an immediate medium of wider communication, i.e., Thai language, for urban refugees to acquiring a globally-oriented foreign/second language, i.e., English language, in a resettled host country, i.e., Thailand. Note that practices of language teaching and learning reported from data in this present inquiry can only be limited to speak the fact for local contexts of some urban refuge shelters in Thailand. They do not meant to be generalize-able for other individuals and groups with similar exiled backgrounds in different contexts.

Conclusions and Recommendations
(Please see Endnote 2.)
結論和對未來研究的建議

This present inquiry concludes with the following analysis: What has held back these humanitarian based language learning programs to prepare urban refugee students ready for resuming and continuing their formal schooling is that with extremely focus on teaching English language only, there has not been an accompanying regular Thai language program to teach Thai language.

Qualitative records from this paper add to our current understandings of young urban refugee's language learning issues and how they are in relation to formal schooling interrupted problems among them in Thailand. This paper urges that Thai as a second language programs should be established by UNHCR in meeting the needs of formal schooling interrupted urban refugee children and adolescents to continue their formal schooling in Thailand. English language only curriculum and English language focused programs accessible to refugee children and adolescents could be problematic, because English language courses alone cannot cover what urban refugee children and adolescents need in other subject areas and skills. Just because these urban refugee children (> 90%, N=80) express a strong desire to only learn

English language does not mean that they do not need to develop other knowledge and skills from a variety of subject contents. These urban refugee children and adolescents are too young to make their own decisions on whether they should be only entitled to learn English language alone or they should be entitled also to learn subjects, especially Thai language, other than English language in helping them end formal schooling interruption. These educational language policy decisions should be given to UNHCR and grass-root religious groups who organize urban refugee services to make. Thus, implications of this study are geared for language policy makers, literacy planners, language educators, foreign/second language teachers and anyone interested in meeting the needs of language, communication and formal schooling continuation for urban refugee children and adolescents. With decreasing social inequality in mind, this article is intended to bring together scholars from a variety of disciplines, graduate students, social workers and anyone interested in helping urban refugee children and adolescents to shorten their length of formal schooling interruption in Thailand by providing their needed Thai language courses.

This present inquiry thus suggests the following words: what remains the core challenge for humanitarian based language learning programs at multiple urban refugee sites in Thailand is the balance that should be made between the necessary regular

Thai language teaching, which is to end formal schooling interruption for urban refugee children and adolescents in decreasing their socio-economic inequalities, and the need to teach English language.

（本文原稿於2011年發表在《語言教學和研究》
第二卷第四期）

For further information about this chapter (if you want to discuss with the author), please contact:

Hugo Lee, Faculty Member
International College
National Institute of Development Administration
18th fl., Navamin Building, 118 Seri Thai Rd,
Khlong Chan, Bang Kapi, Bangkok 10240

Hugo Lee, Consultant Roster Member
United Nations
Economic & Social Commission for Asia & the Pacific
3rd fl., United Nations Conference Center, ESCAP HR
United Nations Building, 76 Rajadamnern Nok Ave
Bangkok 10200

T. 088-607-2560
E. hugoclubheart3@gmail.com   **f** Li Y-h Hugo
W. https://indiana.academia.edu/YuHsiuLee

ENDNOTES

1. The findings derived from the 2010-2011 dataset should be regarded, to a limited extent, to account for Burmese refugee children only, excluding a massive number of refugee children from Congo and Sri Lanka, 2010-2011. It should be noted that the data gathered from refugee children in 2010-2011 does not include children from other countries than Myanmar. It is largely due to the fact that only Burmese migrant children and Burmese refugee children are permitted to enroll in Thai public schools as agreed by the Royal Thai government, along with some (not all) Thai public schools.

2. The Bangkok Refugee Center (BRC) started to offer Thai language courses (2017 or earlier-present) for refugee children aged 6-18. However, Thai language courses were not offered during 2010-2011 when the author (researcher) was gathering data.

Announcement
Consolidation of Intensive Thai Language Course

Please be informed that starting on Wednesday 1 November 2017, Intensive Thai Language classes will be consolidated at Good Shepherd School for operational reasons. All services for refugee and asylum seeking children aged 6-17 will remain the same.

School time • • • 10:00 am - 3:00 pm • • •

4 hours / day, 4 days / week X 6 months (except Wednesdays)
Classes include Thai, English, Mathematics and Cultural Studies.

Transportation allowance, stationery and books, a daily lunch at school and uniforms will be available including facilitation to Thai Public schools for those who passed the relevant examinations.

For Registration and more information, please contact the Bangkok Refugee Center Monday to Friday or call 02-2771753 Ext 103, 108 (except Wednesdays.)

UNHCR and COERR are making all efforts to constantly improve educational services and this consolidation in a location with high-standard educational facilities will be beneficial to all children.

COERR / BRC
13 September 2017

參考文獻　References

1. Adelman, H. (ed.) (1990). Refuge: Canada's periodical on refugees, 10 (2), 1-20,

2. Ellis, N. C. (ed.) (2010). CHAPTER 5: The policies and politics of educating refugee adolescents. Language Learning, 60, pp. 119–145. Ann Arbor, MI: University of Michigan.

3. Huguet, J., & Punpuing, S. (2005). International migration in Thailand [Electronic Version]. Bangkok, Thailand: International Organization for Migration. Retrieved on October 13, 2010, from the Web Site: http://www.iom-seasia.org/resource/pdf/SituationReport.PDF

4. Jesuit Refugee Service (n.d.). Urban refugee program, Bangkok. Retrieved December 18, 2010, from the Jesuit Refugee Service Web Site: http://jrs.or.th/thai/

5. Settlement English (n.d.). ACL settlement English, York Street: Sydney. Retrieved November 11, 2011, from the Settlement English Web Site: http://www.acl.edu.au/

6. UNHCR. (2006). The 1951 refugee convention: Questions & answers [Brochure]. Geneva: Archives of the United Nations.

CHAPTER 7

Issues in Language and Communication faced among Urban Refugee Adults

urban refugees

refugee adults

第七章

成人難民的語言和溝通議題

BY ADOPTING A pluralistic approach to Thailand's urban refugee shelters, this paper yields insights of contextualized factors that hinder Thai-English bilingual and biliteracy practices through English for communication purposes among non-native speaking urban refugees. Interviews, observations and surveys gathered from 80-100 urban refugees revealed that their most dominant second language uses are closely tied with their English medium communication instead of immediate contact of Thai language. That is to say, English for communication purposes among linguistic diverse urban refugees has become apparent, dominant and intensified over oral and written discourses in Thai. Predominantly Thai language environments outside urban refugee shelters have limited influence on participants, whereas English medium communication among linguistically heterogeneous urban refugees has tremendous influence on their second language learning. This study argues how Thai and English as two competing linguistic orientations to everyday language practices that foreground English language over Thai language across urban refugee communities in Thailand. However, these urban refugee shelters are depicted as contrary to the positive development(s) of English language, because confluence of Thai administrators, Thai social workers, refugee adults, children and adolescents speaking non-native and/or non-native like English resulted in mutually reinforced misguided uses of English language, underscoring the *phonologically-, grammatically-, and pragmatically improper use of English one-word-, two-word-, and multiword-utterances the researcher has witnessed via instruments.*

ACKNOWLEDGMENTS

The original study reported in chapter 7 was peer-reviewed by the editorial board of the Modern Journal of Applied Linguistics (ISSN 0974-8741).

PROJECT OBJECTIVES

Introduction 導論

THIS PRESENT INQUIRY provides an empirical grounding, rigor, and update in English for communication purposes among urban refugee communities across Thailand and how English medium communication is in relation to discourage Thai-English bilingual and biliteracy developments. The intertwined role of linguistically diverse urban refugee population and the need for a common medium of communication can be understood by adopting English for communication purposes. The central argument throughout this paper has been the fact that reliance on English for communication purposes among non-native and/or non-native like speaking urban refugees reduces their likelihood to learn Thai language and misguide each other's uses in English L2 utterances, hindering their Thai-English bilingual and biliteracy developments—both their learning of Thai language and English language. This theme frames preceding and subsequent sections in this article.

Introducing transnational asylum seekers and urban refugees resettled in Thailand serves a background review for this study. An increasingly growing migratory trend is frequently through transnational asylum seeking. One of the most actively participating groups in this diasporic trend for decades has been urban refugees resettled in Thailand. A large body of studies in multidisciplinary fields of applied linguistics, sociolinguistics and general linguistic studies has yielded understandings into daily language activities among camp-based refugees (i.e., Burmese and Lao refugees) as well as urban refugees (i.e., Congo, China, North Korea, Pakistan, and Sri Lankan refugees) in Thailand. Nevertheless, very few studies have focused on urban refugees that to what extent their Thai-English bilingual and biliteracy learning might otherwise seem to be discouraged as a result of their English for communication purposes among non-native and/or non-native like speakers.

Two forces seemingly fuel emerging importance regarding urban refugees' second language learning in Thailand. First, local Thai communities demand urban refugees that acquire immediate use of Thai language that is much needed in communicating with them. Second, more and more refugees cannot accept the unequal socio-economic outcomes that have characterized some of them with advantaged English learning opportunities achieving more financial gains than others with fewer means to access English language. On the one hand, an increasingly transnational migratory trend among urban refugees presumably leads to heterogeneity and linguistic diversity in Thailand with regard to multilingual, multiliterate and multicultural developments. On the other hand, most probably, transnational refugees' exposure to a predominantly Thai language environment can facilitate their Thai oral discourse acquisition. However, this study has found otherwise in Thailand. Consistent with interviews, observations and responses from questionnaires conducted among urban refugee communities in Thailand, this paper discloses how urban refugees enacted and employed daily language activities resulted in 2 divergent and yet intertwined pattern termed Thai-English bilingual and biliteracy, which is evident from data in this study indicating its destined failure resulted from non-native and /or non-native like English medium communication.

Issues of English for communication purposes among urban refugees in Thailand

The rise of United Kingdom (UK) of Great Britain, followed by the rise of United States of America (USA), accompanied with other factors has jointly created English language to become the most widely-spoken lingua franca in our time (McCrum, 2010). It has replaced rivals such as French to become the language of diplomacy and defeated rivals such as German to become the language of science. Though many more people speak Mandarin-Chinese on the earth at this moment today, Mainland China itself has vast numbers of English as a foreign language learners. In India, likewise, the biggest English-speaking middle class is considered a big asset to help the country grow. Some assumed that English is the last lingua franca until the return of Babel (see Ostler, 2010). This biblical account documents a period of time prehistorically when all humans on earth were united with the same language. A common medium of communication not only influenced people's speech, but also their thoughts, ideas, cultures and so on during that time. This implies that one can more easily influence others, given the fact that they did not have communication barriers linguistically and culturally.

Nonetheless, can English for communication purposes in the 21st century unite linguistically diverse population(s) on the earth back to the Tower of Babel? One problem with such bold vision is that data from English medium communicators among ethnically and linguistically diverse non-native speakers in this paper show discouraging results. Evidenced by data, this study claims that deficiency in learning Thai L2 and failure in learning English L2 is resulted from English medium communication among nonnative- and/or non-native like English speakers who are heterogeneous urban refugee adults in Thailand. In other words, convincing arguments derived from data in this article asserted limits and boundaries to the ideal of effortless English for communication purposes among linguistically diverse groups. To claim that English medium communication can solve communication problems among linguistically diverse people such as urban refugee groups in Thailand is actually to neglect constrains created by non-native and/or non-native like speakers that not only hinder their English language learning, but also prevents them from learning Thai language.

This chapter gave a sobering observation in following accounts particularly in regard to difficulties in learning Thai and English language faced by transnational urban refugees in Thailand. In addition to their unspeakable trauma fleeing home countries and resettling in a strange country they never knew before, language and communication issues add more obstacles to unwilling migrants such as urban refugee communities in Thailand. Thai and English language are much needed for transnational urban refugees in Thailand. Nonetheless, Thai-English bilingual and biliteracy developments among urban refugees are at risk. Mainly through English for communication purposes, urban refugees are socialized into an isolated language boundary. This relatively isolated language boundary via English medium communication within urban refugee communities in Thailand greatly reduces their opportunities for their social- and daily use of Thai language, hindering both urban refugees' efforts to learn Thai language for immediate use and their possibilities to learn English from native and native-like English speakers outside their constrained shelters.

However, there are some exceptions when very few urban refugees marry Thai wives and attempt to settle in Thailand for good. In addition, exceptions too are urban refugees/illegal migratory workers brought into Thailand from bordering countries such as Burma, Cambodia and Laos by human traffickers to beg money through team works and engage in more language contacts with Thais. Without learning to speak Thai and English language with adequate learning resources, there is no way urban refugees can express themselves clearly unless they only hang out with their homogenous groups of refugees fleeing from the same countries of origin.

Multiple field-site experiences in this study also asserted that some urban refugees are not able to use English for communication purposes and thus cannot communicate clearly to receive medical benefits they are entitled with. When urban refugees go to hospitals and clinics for medication, they may not understand instructions explaining to them a proper use of prescription drugs and medicine in Thai or English language unless they can go with volunteer interpreters/translators.

However, duties of volunteer interpreters/translators usually exclude translation assistances in hospitals and clinics for urban refugees who do not speak Thai or English language. Grass-root religious organizations in collaboration with United Nations High Commissioner for Refugees (UNHCR) fall short to provide resources and services necessary to maintain a permanent team of bilingual/biliterate interpreters and/or translators for linguistically diverse urban refugees resettled in Thailand.

But for most urban refugees, the problem of translation/interpretation is usually solved informally by using bilingual urban refugee family members or friends to interpret/translate for those who cannot speak Thai and English language. This informal bilingual/biliterate interpretation and/or translation practice can lead to serious communication problems as data from this study pointed out. Frequently urban refugee children and adolescents become bilingual speakers in their native or heritage languages and non-standard English in Thailand after receiving non-formal humanitarian based educational assistance taught by local refugee English teachers instead of native speaking English teachers. After urban refugee adults bring bilingual children or refugee friends' children to a hospital or a clinic, urban refugee children may not understand what medical doctors say and may not have an adult level understanding beyond language competencies to translate and/or interpret things accurately.

Issues of non-native and/or non-native like English medium communicators

Literature document an unbridgeable division in English language competencies and proficiencies between native speakers and non-native speakers (Medgyes, 1992). A disadvantage of linguistic globalization through English medium communication is that somehow English language is liberated from its owners of UK and sub-variants are created from Estglish spoken in Estonia to Singlish spoken in Singapore: the key words are recognizable; nevertheless, many novel words dot the lexicon, idiosyncratic language rules, and sentence structures to make these English variations hard to understand (McCrum, 2000). English language spoken by non-natives is dissimilar to each other. The nuanced-, daily life rooted-, and colloquial English of Singaporeans, Filipinos and Indians can be incomprehensive to Americans, Australians, British, Canadians and South Africans. Spoken English language is thus fractured by differences and variations in pronunciation, intonation, pragmatics, politeness strategies and syllable stresses. As non-native speakers of English are contrasted with their native speaking counterparts in demonstrating their competencies and proficiencies performed in English language, the difference is striking because the former has unbreakable constrains and inabilities created by their late bilingual and/or late biliteracy developments in regard to phonological-, grammatical-, syntactical-, pragmatic- and other different areas of English language than the latter. In sharp contrast, non-native pronunciations of English tend to carry their pronunciations and intonations from their native languages to interfere with their English speech (MacDonald, 1989, p. 224). Speaking English language with a slightly different accents and intonations may lead to speech that is not understandable to ears of its native speakers and thus obscures meanings. For example, when you listen to a Malaysian businessman negotiating with a Thai businessman from Bangkok in Malaysian English language and Thai English respectively, you will hear the differences: the entire conversation sounds a mix of Cantonese, Southern-Min and Central Thai; the English parts are abrupt, emphatic, last syllables omitted, and stripped-down.

However, just because non/native and/or non-native like English language speaking teachers are different in competency and proficiency level does not mean that they cannot benefit English as a foreign and second language learners. But when the division between native and non-native is treated as rigid rule and policy to recruit English language teaching staffs, non-native and/or non-native like English speaking teachers might have little room for them to contribute their knowledge of English and pedagogical skills that can have potentially helped English as foreign and second language learners (Medgyes, 1992, pp. 340-349; Moussu, 2000).

Note that the scope and aim of this present inquiry has been limited to not include formal analysis on what non-native English teachers and peers can do to help English as a foreign and second language learners in urban refugee shelters in Thailand develop their English competencies and proficiencies. This will be the next inquiry. This current study, however, allows data to speak and defend for themselves regarding disadvantages and negative effects of English medium communication among non-native speakers of English.

Methodology 研究方法

Research Questions and Research Instruments
探討的問題和研究工具

This work on English for communication purposes among non-native- and non-native like speakers that discourage urban refugees' developments in Thai-English bilingual and biliteracy presents recent theoretical and empirical-based findings that have been generated by pursuing this question: what is the current state of English for communication purposes in relation to Thai-English bilingual and biliteracy developments among transnational urban refugees in Thailand and what are contextualized factors that affect its developments. This study is aimed to help construct bridges between English for communication purposes in relation to bilingual and biliteracy theory and their grass-root practices among urban refugee communities at multiple sites across Thailand. Participants were measured by their proper uses of one-word, two-word and multiword English utterances linguistically, \grammatically and pragmatically during interviews and spontaneous conversations occurred in natural- and non-manipulated settings under observations, assessed and evaluated by a Ph.D. holder in English as a foreign and second language education from a leading research-based university in USA, accompanied with a certified assistant in the highest level of English language proficiency from a leading research university in Australia.

Multiple urban refugee sites across Thailand

Thailand is a prominent refugee receiving country in almost world-wide scale. Throughout Thailand's history, immigrants and refugees, in searching of opportunities and liberations, have settled in this kingdom with little more than their ambitions and hopes. Some illegal human traffickers promised some urban refugees to bring them to Europe, but dropped them in Bangkok, said by an anonymous administrator in an urban refugee shelter. Other urban refugees fled from cruel political- and religious persecution in their home countries to Thailand, because they can meet tourist visa or visa on arrival requirements easier in Thailand than some other countries (Jesuit Refugee Service, n.d, online).

Urban refugee communities in Thailand have maintained their many unique features. Data in this study were gleaned from a wide variety of data sources including administrators, social workers and religious groups that organize urban refugee shelters, local refugee English teachers who provide humanitarian based educational assistance for urban refugee children and adolescents, and urban refugee individuals as well as urban refugee families that fled Congo, Mainland China, Pakistan, and Sri Lanka to resettle in Thailand. Many groups of 80 refugees from multiple urban shelters participated in this study. However, multiple research sites in this study constantly have new urban refugee members coming in and leaving out from time to time, so the total urban refugee population is fluctuating.

PROJECT OUTCOMES

Results and Discussion
研究成果和討論

Things in local contexts may not always go the way leading scholars have speculated. Bilingual and biliteracy studies have been significantly expanded by Nancy Hornberger's continua model of biliteracy (Hornberger, 1989, 2003, 2004). Conversely, urban refugees in Thailand have challenged existing notions of biliteracy developments advanced by Hornberger's model by revealing that urban refugees show little hard evidence to draw on linguistic resources from native languages in facilitating acquisition of Thai-English bilingual and biliteracy, because they fail to develop Thai-English bilingual and biliteracy to a great extent. In other words, it has become evident from data in this paper that English for communication purposes among heterogeneous and linguistically diverse urban refugees, non-natives of English language, enormously hinders both their English language learning and Thai language learning.

Bilingual and biliteracy studies, models and theories that document urban refugee learners are by no means one-size-fits-all. These above fields need to be tailored to fit socio-cultural- and political- contexts in which urban refugees learn and develop bi/multilingual and bi/multiliteracy in their dynamic political, socio-cultural, multilingual and multicultural settings. A well-established model that is a great success in accounting for bilingual and biliteracy might fail in some local contexts. Urban refugee communities in Thailand might be one of these worst cases. Transnational urban refugees in Thailand typically have a wide range of goals they intend to achieve in their second language learning. However, evidenced by empirical data they are frequently not skilled at developing their English language competencies and often fail to acquire their immediate needed Thai language. Though most participants were excited to learn English language and some are of interest to learn Thai language, when it came to examine their Thai-English bilingual and biliteracy learning outcomes, almost 90% of them admitted that they cannot do both well. In discussing with informants, the researcher discovered that several contextual factors are at play.

Two main themes emerged from data analysis are examined in detail: failure in acquiring English language and failure in learning Thai language. That is to say, failure in acquiring Thai-English bilingual and biliteracy is occurring to urban refugee communities at multiple shelters across Thailand. The explanations this paper would like to advance lies in the fact that it was primarily a consequence of non-native and/or non-native like English speaking Thai administrators, Thai social workers, multi-linguistic refugee teachers and refugee peers that hinder their Thai-English bilingual and biliteracy learning among and within themselves. Most of their local urban refugee English teachers never get certified in TESOL (Teaching English to Speakers of Other Languages) and/or ESL/EFL pedagogy. Neither do they study overseas before in English speaking countries, i.e., USA, UK, Canada and Australia. Non-native and/or non-native like English uses by fellow urban refugees and Thais who provide humanitarian based services are effective in forcing worse changes onto mixed non-native accents and mistaken utterances among English speaking refugees. Though an individual urban refugee can surely affect his/her Thai-English bilingual and biliteracy learning in isolation, there is more powerful to hindering bilingual and biliteracy acquisition among linguistically diverse refugees living together as a whole linguistic community. Thus, rather than draw on available linguistic resources from native languages to develop toward independent Thai-English bilingual and biliteracy, suggested by Hornberger's influential continua model of biliteracy, participants from this study show their evidence of counter effect against both Thai and English language learning.

Evidently, non-native and/or non-native like speaking refugee English teachers have the most direct impact on their students' English language learning. Urban refugee children and adolescents' English learning depends on their local refugee English teachers' competencies in English and their teaching skills. This study shows that it is unfortunate but true that no native- and/or native-like English speaking teachers are available for urban refugee children and adolescents who are entitled with humanitarian based language education assistance.

Thai language immersion might be an intensive second language learning experience for transnational refugees in Thailand. Nevertheless, data from this study show otherwise. Thai language courses are provided occasionally for urban adult refugees, but not regularly in these shelters. Urban refugee children and adolescents are entitled with non-formal humanitarian based education assistance in English language learning taught by non-native English speaking refugee teachers. However, no Thai language courses are regularly offered in their non-formal educational programs.

It is impossible to underestimate the impact of linguistic cultures on urban refugee communities in Thailand. Linguistic cultures in Thailand and in global level figures heavily in the selection of second language learning among urban refugee communities. Urban refugees determine which second languages they use to speak, read and write. Their desire to speak, read and write in English language are encouraged, fostered and supported by fellow urban refugees, Thais and linguistic cultures in Thailand.

The degree of language contact between refugees and Thais enhances urban refugees to see a need in learning Thai language. Nonetheless, when linguistically diverse urban refugees become English medium communicators— employment of English for communication purposes, they skip their immediate need of learning Thai language for communication and their reliance on English language learning to a great extent suffer from their non-native and/or non-native like English speaking Thai administrators, Thai social workers, refugee teachers and refugee peers.

TABLE 7.1:
Daily language practices claimed by urban refugee informants

Infor-mant	Ethnicity of informants	1	2	3	4	5	6
A	Cambodia	L1	L2E	L2E	L2E	L2E	L2E
B	China	L1	L2E	L2E	L2E	L2T	L2E
C	Congo	L1	L2E	L2E	L2E	L2E	L2E
D	Congo	L1	L2E	L2E	L2E	L2E	L2E
E	Congo	L1	L2E	L2E	L2E	L2T	L2T
F	Congo	L1	L2E	L2E	L2E	L2E	L2E
G	Congo	L1	L2E	L2E	L2E	L2E	L2E
H	Lao	L1	L2E	L2E	L2E	L2E	L2E
I	Middle East	L1	L2E	L2E	L2E	L2T	L2T
J	Middle East	L1	L2E	L2E	L2E	L2E	L2E
K	Nepal	L1	L2E	L2E	L2E	L2E	L2E
L	Nepal	L1	L2E	L2E	L2E	L2E	L2E
M	North Korea	L1	L2E	L2E	L2E	L2E	L2E
N	North Korea	L1	L2E	L2E	L2E	L2T	L2T
O	Pakistan	L1	L2E	L2E	L2E	L2E	L2E
P	Pakistan	L1	L2E	L2E	L2E	L2T	L2T
Q	Pakistan	L1	L2E	L2E	L2E	L2E	L2E
R	Pakistan	L1	L2E	L2E	L2E	L2E	L2E
S	Pakistan	L1	L2E	L2E	L2E	L2T	L2T
T	Sri Lanka	L1	L2E	L2E	L2E	L2E	L2E
U	Sri Lanka	L1	L2E	L2E	L2E	L2E	L2E
V	Sri Lanka	L1	L2E	L2E	L2E	L2E	L2E
W	Sri Lanka	L1	L2E	L2E	L2E	L2T	L2T
X	Sri Lanka	L1	L2E	L2E	L2E	L2E	L2E
Y	Vietnam	L1	L2E	L2E	L2E	L2E	L2E
Z	Vietnam	L1	L2E	L2E	L2E	L2T	L2T
No. of informants=26							
1=communicate with homogenous urban refugee peers				L1=Native languages L2T=Thai L2			

2=communicate with heterogeneous and linguistically diverse urban refugees 3=communicate with Thai administrators 4=communicate with Thai social workers 5= communicate with Thais in public language domains, i.e., grocery stories. 6= communicate with Thai medical doctors in hospitals or clinics	L2E=English L2 N=No opinion/unclear/neutrality

Note that due to space constrain, table 1only reports responses from 26 informants. Information about informant's age(s) does not reveal in this report to keep their confidentiality. There are more than 10,000-20,000 urban refugees coming in and out several urban refugee shelters across Thailand daily. Though the researcher is aware of more variations that could have been occurred from a larger sampling size, this study has been limited to document a smaller sample size of 80-100 urban refugees.

Conclusion and Suggestions
結論和建議

Though the researcher is open to alternative explanations to interpret data, any insights and comments other than non-native and/or non-native like English speakers utilizing English for communication purposes that lead to unsuccessful Thai-English bilingual and biliteracy developments will go beyond the scope and aim of this present inquiry. This study does not encompass formal analysis of what exactly makes non-native English speaking urban refugees different than their native speaking counterparts with regard to English phonological processes, intonation variations, and pragmatics and so on. More future inquires are much needed to undertake in a variety of urban refugee sites to ensure more comprehensive understanding. As for now, limited salient findings emerged from analysis in this study reported in this paper is included in this contribution.

Data gathered for this chapter would conclude that one main factor causes unsuccessful learning in Thai-English bilingual and biliteracy—both English language learning and Thai language learning—among transnational urban refugees in Thailand. Deficiency in learning English and Thai language is not brought by English for communication purposes alone, but also accompanied with non-native and/or non-native like English speaking Thai administrators, Thai social workers, refugee English teachers and refugee peers. Despite other scholarly works might document positive effects on non-native English teachers and how they improve English as foreign and second language learners' achievements, competencies and proficiencies (Moussu, 2000), data gathered for this study do not show any explicit messages and convincing arguments to support non-native speaking English teachers and English medium communicators. Data cannot go beyond themselves to claim any positive effects on non-native and/or non-native like English medium communicators, because analysis shows discouraging results that nearly all participants (>95%) failed English language assessments and evaluation regarding proper uses of their one-word-, two-word- and multiword-English L2 utterances in phonological, grammatical and pragmatic levels. But as far as basic communication and mutual understanding are concerned, linguistically diverse urban refugees seem to be content with their varied English competencies and proficiencies.

To avoid above pitfalls, several implications and suggestions surface. This article adds to literature and advances our current understanding regarding a dynamic relationship between Thai and English language in transnational trajectories by focusing on multiple and context-specific discourses in urban refugee shelters. Several research results yielded from this article are that Thai-English bilingual and biliteracy development(s) is an unrealistic goal unless heterogeneous urban refugees stop non-native and/or non-native like English for communication purposes, outsourcing more qualified native and/or native-like English language teachers and entitled with regular Thai as a second language education. Nevertheless, to stop non-native and/or non-native like English for communication purposes among heterogeneous and linguistically diverse urban refugees is not feasible at the moment, due to the fact that there is lack of an existing common medium of communication but English—even they are non-native speakers. Taking stock of the English for communication purposes among non-native and/or non-native like speakers as in relation to failing Thai-English bilingual and biliteracy developments, interventions are recommended to take initiatives in meeting needs of English as a foreign language teaching by filling in native speaking English teaching staffs, jointly with Thai as second language teaching programs provided on regular basis within urban refugee shelters. Perhaps possible implications and contributions from this inquiry is to inform us that we at least are aware of the limitation of non-native English medium communication that could potentially lead to unsuccessful developments in bilingual[ism] and biliteracy.

(本文原稿於2011年暑假發表在《現代應用語言學期刊》第三卷第二期)

For further information about this chapter (if you want to discuss with the author), please contact:

Hugo Lee, Faculty Member
International College
National Institute of Development Administration
18th fl., Navamin Building, 118 Seri Thai Rd,
Khlong Chan, Bang Kapi, Bangkok 10240

Hugo Lee, Consultant Roster Member
United Nations
Economic & Social Commission for Asia & the Pacific
3rd fl., United Nations Conference Center, ESCAP HR
United Nations Building, 76 Rajadamnern Nok Ave
Bangkok 10200

T. 088-607-2560
E. hugoclubheart3@gmail.com   f Li Y-h Hugo
W. https://indiana.academia.edu/YuHsiuLee

參考文獻 References

Nancy Hornberger

1. Hornberger, N.H. (1989). Continua of biliteracy. *Review of Educational Research. 59 (3)*, 271-296.

2. Hornberger, N.H. (eds.) (2003). *Continua of biliteracy: An ecological framework for educational policy, research, and practice in multilingual settings.* Tonawanda, NY: Multilingual Matters.

3. Hornberger, N.H. (2004). Continua of biliteracy and the bilingual educator: Educational linguistics in practice. *International Journal of Bilingual Education and Bilingualism. 7 (2&3)*, 155-171.

4. Jesuit Refugee Service. (n.d.). Urban refugee program, Bangkok. Retrieved December 18, 2010, from the Jesuit Refugee Service Web Site: http://jrs.or.th/thai/

5. MacDonald, M. (1989). The influence of Spanish phonology on the English spoken by United States Hispanics. In Bjarkman, Pe.; & Hammond, R. American Spanish pronunciation: Theoretical and applied perspectives (pp. 215–236). Washington, DC: Georgetown University Press.

6. McCrum, R. (2010). *Globish: How the English language became the world's language,* New York City: The Viking Press.

7. Medgyes, P. (1992). Native or non-native: Who's worth more? *ELT Journal, 46* (4), 340-349.

429

8. Moussu, L. (2000). Native versus nonnative speakers of English: Students' reactions. Retrieved December 22, 2010, from the Web Site: http://www.moussu.net/TP/540.pdf

9. Ostler, N. (2010). The last lingua franca: English until the return of Babel. Retrieved December 21, 2010, from the Web Site: http://www.tnr.com/book/review/tongues-twisted?id=N8UeBtb2T6eBU9eRM1p5oUWLu3uRjQoniM5RCp KvWgOc+iWwMn   X40JIlvKE+urPI

Concluding Remarks of The Book

For these disadvantaged groups studied, access to English and other dominant languages is helpful in both their battle against poverty and their effort to achieve economic and social sustainable development. Nonetheless, there is a limited extent for upward social mobility across the urban poor populations researched, largely because English skills and proficiency in dominant languages (other than English) may or may not change the social status of these marginalized groups.

The book has utility for a fairly wide audience.

Implications of The Book

TOWARDS THE 2030 AGENDA:

 SUSTAINABLE DEVELOPMENT GOALS

How bi-/multilingual (foreign/second) language ability contributes to achieve key sustainable development goals for minority peoples in individual, group & national levels?

SD1: No Poverty (See Chapter 2-5)

It is increasingly evident that foreign/second language competence (bi/multilingual ability) in individual levels can increase a person's competitiveness in the job market, thereby one's increased income results in poverty reduction. Increased income might be used to purchase food (SDG 2: Zero Hunger).

SD2: Zero Hunger

Foreign/second language competence (bi-multilingual ability) can create better opportunities for employment and economic development in individual, group and national levels.

SD3: Good Health and Well-being

If a person's income is increased largely because of his or her foreign/second language advantage in the job market, s/he is more likely to have budgets to access medical cares and medicines. As a result, there is an indirect link from bi-/multilingual ability in individual levels to SD3: Good Health. Subsequently, one's good health may in turn contribute his or her sense of well-being psychologically and physically.

SDG 5: Gender Equality (See Chapter 4-5)

Women, in general, are empowered by their foreign/second (bi-/multilingual) language competence, particularly their ability to speak more global languages such as English and Mandarin (Chinese). Being able to speak a dominant language increases opportunities for women's employment and income. This leads to women's long-term sustainable development.

In the individual and national level and at the global level, English, i.e., English-speaking ability, (other dominant languages as well), can be used as a proactive tool to achieve poverty reduction for women across different sectors in an export-oriented economy (e.g., service sector such as tourism, export sector such as international trade).

SDG 8: Decent Work and Economic Growth (See Chapter 1-7)

Foreign/second language competence (bi-/multilingual ability) in individual, society and country levels is central to achieving one's economic growth goal.

SDG 10: Reduced Inequalities (See Chapter 2-3)

Foreign/second language ability (bi-/multilingual competence) plays an important role in individual levels in supporting minority peoples to compete with those who are more advantageous in the job market, decreasing inequality between those fortunate and those marginalized. Ultimately, a more equal opportunity for minority peoples leads to a more just society.

SDG 16: "Promote peaceful and inclusive societies for sustainable development, provide access to justice for all and build effective, accountable and inclusive institutions at all levels".

Epilogue: FUTURE FOCUS

This book identifies the following strategic ways, suggestions and recommendations, and policy implications, which would help minority peoples accelerate their progress in increasing incomes and achieving economic and social development goals.

1. Governments in national & regional levels and the United Nations should recognize foreign/second language competence (bi-/multilingual ability) in individual and group levels as a means of implementation of the 2030 Agenda.

2. Mainstream English and other dominant languages such as Mandarin (Chinese) into the basic educational curriculum and the school program in the national level

3. Continue offering language-support (English and other dominant languages) programs to orphans with and without disabilities in orphanages. Short-term summer English programs do not work well. long-term English program solution is needed.

4. Provide language-support (English and other dominant languages) pre-service and in-service trainings to service-industry workers in massage parlors and bars.

5. Further efforts to reform the humanitarian-based educational programs for refugee children

6. Provide language-support programs (e.g., translation services) and language educational programs (e.g., teach English) for refugee adults

7. Enhance the refugee center's service by improving staffs' English ability for effective communication with refugees

8. Ensure that language is not a barrier for refugees to access essential services

The Top

Bi-/Multilingual

Urban Poor

from Bangkok

AT A GLANCE:

No. 1

Coordinators in the Seladeng district
to introduce massage parlors
to potential male customers
WHO ARE THEY: *Thai males who speak English, Chinese, Thai, Japanese and more*

No. 2

Survivor shop staffs in Baiyoke Tower's district
WHO ARE THEY: *Ethnic-Nepali Myanmar nationals who speak Burmese, Nepali, English, Thai, Hindi and Iranian. They generally learn to speak Hindi from interactions with Indian customers and watching YouTube TV series from India. They also learn to speak Iranians from their Iranian customers.*

No. 3

Freelancers
WHO ARE THEY: *Rental Thai wives who speak fluent English, catering for male expats and male tourists*

There is, of course, a **paradox** here:
They earn a living by their incredible language ability and by services they provide to expat customers.
It is strange to see that despite their multilingual ability, they continue to work in the same service sector (the tourism sector

and the love industry). It is seemed that there is no upper social mobility for them.

The least bi-/multilingual is the majority of massage therapists.

Reference: Databank, complied by the author
| Hugo Yu-Hsiu Lee, PhD

APPENDIX II.

WISDOM *for* Change

Consulting Services 作者的諮詢服務
Available at the International College
the National Institute of Development Administration

Consultation on Language and Sustainable Development
Consult with Hugo Yu-Hsiu Lee. Ph.D.

He can be reached at: *hugoclubheart3@gmail.com* 請發電子郵件預約

18th Floor, Navamin Bldg. | Faculty Office, ICO-NIDA | 18 Seri Thai Rd,
Khwaeng Khlong Chan (sub-district), Khet Bang Kapi (district), Bangkok
Thailand 10240

Call for Papers

Journals & Books:

We will submit to, for example, Bloomsbury, Palgrave Macmillan & Springer for publication.

Edited by the Author

Titles in the Minority and
Language Studies Series

The Author (Hugo Yu-Hsiu Lee, PhD | hugoclubheart3@gmail.com) promotes better mutual understanding between modern-day minority peoples (e.g., urban poor, street teen workers, orphans with disabilities, bargirls, asylum seekers and refugees), research communities (e.g., researchers and graduate students in applied linguistics, sociolinguistics and development studies) and the non-profit sector (e.g., nongovernmental organizations) through academic conversations, formal and informal dialogues and cooperative research projects. One way of achieving this is by mobilizing experts from applied linguistics, sociolinguistics, anthropology and development studies (in the government sector and the non-profit sector) to jointly write a special journal issue together and write a book together.

Topics that address Issues in Language-related Matters

among Minority Peoples are Welcome

Language and Poverty | Language and Development

| Language and Economic Growth | Language and Asylum Seeking

This book is available in the following libraries after November-December 2019:

United Nations ESCAP

United Nations Library

(ESCAP Library, Bangkok)

https://www.unescap.org/library

The United Nations Building

Rajadamnern Nok Avenue

Bangkok 10200 Thailand

聯合國圖書館
聯合國亞太經社會
（聯合國亞洲總部——曼谷）

Indiana University (Bloomington)
Education Library

(IU Education Library)

https://libraries.indiana.edu/libeduc

201 North Rose Street

Bloomington, IN 47405 USA

美國印第安那大學
——博民頓校區（花開鎮）
教育學院圖書館

Asian Institute of Technology Library

(AIT Library)

http://www.library.ait.ac.th

Asian Institute of Technology

Klong Luang, Phatum Thani, 12120 Thailand

亞洲理工圖書館

ASEAN Library

(Thanat Khoman ASEAN Library)

https://www.facebook.com/NidaAseanLibrary/

21st floor of Navamin Building, NIDA,

118 Moo3, Serithai Road, Klong-Chan, Bangkapi, Bangkok Thailand

10240

東盟（東協）圖書館

National Institute of Development

Administration Library

(NIDA Library, Bangkok)

http://library.nida.ac.th/2015/index.php/en/

https://www.facebook.com/NIDA-Library-474196622700286/

118 Moo3, Serithai Road, Klong-Chan, Bangkapi, Bangkok Thailand

10240

國家發展研究院圖書館（泰國）

APPENDIX IV.

Book Back Cover Text

We are living in the world of globalization, migration, regionalization and nationalism, among other trends.

"Are we making a more just world by our contemporary linguistic practices in political, economic, educational, societal, global and regional levels?"

"Our linguistic privilege and disadvantage, as well as linguistic deprivation, affect the ways in which we access educational, economic, political and social institutions."

"Many linguistic minorities cannot access resources necessary for succeeding linguistically in their societies."

"How to achieve linguistic justice and ensure linguistic practices for economic development and social inclusion is a pressing concern."

This book aims to address language-related issues pertaining to economic and social development, linguistic justice and social inclusion. It tackles some of the biggest challenges facing linguistically disadvantaged communities in developing countries.

"First/foreign/second language ability has a direct impact on our upper social mobility and our country's economic. "

"It is unfortunate that resource-constrained populations in the margins are less likely to master first/foreign/second languages (in both developed and developing countries) and are less likely to be competitive in the global professional workplace and the labor market. "

"For a multitude of reasons, the linguistic disadvantage populations are often excluded from the mainstream society. "

"Despite the inequity persists, it is possible to use modern-day applied linguistics and social work (nonprofits) to help the linguistic disadvantaged minorities learn a first/foreign/second language and literacy for the purpose of economic and social development, linguistic justice and social inclusion. "

國家圖書館出版品預行編目資料

Language and Minority Peoples in the Making of Modern
Thailand 泰國庶民和弱勢群體的草根式語言學習和語言
使用／李育修 著. – 初版. – 臺中市：白象文化，2019. 11
ISBN 978-986-358-895-5（平裝）
1. 語言教學 2. 泰國
800. 9382   108015692

Language and Minority Peoples
in the Making of Modern Thailand
泰國庶民和弱勢群體的草根式語言學習和語言使用

作　　者　李育修 *(Hugo Yu-Hsiu Lee)*

校　　對　李育修 *(Hugo Yu-Hsiu Lee)*

專案主編　陳逸儒

出版編印　吳適意、林榮威、林孟侃、陳逸儒、黃麗穎

設計創意　張禮南、何佳諠

經銷推廣　李莉吟、莊博亞、劉育姍、李如玉

經紀企劃　張輝潭、洪怡欣、徐錦淳、黃姿虹

營運管理　林金郎、曾千熏

發 行 人　張輝潭

出版發行　白象文化事業有限公司

　　　　　412台中市大里區科技路1號8樓之2（台中軟體園區）

　　　　　出版專線：（04）2496-5995　　傳真：（04）2496-9901

　　　　　401台中市東區和平街228巷44號（經銷部）

　　　　　購書專線：（04）2220-8589　　傳真：（04）2220-8505

印　　刷　普羅文化股份有限公司

初版一刷　2019 年 11 月

定　　價　450 元